MY VIKING VAMPIRE

Sanctuary, Texas Book One

KRYSTAL SHANNAN

My Viking Vampire

Sanctuary, Texas Book 1

Copyright © 2014 KS Publishing

ISBN-13: 978-1945417054

ISBN-10: 1945417056

All rights reserved.

Cover Design by Clarise Tan - CT Cover Creations

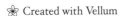 Created with Vellum

PRAISE FOR SANCTUARY, TEXAS

"Wonderfully imaginative. Vampires have never been so sexy or dangerous." ~Liliana Hart, NYT Bestselling Author of the Rena Drake Series

"I couldn't put it down, action packed and sexy!" - Amazon Reviewer

"steamy love scenes, danger, friendship, magic, vampires, werewolves, adorable pixies and more!" - Amazon Reviewer

"Shannan weaves a sexy, action-packed tale sure to keep you turning the pages late into the night." ~~Liliana Hart, NYT Bestselling Author of the Rena Drake Series

"The dialogue is intelligent, exceptionally

well written and flows effortlessly. Ah, the characters....they are the main component, the heart and soul of this story. Each and every character is fascinating, captivating, intriguing, engaging and sexy as sin." - Judy Lewis

PROLOGUE

2096

F<small>IFTY</small> <small>YEARS HAVE PASSED SINCE THE</small> O<small>THERS' EXISTENCE</small> *was discovered on earth. They say the United States was torn apart by riots, and that until the government took control, people were being murdered in their beds by supernatural creatures. At least that's what we were told in school.*

Information about that time period is carefully guarded. Life before the riots lives on only in the whispers of our elders and the few scattered books that escaped the burnings. Even information on the Internet is carefully monitored and filtered. The government sees everything.

Questions only lead to death.

"What the hell?" I screeched, stepping onto soggy carpet. Putrid water squelched and flowed around the soles of my battered tennis shoes, staining them a very nasty brown. My living room was a swamp of filth and muck. I covered my mouth. The smell was worse than the dumpster behind the Seafood Shack. And that said a lot.

"Miss Bailey!" George, the maintenance man for the apartment complex, poked his head out of my closet-sized kitchen. "Miss, you can't be in here. We're trying to get the water shut off. But this is dirty water. It's not safe."

He wore black rubber waders and gloves and held a giant wrench in one hand and a radio in the other.

"What happened?"

"The sewage line in the apartment above yours. It leaked."

"A leak? This looks more like an eruption."

"I'm very sorry. Everything here is ruined."

No shit. My living room ceiling was now in the middle of my floor. Water dripped from the edges of the still-remaining pieces of sheetrock onto the couch I'd found on a curb down the street. Not a huge financial loss, but it was my only piece of furniture other than my bed. I moved so often, I didn't have the money or the time to collect any other decor.

Sooner or later, *he* would show up. He always did. This time it had been sooner. Thankfully I'd spotted his car outside the restaurant before I'd gone in for my shift this morning.

My abusive ex Kevin Holt was an investigator for the SECR (Southeast Coast Republic), and the good ol' boys there always seemed to help him figure out where I'd gone. I'd changed my last name a half-dozen times, but it didn't seem to matter. His tenacity was an admirable trait for a man in his profession, but exhausting in a stalker.

So I just kept moving. Eventually he would get tired of chasing me. Right?

Four years and he hadn't tired yet. I thought running to the Texas Republic would slow down his hunt. Maybe even make him give up on ever finding me.

He hated Others and Texas was full of them. The other three republics had banned Others from becoming citizens. Texas, joined by Louisiana, New Mexico, and Colorado, opened its doors to all, avoiding both riots and economic turmoil. It went about its business while the rest of the states were nothing more than dictatorships under the guise of republics. At least that's what my tenth-grade history teacher told us before he was removed from his position for being a sympathizer in the SECR. It also helped that Texas was a major supplier of oil and gas. The other three republics depended on those shipments.

Someone hollering from my kitchen distracted George long enough for me to tiptoe as best I could around the mess and into my bedroom. More of the ceiling looked like it was about to come down, so I had to move quickly.

Other than the stuff on the floor—which unfortunately was almost everything—nothing else was wet. It was tough to keep things off the floor when you didn't have money for a dresser.

After stuffing my purse with a few of the dry clothes hanging in the closet, I darted to the bathroom, but gagged at the stench and quickly closed the door on that disaster. If it smelled that bad, I didn't need it.

The mucky carpet sucked at the soles of my shoes, threatening to steal them off my feet as I hurried out the front door. It was the end of most of my meager belongings. I tried not to think about it. I had to get moving.

Out of habit, I studied the parking lot for Kevin's large, blue pickup truck.

Nothing. At least he hadn't tracked me here...yet. Maybe I still had a chance to shake him.

Fate was giving me a double kick in the ass out of Fort Worth. I just wished I'd had more than three months to recoup from the last move. I didn't even have enough money for a bus ticket.

There had to be a better way to survive in this world.

I made it safely to the park behind the complex and stopped for a moment to catch my breath.

A warm breeze tossed my long bangs back and forth across my face. I was trying really hard not to wallow, but despair crept in. He'd gotten so close. What if I hadn't seen his truck? I wiped a tear from my cheek and shuddered. My hand rubbed my shoulder, remembering the pain I'd been in when I ran the first time. He'd been so angry.

I never saw the bat coming.

࿇

A STORM LOOMED ON THE HORIZON.

The sun was setting, turning the sky fiery shades of orange. And the wind had picked up, too. I could smell the rain in the air. Sticky. Hot. It curled around me, squeezing like a boa constrictor, threatening to choke the last spark of life from my tired, worn body.

My eyes fluttered closed and my head did the nod thing, jolting me back awake. I couldn't afford to fall asleep. Not out in the open. Gravel crunched behind me and I stumbled to my feet. A burly giant of the Fort Worth Sheriff's Department was about ten feet away.

"You can't sleep here, ma'am."

"I know." I hurried down the path away from him. I wouldn't be the only homeless person he chased out of the park that night. The coming storm would do most of the grunt work for him, though. The homeless would flock to the train yard and overpasses to avoid the coming downpour.

I didn't have that luxury. Hitting the road was my only choice, but walking the highway at night was stupid. I needed a safe place to rest until morning.

My stomach growled as I hurried along, reminding me

I hadn't eaten since the night before. I usually ate at the restaurant for free after working my shift. The tantalizing scent of hamburgers and fries drifted on the breeze from the restaurants up the hill and I sighed.

I had avoided Kevin for now, but a strange guy in a suit had been following me for the last few minutes on the park path. I'd only noticed him because he seemed so out of place. No one walked through the park in a full suit. Especially not in the sweltering heat of a Texas August.

I looked over my shoulder again and saw nothing. Strange, he'd been there only a few moments ago. The sound of his dress shoes on the concrete had been very distinct.

Throwing the strap of my large purse over my neck, I started jogging again. Sweat ran down my face, between my breasts and soaked the back of my shirt. Everything clung and rubbed uncomfortably in the nearly unbearable humidity.

There was a huge bus station only a couple blocks away. It was grand central for the city of Fort Worth. I should be able to get a little catnap and a snack from a vending machine. Plus, it was public. Maybe the creepy-suit-guy would wander off for an easier target. I might be having a shitty day, but I knew how to run and he shouldn't be able to keep up in that heavy wool.

The stairs leading up the hill and out of the park were only a few yards away. I never looked back. Taking them two at a time, I cleared the two-level flight in only a couple of minutes. Another glance over my shoulder assured me the staircase was still empty.

There were street lamps along the sidewalk from here

to the bus station, lots of cars and some foot traffic. People and cars meant safety. Black market traffickers wouldn't snatch someone on a busy road.

A nice-looking Mustang pulled up alongside me, but I kept walking, focusing on the large bus station straight ahead. The soft whir of the passenger window sliding down made my heart race.

Only one more block.

I could make it one more block.

I had to.

"Hey, baby. You need some money? I could really use a drink and you look delicious."

A vampire. Great. I wasn't some common blood whore. I'd never been that desperate and I still wasn't. "Not interested." I turned away from him and focused on the bus station doors.

"Your loss, baby. I could rock your world."

Yeah, right into the grave or into a cage. Girls who hooked on the street were the ones who always went missing. A good whore knew to find a brothel to protect her from being sold as a slave.

The black Mustang peeled out, and I released the breath I'd been holding.

A few more steps got me to the sparkling glass doors of the bus station. I waited for them to slide open and then I slipped inside, shivering at the blast from the AC. The cool air conditioning felt like the restaurant's walk-in freezer compared to the hot sticky mess outside, and all the sweat on my body and clothes crystalized instantly. It would be a long night in these arctic-like temperatures. I didn't have anything in my bag but a couple of extra tank tops, a few pairs of underwear I'd snatched from my bed, and a pair of yoga pants. The smelly jeans I wore were the warmest thing I had. Too bad my sweatshirt had been in my flooded bathroom.

It was crazy that I had to worry about being cold in Texas—in August.

I crossed the lobby to the snack machine and put in a few quarters. It was the last of my cash after paying my rent yesterday. One lonely bag of animal crackers fell into the basket. I took my snack to the nearest bench and tucked my legs under my body. People were less likely to sit down next to me with my legs taking up so much space. Plus, the putrid smell from my apartment still lingered on me and was less than desirable. *I* didn't even want to be next to me.

As my head did the nodding thing again, I let myself drift a little this time. I needed a few naps this evening if I was walking out of Fort Worth tomorrow.

My eyes opened and refocused every time I heard the front doors slide open, making napping very difficult. But being surprised by someone was not on my agenda. Survival meant not being caught unaware.

People came and went. No one bothered me. No one asked me why I was there. The doors opened again and a sense of dread spread through my being, not unlike the sickening feeling I used to get when Kevin came home from work.

Into the station walked creepy-suit-guy. Brown curls brushed against his shoulders and his skin was dark. His eyes glistened an inhuman shade of lavender in the florescent light. *Holy shit!* He was a Djinn. No wonder I'd lost him in the park a couple of times. Teleporting, creepy psychopaths. They were always on the governments most wanted lists. I would've stood a better chance with the horny vampire in the Mustang.

A few people looked up when he walked in, but no one said anything. Most of them moved to the opposite side of the lobby. Djinn weren't on the list of friendly Others. They were diabolical and evil and most everyone knew to avoid them. Their lavender eyes, if not hidden by contacts, made them easy to recognize. Though most didn't even try to hide what they were. They enjoyed the fear their presence elicited—fed off of it.

A moment later, the door opened again and the picture of male perfection entered the bus station, right behind the creep. He had wavy, blond hair, unnaturally bright jewel-blue eyes, and broad shoulders. His chest tapered to a narrow waist and what could only be washboard abs hidden beneath a casual polo shirt. As much as I avoided men, this one was worth a double look, even if he was a vampire.

I liked him even more when he glared at the Djinn and walked straight toward me.

The Djinn frowned and turned away from me, focusing his gaze toward the giant map on the wall to his right.

I turned back to the blond giant who'd settled himself on the bench next to me and smiled. His grin melted right through my frazzled nerves. Why were all these guys coming out of the woodwork when I was just trying to get away from one?

"Where are you headed, *kjaere*? You know it's dangerous to be out at this hour alone and so upset. Your pheromones are broadcasting your location to the entire area, especially after that jaunt through the park."

Pheromones? *Shit.* I'd heard Djinn were attracted to human anxiety, but I thought vamps just smelled blood. I moved away from him a few inches. It didn't really help, but it made me feel better.

He was dressed like an average human, loose jeans and a white polo. Nothing fancy or out of place. His accent indicated a little something foreign mixed into his Texas twang. But those eyes gave him away. All vampires had bright, teal blue eyes—like rare gems that could've been cut from photos of a tropical ocean paradise.

"I'm fine, thanks." I hoped he didn't hear the tremble in my voice. I didn't want to end up kidnapped and on my way to some foreign slave auction on the black market. Although, being his personal slave might not be so bad. He couldn't be worse than my ex.

This sexy giant sitting next to me oozed sexuality and dominance—most vampires did. The waitresses at the Seafood Shack were always saying it was the vampires' confidence that made them attractive. Maybe. Mostly I just appreciated the fact that he acted as Djinn repellant for the time being.

I did my best to stay away from everyone, including the supernatural population. Texas was the only republic of the former United States that allowed Others to be citizens—equal rights and whatnot. I'd lived in both the SECR and the Washington Republic, but the Texas Republic was my favorite so far. People stayed out of your business, for the most part. And there were fewer restrictions on the citizens here than in the other republics.

"Is your bus leaving soon, *kjaere?*" He was questioning my travel plans again, stretching his arm along the top of the bench behind me. His gaze scanned the room, and I followed it across the lobby to the Djinn, who hadn't left the map area.

I didn't think the vampire would try anything out in the open, but his nearness made me nervous all the same. I'd lived in the worst of the worst neighborhoods and people got attacked all the time. Vampires were just careful enough to make the attacks look like human violence now that they were out in the open.

Still, I was a less-than-desirable target for either of these supernatural predators. I smelled terrible and looked worse. My long bangs were plastered to my temples and me and my bag held just enough of the sewage stench from my apartment to make even my human nose wrinkle in disgust. Why the hell were these guys following me?

I'd had just about enough, but when I moved to get up, his deep voice hissed in my ear and I froze. "Be still."

The command struck a dormant chord within me, making me shiver. But it wasn't fear I felt. It was something else, but I couldn't put my finger on it.

"He is stalking you."

I knew that. But it's not like I could pretend the entire day hadn't happened. I was homeless, still starving, and had no other options than to sit in this freezing cold bus station until the Djinn decided to leave me alone.

"You don't have a ticket, do you?" his voice rumbled. My jaw quivered and he leaned back, giving me a little breathing room.

I shook my head and stared at the floor. My mind

processed through a thousand ideas a minute. Maybe I could slip out a bathroom window and lose them both. I already had Kevin chasing me. Why did these guys have to show up and add more stress to my imploding day?

"Do you have family?"

Again with the personal invasion of privacy. "Who are you?" I snapped. Why did he think I would tell a perfect stranger, a vampire nonetheless, if I had a family who would miss me after he grabbed me. I might think he was drop-dead gorgeous, but I wasn't born yesterday.

Then he completely surprised me.

He smiled. Again.

Not a little grin. A whopping ear-to-ear smile, like a guy who'd just found out he was getting laid. My heart did a little pitter-patter and some of my resolve melted away, along with my fear. But I was feeling confused, too. Why did he care?

"You remind me of someone I knew a long time ago. She was brave like you, *kjaere*. I admire that. My name is Erick Thorson. I'm headed home after a long overdue visit to my sister in Dallas. When I realized Darius was tracking you, I followed as well." He nodded toward the Djinn.

His admission seemed quite open, but my inner skeptic still took rein. "So what, you intend to share me with your pal?"

He growled and I saw just a hint of his fangs. "I have no such intentions. I would never share you with any man."

"I'm not yours to share." Jerk!

He cocked his head to the side and stared. "No of course not, I meant *if* you were mine, *kjaere*."

The twinkle of amusement in his eyes confused me further. I'd said nothing to amuse him. Nothing to make him think I was his. And yet ... I couldn't erase the thought of *being* his. Something was terribly wrong with me.

"Where are you going?" The question just slipped out. What did it matter where he was going? I needed to get as far away from Fort Worth as possible, and I didn't intend to go anywhere with him. But a part of me felt like I could.

I had a feeling he wouldn't let Kevin or anyone else near me. Maybe he could just eat Kevin for me and ... what am I thinking? I can't ask some strange vampire to eat my ex and not expect him to want something in return.

Me, for example.

I took a deep breath and tried to clear the murderous and selfish thoughts from my head. When I looked up, he was still staring. His gaze alone felt all-consuming. Hungry.

My head told me to get away, but the tired, lonely, and beaten woman inside me wanted to trust the kindness I heard in his voice.

"I'm going home to Sanctuary," he whispered, glancing over at the Djinn again.

That sounded nice. A sanctuary. Somewhere to rest. Maybe a small town would be a good place to stay for a little while. Wait? Was I seriously considering following this vampire home? What if he was crazy? Or hid me away in his place and drank my blood? Or killed me?

His beautiful blue eyes caught my gaze and my worries

seemed to vanish into their depths. If he offered, I would totally follow him home.

Please offer.

"What is it like there? Is it small?" I asked.

"You could say it's on the small side. Less than a thousand souls." He paused and glanced around the lobby again.

I followed his gaze and noticed the Djinn was gone. A sigh of relief slipped from between my lips.

"He will be back. Darius doesn't give up that easily."

"What?" I sucked in a breath. "You know him?"

"We have an unpleasant history." He reached out and tucked a loose strand of my wayward hair behind my ear.

His touch sent a shiver of excitement racing through my body. When had my fear morphed into arousal?

"You will be safe in Sanctuary."

I looked down at the floor again and then back up into his mesmerizing eyes. The last of my resistance melted away. I was so tired of running. Maybe it was time to take a chance on a man again, even a supernatural one.

"Won't he just follow us there?" It sounded too good to be true. Skepticism and an inability to trust anyone had kept me safe from Kevin for four years. Was it wise to give away that control to a stranger? To a vampire?

"The Djinn are not welcome there. He would not dare follow you."

"How do you manage that?"

"An old enemy of theirs calls Sanctuary home."

"There's something worse than a Djinn?"

He chuckled. "There are things much, much worse, *kjaere*. But nothing you need to fret about."

Nothing I needed to fret about? Who talks like that? How old was he? No. I didn't want to know that. It didn't matter.

"I don't have money for a ticket, much less a place to stay." I hated to ask for charity, but there was a first time for everything and I was in a desperate situation. Kevin would be checking bus stations soon and I needed to be gone by dawn, if not before.

He raised an eyebrow and stared for a moment before answering. "I will cover the ticket and you are more than welcome to stay with me or at the Castle. The Sisters are quite hospitable, though you might find their version of entertainment a bit over-stimulating."

Now what was that supposed to mean? Over-stimulating? And what were the Sisters? Some kind of sex cult? Exhaustion always caused my mind to swim in the gutter.

"Rose can always use help at the café. I'm sure she'd be willing to let you work some shifts."

A café. That sounded cute and quaint and non-threatening. I could work with that, but there had to be a catch. "Is she a vampire, too?"

"No. She's a ..." He paused. "She would probably rather tell you herself. She's very protective of anyone we bring into town. You'll be safe."

Safe. I craved that word. But it was an illusion. I would never truly be safe from Kevin until one of us was dead.

Erick's smile faded and a frown replaced it. "Don't worry about the Djinn. I will keep him away from you."

Again with the mind reading, though it hadn't been the Djinn I was worried about that time. What was this guy's deal? "How do you know what I'm thinking?"

"Humans emit very different pheromones depending on their thought patterns. My sense of smell can pick up on those tiny fluctuations."

"Can all vampires do that?"

"Only ones who've practiced for a long time."

"This Rose ... she won't care that I'm human?"

"You will be my guest." He shifted in his chair and his eyes drifted to the floor for just a second.

"What aren't you telling me?"

"There are very few humans in Sanctuary, but I promise you will be safe."

A small town full of Others. It would certainly be the last place Kevin would look for me. For that I could get on board with just about anything. "All right. But, if someone cats me, I'm holding you personally responsible."

His blue eyes darkened and just a hint of red ringed the irises. "I can assure you, I have no intention of allowing anyone but myself that close to you."

I shivered, wondering if he was implying what I thought. Didn't matter. I would let him fight my battles until I could get on my feet again.

This sex-god of a vampire could have me any which way he wanted, at least until I had to run again.

CHAPTER 2

"Come." He took my hand and led me to the ticket window.

I tugged his six-foot-six frame down into the atmosphere where I lived. He bent, putting his face so close to mine I could smell the faint scent of peppermint, my favorite candy. It made my mouth water.

"What is it, *kjaere?*"

The word he used made me pause. It dripped with affection, like something a man would say to his lover. My body agreed with my mind's observation. Heat curled in my belly and moisture began to pool between my legs. I tugged my hand free and he spoke again.

"Do not move from my side. The Djinn is not gone. If I'm touching you, he can't jump with you."

Jump with me? *Shit*. Fear snaked its way to the forefront of my thoughts again, pushing aside my hunger and arousal.

The guy in the suit had vanished from the bus station.

Of course he was gone, right? He wouldn't just wait outside for me. Or would he?

Nausea chased away every shred of calm I'd mustered, replacing it with terror. I'd merely needed to go use the ladies room, but now ... now I was afraid to leave Erick's side. What if the suited creep was hiding in there and somehow stole me from the bathroom?

This day was getting shittier by the hour. Actually, it was morning now. So the shit was just carrying over into the next day. What was I going to do when the sun came up and Erick had to go hide, or whatever vampires do during the day? There were only a few hours left before sunrise. I glanced out the front doors, sucking in a quick breath of relief at the still-black sky.

"What about when the sun comes up?"

He squeezed my hand and took the tickets from the clerk behind the thick glass window. "I can walk in the sun, *kjaere*."

"What does that mean?" I asked, ignoring his crazy answer about walking in the sun.

"It means I will not leave your side, even when the sun rises."

"No." I shook my head. "I mean that strange word you keep calling me."

"It means beautiful."

Beautiful. That was hard to believe. I was a mess. There was nothing beautiful about my bright blue Seafood Shack t-shirt, ratty jeans, and old gray tennis shoes. On top of everything, I smelled like something that might crawl out of a sewer.

"You are," he added, again acting like he could read my

thoughts. "You will feel better after a shower and a good meal."

As he led me back to the bench, my bladder reminded me of its desperate need to relieve itself. I gestured to the bathroom and he redirected our path. He stopped in front of the family single restroom, opened the door, and stuck his head inside before letting me go in.

The bathroom was dingy and smelled like pee and bleach. I turned on the light and gasped at my reflection in the mirror. My normally silky brown hair was stringy and hung limply in a sagging ponytail. All my makeup had melted away during the course of the day and my face was flushed pink. I didn't have anything in my bag—no powder, nothing. I'd left everything behind in my toxic apartment.

I closed the door and washed up the best I could, redoing my hair into a tighter ponytail. It helped alleviate the homeless vibe I gave off. Then I pulled off the blue Seafood Shack t-shirt and tossed it in the trashcan. The only clean shirts I had rescued from my closet were a black tank or a bright pink one. Black it was.

I unlocked the door and stepped out, colliding with Erick's chest. He wasn't taking the whole protecting thing lightly. Strangely, it made me feel safer instead of more worried. He wasn't warm, but he was a wall of muscle. I'd never had something or someone as strong as he was on my side before.

We walked to our idling bus along with a half-dozen others. As small as he'd made the town out to be, I was surprised by how many were headed the same way. As we shuffled down the aisle of the bus, I noted several nicely dressed businessmen, a red headed young woman, and a handsome man whose gaze lingered a little longer on my body than I appreciated.

I followed Erick to the back of the bus and settled on the bench next to him. No one gave me a second look after we sat, though several did cover their mouths. I couldn't blame them.

I was a hot mess. The smell alone should've cleared the bus, but no one spoke. Not even the bus driver.

"Why are you helping me?" It really didn't make sense. What did he want? Would he sell me? Drink from me himself? My emotions began clouding my brain and panic threatened to claw its way out of my stomach and drag the rest of me into the dark pit my fear had created. I was on a bus, alone with a vampire and who knew what other kinds of supernaturals.

What was I thinking?

"You are safe now. The Djinn can't jump into a moving target. Just try to get some rest. It's about a two-hour ride to Sanctuary." The calmness in his voice transferred to my terrified body and my muscles slowly began to relax.

One guy, the one who had stared, turned and glared straight at me. His eyes flashed a bright gold and I saw just a hint of fangs beneath his top lip. "You could at least wash what you plan to eat before subjecting the rest of us to such a stench." His voice was low, but I could understand every cruel syllable.

One second Erick was beside me and the next he wasn't. The asshole complaining about me coughed and I sucked in a quick breath.

Erick had him by the throat and growled something I

couldn't understand. It sounded like more of his native language. Whatever it was, it didn't drip with affection like it had when he'd called me beautiful. This time it sounded like a knife and he used it to cut the jerk down to size. The guy seemed to understand and apologized profusely.

The rest of the bus fell silent. No one moved to help the man or hinder Erick.

A flick of Erick's wrist sent the groveling male sailing toward me. I barely held in a shriek when he landed only inches from my feet.

"Apologize." Erick's voice was soft but carried over the rumble of the bus with absolute authority.

Every head bowed, and still no one spoke.

The guy below me prostrated himself on the floor of the bus. "Please forgive me. I spoke out of turn. I should've been more respectful."

An "I do" squeaked out of my throat as I pulled my legs up under my body away from the stranger's face. The terror in his yellow eyes surprised me, but I wasn't the one he feared.

Erick stood calmly in the center of the aisle. His blue eyes sharp as glass and his mouth open in a snarl, fangs bared menacingly. I couldn't help but shiver.

He caught my stare and everything about him changed back. His face softened. Fangs disappeared. Even his stance relaxed. He moved toward me as the other man backed away.

I wouldn't have to ask him to eat my ex. Kevin would bring it on himself if he ever came around.

Maybe my identity would be easier to hide in a small town. I hoped so. I needed a chance to rest. A chance to live without fear of being caught and dragged back into the hell I'd experienced with him—beaten until my spirit wilted at the very sound of his voice and sexually used every day before being chained or caged for the night. Dying was preferable to being caught by that sonofabitch.

Erick settled in next to me. He wrapped an arm around my shoulder and pulled me closer, surprising me with a soft kiss on the crown of my head.

"You are safe with me, *kjaere*. Always."

Maybe it was my exhaustion, but I nodded my head and leaned against his chest. An unfamiliar silence greeted my ear. No heartbeat. Still, I found comfort in his strength, and I believed him.

"My name is Bailey Ross," I mumbled as my eyes closed and I began to drift off. At least, that's what my name was right now.

"It's nice to meet you, Bailey Ross."

My name slipped from his lips slowly, like he was tasting a sweet treat. Maybe he'd be tasting me later ... I found myself not caring as the vibrations of the bus on the highway and his pleasant scent lulled me to sleep.

THE SCREECH OF BRAKES ROUSED ME FROM MY DEEP SLEEP and I opened my eyes to find Erick typing in a number on his cell. He put the small glass screen to his ear and then looked at me.

"I need you to remain calm and still."

Fear clenched in my belly again and I nodded.

"Rose, we're on the bus in. Darius is on the move

again." He pressed the screen again and slipped the phone into his pocket. "Garrett," he pointed at the man with the yellow eyes, "sit next to her and hold tight. I'll take care of the Djinn."

"B-but." My brain raced, trying to understand but I was still groggy. Darius was back? We were in the middle of a highway. He asked the man who'd been mean to me to watch over me?

"Calm and still." Erick repeated and held my face for a moment with his free hand. I met his gaze again, trying to scrape up enough courage not to start bawling like an infant. Nothing I did could hide the tremor in my lip, though.

"You are safe, Bailey, but whatever happens while I'm gone, do not let go of Garrett."

His claim reassured me and terrified me at the same time, but then he leaned down and pressed a kiss to my dry, trembling lips. It was soft and reminded me of the kindness I heard in his voice. I nodded against his mouth. He pulled back swiftly and exited the bus before I could speak. At least he'd confirmed he was interested in more than just drinking my blood.

Garrett moved nearly as fast, replacing Erick by my side and wrapping an arm around one of mine. His breathing was heavy and I could hear a rumbling growl coming from his chest. He was tense, but in control.

"I'm sorry about before. I can't believe I missed that tattoo when he got on the bus. I shouldn't have opened my mouth and said what I did about you. It's been a rough couple of days."

"Join the club. Mine went from shitty to nuclear," I

replied, a heavy sigh slipping from my chest. Two men were hunting me and both would do horrible things if they caught me.

"I'm sorry." He tightened his hold on me. "No one should have to suffer the way you have. I'm truly sorry."

Again with the mind reading. Could they all smell pheromones the way Erick had mentioned?

"Nope, I can actually read your mind."

I tried to jerk away, but he tightened his grip. "If Darius is here, he can't snatch you away if I'm hanging on to you. Djinn can only jump with one extra body in tow."

Good to know.

"What are you?" I stopped trying to pull away and glanced out the window. Morning sunlight began to warm the blue skies, from a dark navy to a soft lavender, but Erick said he could walk in the sun. He'd said he wouldn't leave me.

"Lycan," Garrett answered.

"A werewolf." They were the ones who'd been caught on video first. The very first riot happened after a half-dozen werewolves tore up downtown Los Angeles in 2046.

"We prefer to be called Lycan."

A thud outside rattled my nerves. I held my breath and closed my eyes.

Garrett's grip on my arm tightened more and a terrifying growl ripped from his throat.

"You'll pay for helping the Protector," a silky male voice spoke from the middle of the bus. "She was mine first. He stole her from me."

Oh, shit. It was creepy-suit-guy ... Erick had called him Darius. Where was Erick? I wanted him. He calmed me.

I dug my fingers into Garrett's jacket and hung on, praying he'd spoken the truth about Djinn not being able to jump with more than one passenger.

"Possession is nine-tenths of the law, asshole." Garrett snarled and pulled me into his lap. I didn't object and wrapped my arms around his neck.

Darius charged and Garrett ducked to the floor with me stuck to his chest like a baby in a sling.

A loud snarl from the doorway preceded Erick's voice. "Get out."

The bus driver and all the other passengers fled, except one.

A female voice began chanting something in Latin and Darius screamed in pain before teleporting away. Erick left the bus again and Garrett moved me back to the seat, still keeping a heavy hand attached to my arm. He peered out the window and then over at the redheaded female near the front.

Erick reappeared at the door. "Thank you for your assistance, Meredith." He bowed his head.

"I'm just glad I was here," she said.

The bus driver climbed up and stopped next to Erick. "Is it safe to start again? I nearly lost it when I saw that man just standing in the middle of the highway. Then that witch started jabbering back there."

"There was no man. You saw a deer cross the road and stopped the bus to avoid killing it. There was no witch, no fight. This run was as uneventful as your last." Erick's voice was low, but I could hear every word.

The driver had seen and heard everything—people

screaming, growling, showing fangs. He couldn't possibly think the man would just forget.

"Yeah, this is a problem area for deer crossing." The driver nodded his head and returned to his seat, ready to continue the run.

"What the hell?" I whispered.

"Don't ask," Garrett answered.

"He influenced him somehow. How?" My mouth just kept moving of its own accord. "Why doesn't anyone know they can do that?"

"Hush," Garrett hissed.

I snapped my mouth shut, but my brain kept turning. Mind control?

The bus rumbled to life and Erick made his way down the aisle. "Thank you for protecting Bailey."

"I am at your service. I'm visiting my brother, Travis, but if you need me for anything, I'll be there. I hope we can look past my previous crudeness."

"You are forgiven. No debt is owed."

Garrett stood and moved past Erick, leaving the bench next to me empty.

Sitting next to Garrett had been like sitting in the center of an asphalt road at noon in the Vegas desert. He put off heat like a hot oven. In this Texas heat, Erick's cool skin was a beautiful thing. I leaned against him as he settled on the seat next to me.

He'd protected me. Garrett had, too. I was safe with these men. At least for now. It was a strange feeling to be indebted to men, but almost anything was better than Kevin or a psychopathic Djinn bent on torture. The news media didn't spare any gory details when it came to reporting about the most dangerous Other known to exist.

Erick's mind control ability had me concerned, but he hadn't given me any reason not to trust him. Garrett's mind reading had me a little unnerved as well. Then there was the little, redheaded witch halfway up the aisle who'd somehow forced Darius to leave.

I was somewhat aware of the supernatural powers that Others possessed, but I'd never heard of vampires influencing memories or Lycans reading minds. This type of information, if known at all, was not public. The news that *was* reported talked about vampires and werewolves like they were animals. Sometimes they even mentioned cleaning out a coven of witches.

Cleaning? Like they were a dirty closet that needed to be gone through and the trash tossed out. Weren't they just people? She sure looked like an average person I might've served at the Seafood Shack.

The young woman leaned out of the seat and glanced at me as if she knew I was contemplating her existence. Her hazel eyes met my gaze and she smiled and leaned back. Darius had called Erick a Protector. I'd never heard that term used in school. Supernatural Studies had been a required class in high school since the riots. It gave a broad overview of all known species, their weaknesses and their strengths.

Apparently not all the strengths were known. Probably not all their weaknesses, either. I sat with a vampire while the early rays of morning light caressed the bare skin of his arm. No smoldering. No burning. He even looked like he had a pretty good tan.

My brain jumped back to the mind control. Garrett told me to be quiet. And it would make sense that vampires would want to keep that sort of thing a secret. I couldn't even imagine what the governments might try to force on them.

As of right now, they were lucky to be alive anywhere outside of the states of the Texas Republic. In a lot of places, it was legal to shoot a vampire on sight or any Other, for that matter. They weren't even arrested. Just killed ... like vermin.

Vampires weren't singled out, though. In the other republics, it was legal to shoot and kill any supernatural being without cause or provocation. Old billboards along highways touted their slogans every few miles

Humans have rights. Others don't.

Some extremists took those words to heart, but the average person didn't go around shooting anyone. The police, on the other hand, were a different matter. I'd seen more than one Other executed on sight by a police officer.

"Your mind is spinning, *kjaere*. What's bothering you?"

"If you can influence a human the way you did the bus driver, why ... why don't you do that to more people to make it easier for you to live?"

He sighed and pulled me tighter to his chest. "Is it our place to tell everyone what to think? How to feel?"

"No, I suppose not."

"There are vampires that misuse the ability, but the majority use it sparingly and always have. Thus, the general public and governments are unaware."

I nodded. "I won't say anything. But, did it hurt the bus driver?"

"If used numerous times on the same human, their brain can suffer. But a mental push now and then does no permanent damage."

"Can a person be uninfluenced?"

"Yes."

"Will Darius come after me again?"

"Yes."

Damn. No hesitation in that answer.

"But, you said he couldn't come to Sanctuary."

"He probably will not," Erick answered. "Not that he couldn't."

Okay, fear was creeping back in again. That Djinn had been pissed and Erick had already said they had a history. I didn't need more anguish in my life. Kevin brought me enough as it was.

"What am I supposed to do with that? I've already got one psycho ex. I don't need a Djinn hunting me to the ends of the earth, too. How do we get rid of him?"

Crap. Crap. Crap. I hadn't meant to mention Kevin. Way to go, Bailey. Pile on the baggage. Push away the only man who'd been genuinely nice to you in years.

Every friendship I'd ever tried to have in the past had been ruined by Kevin. History was doomed to repeat itself. Eventually he would find me. Even in a small, out-of-the-way town.

"You were running from a human? An ex?"

I swallowed a sob. "I don't want to talk about it. I just need a place to take a shower and maybe eat a hot meal. I'll be out of your hair ASAP. I promise."

"You don't have to talk about it, *kjaere*."

Tears ran down my cheeks. His tenderness tore at the

walls I'd built around my heart. Why did he care? No one had truly cared for me in years. Of course, I hadn't slowed down long enough to let anyone get close, either.

"But, you should reconsider staying in Sanctuary a while. You will not be 'in my hair' as you put it." A gentle chuckle rumbled in his chest. "I will watch over you for as long as you need. Don't worry about your ex or Darius. Both would be fools to step a single foot into Sanctuary."

"He's right, you know," the redhead called out from several rows up. "Darius might come to Sanctuary, but he'd be a fool to stay for more than a minute or two. The Sentinel would make sure of that."

I shifted and looked up into Erick's tranquil blue eyes. "What is the Sentinel?"

"Rose is the Sentinel."

CHAPTER 3

"I thought you said Rose owned the café." Sentinel sounded like some kind of warrior or guard. Why was the owner of a small-town café the one who would make sure the Djinn wouldn't stick around?

"She does." He smiled down at me and squeezed my shoulder.

"Why did they call you a Protector? Like it's an official title?"

"It *is* an official title. There are only four of us and we help protect the town."

"From Djinn?"

"From anyone or anything that would threaten it."

I lay my head on his shoulder and yawned, exhaustion and lack of sleep catching up to me. Erick moved his hand from my shoulder to the curve of my waist and pulled me even closer to his hard body. The touch was sensual and comforting, reassuring me it was okay to rest.

My mind wouldn't slow down enough to let me slip

away, though. Everything I'd seen today kept swirling around, prompting more questions, more fears, anxiety about Kevin, anxiety about Darius. Even a little anxiety about Erick's expectations of me. What did he want from me? There weren't many good Samaritans left in the world. At least not in the places I'd visited.

People these days were afraid if they held out a hand, it'd get bitten off. And most of the time, it did.

۞

"BAILEY."

His voice was dark and velvety. The dream I was having put both of us in a giant bed with satin sheets and no worries in the world. The things he was doing to me would even put the slutty bartender at the Seafood Shack to shame. The last thing I wanted to do was come out of my euphoric dreamland.

"Bailey. We're here."

Here? Where?

I popped my eyes open and my cheeks burned. My head was in his lap. *Holy shit!* I pushed myself up, off his muscular thighs, and just sat for a moment, open-mouthed. Words wouldn't form. I didn't know what to say. No wonder I'd been having naughty dreams.

"I'm glad you finally got a little rest."

I snapped my jaw shut. "Um, yeah. I ..."

Rest? I'm not sure what I'd gotten could be called rest. My heart raced and my core clenched, suddenly very aware of his maleness. The handsome curve of his jaw. The way the tip of his tongue ran across the seam of his lips. The mischievous sparkle in his dreamy, blue eyes.

Wait! Lips. He'd licked his lips and now he smiled at me. He knew what I was thinking. Or feeling. Or something. Hadn't he said he could smell human pheromones? Embarrassment darkened my cheeks further. They had to be beet red by now.

Could he sense my attraction to him? How could he not? My own body had turned against me. I didn't need this—a third guy to juggle through this mess, even if he was hot and acting as my personal bodyguard.

A chuckle from halfway up the bus distracted me and I caught a smirk from Garrett before he turned and walked to the front. Damn it. The wolf could probably smell my traitorous pheromones, too. Wait. No. He could hear every single naughty thought. How could I live surrounded by these dangerous, intimidating men who could sense everything I thought and felt?

When I looked back at Erick, he'd narrowed his eyes and stared with an intensity that made me shiver. Jealousy? A whimper slipped from my throat without my permission and I covered my mouth—as if that would help cover the sound. He could probably hear things a half-block away. Vampires were supposed to have extraordinary hearing.

His demeanor softened again as he gestured toward the front of the bus. "Would you prefer to meet Rose now and get some breakfast or get cleaned up first?"

I stood and walked down the aisle of the now empty bus. Everyone else had disembarked. "I'm starving, but I think it would be better for everyone if I took a shower first." My stomach rumbled embarrassingly at the mention of food, but my desire not to smell like a sewer rat was stronger.

The sun still hung low in the Texas sky. But, I had no idea what time it was, maybe eight-ish. I stepped down from the bus onto a concrete sidewalk. I glanced across the street, taking in the small-town charm. Worn brick and battered, wooden signs gave an antique look to the town. Rose's Café lay just a few buildings to my right. Flanking the café was the sheriff's and fire marshal's office. They appeared to share the small space. And I didn't see a bay for a fire engine.

Strange.

I walked a few steps away from the bus and continued to examine my surroundings. It was quiet. A few people were making their way along the sidewalks toward the café, along with all the other passengers from the bus.

I didn't see any other restaurants in the circle. There was a clothing boutique, a library, a hardware store, a pawn shop, and a farmers' market.

Then I stopped and swallowed.

Directly across from the café was a castle—albeit a modernized version, but a castle nonetheless. Square with rounded towers on each of its four corners. Turrets, parapets, and archery slits abounded. The only things missing were a moat and drawbridge. I knew it was a castle because when I'd holed up in a barn in Tennessee, I'd found boxes of contraband books hidden in the cellar.

Who could have imagined there would be a castle in some little town in West Texas?

"It's nice, isn't it?" Erick's voice was closer than I expected.

"It's a castle." That came out sounding stupid, but he just nodded.

"Yes, the brothers insisted. They are a bit set in their ways. The Castle shelters The House of Lamidae and is very private. Only guests willing to keep their secrets are allowed to remember ever seeing it."

"So you influence memories, like you did with the bus driver?"

"When necessary." He placed his hand on the small of my back and guided me toward one of the many streets leading away from the circle. Warmth spread through my body from the point of his touch. "My apartment is this way."

We walked past the café and I couldn't help but peek inside the large glass windows. It looked like any other café—bright and busy. Nothing about it seemed supernatural.

I took one more look around before we turned the corner.

In the center of the town circle was a grassy field with a raised stone platform in the middle—like a stage of sorts. There were markings on the side of the stone, but nothing I could read.

Weird.

"So the House of Lamidae ... or should I call it the Castle? What is it? If I am allowed to ask, that is. It sounds like a church or a cult." Or both...

He chuckled. "It's a fetish club."

I coughed, stopped, and turned to meet his gaze. "Like, a *sex* club?" I squeaked. "Like for spanking and whips and stuff?"

"It depends on the partners, but yes." He winked. "There are plenty of spankings, whips, and *other* stuff."

I was terrified and curious at the same time. Was it just for Others or did they let humans in, too? Also, what had he meant by *other* stuff? My gut said there was a lot more to the House of Lamidae than he was letting on. Who would build a whole castle just to be a sex club? A castle was meant to protect something. At least that's what those old history books had said.

"I had hoped you would stay with me, but the Blackmoor brothers have plenty of spare rooms. They don't mind housing the occasional guest." He pushed me into a slow walk again. "It's your choice, *kjaere*."

The tone of his voice sent delicious shivers down my spine. There was a first time for everything, but I was nowhere near ready to see the inside of a fetish club. Though, if he asked, I had a feeling I would follow him anywhere. I just hoped he'd give me time. A lot of time.

We turned another corner and came to a stop in front of a stone and red brick townhome. A small stairway with eight steps led to the front door. To the left, a bay window jutted out, its curve reaching to the second floor. The architecture was beautiful and familiar—similar in style to the brownstone apartments I'd cleaned in New York. I was able to hide in that big city for almost a year before Kevin had found me.

Erick climbed the stairs ahead of me and opened the door. I walked in and stopped in the middle of his foyer, fearful of tracking in the dirt and stench I knew clung to me.

His place was immaculate. White carpet, accented by

black slate tile beneath my feet in the entry and again across the apartment in the kitchen. Black and white leather furniture was perfectly arranged through the living room. A few picture frames had been placed on the mantle above the brick fireplace. A grand staircase with a beautifully ornate wooden handrail lay to my right, leading to the second floor.

He walked past me and turned on a lamp next to one of the large, white couches. "Come, the shower is in the bedroom upstairs."

His bedroom? Didn't he have a nice hall bathroom somewhere? I moved across the room toward him, but detoured into the kitchen. Spotless. Why wouldn't it be? He was a vampire. No need to cook.

"Bailey."

I jumped, startled from my thoughts.

He leaned against the doorway between the living room and the kitchen.

"I didn't touch anything." The words fell out of my mouth before I could think. He liked things clean and I was the furthest thing from that right now.

"I don't mind you looking around." His voice was calming, reassuring me he wasn't angry over my little side-step into his kitchen."

"You have a beautiful home," I offered.

"Not nearly as beautiful as the woman standing in the center of it."

Heat rose in my cheeks. He had an uncanny way of making that happen. And there he went, complimenting me when I resembled a trampled, worn-out, dishrag. I might actually feel sexy and beautiful if he would just let me take a shower. Preferably not the shower in his bedroom. Of course, all I had to change into was a bright, neon pink tank top and some yoga shorts. Yeah, that would make a great impression on the townspeople.

He moved forward from the door jamb with the grace of a lethal predator. My breath caught in my chest. He reached up and caressed the side of my cheek as he leaned forward and pressed his lips gently over mine. They were so soft and tender, completely taking me by surprise. He smelled good and tasted even better—sweet with just a trace of the peppermint I'd smelled earlier.

I ran my tongue along the seam of his mouth and he met my tease with pure hunger. He pressed harder against my mouth and plunged his tongue inside, tasting every corner and nipping gently at my bottom lip.

Trembling against him, I moaned into his mouth. My arms moved to encircle his neck and his slipped around my waist, pressing my belly more firmly against his hard cock. I ground my hips against it before my brain registered what I was doing. He growled into my mouth and suddenly I remembered he wasn't just a man.

Panic set in. He was a vampire.

But he *was* also a man.

He smelled like a man. Felt like a man. He kissed better than any man who'd ever kissed me before. Not that there had been many.

He pulled away suddenly. I met his intense stare and my bottom lip trembled. I knew he could sense my fear, but I really wished his face was a little easier to read.

"I'm sorry. I didn't mean to frighten you." He gestured past him, back across the living area and up the stairs.

"I'm not scared of you, I just ..."

"It is all right to be frightened, *kjaere*. It's a natural preservation instinct. It's been a long day and I shouldn't have pushed. Please forgive me."

I nodded.

I did forgive him.

Frightened as I was, I still trusted him to keep me safe. Plus, the kiss hadn't been bad. In fact, it'd been quite the opposite and a spark ran through my body as I remembered the feel of his lips on mine.

He smiled and slipped his hand down to the small of my back, pushing me gently toward the stairway. He knew I was aroused.

I couldn't help the stupid smile that tugged at the corners of my mouth either. My brain needed to have a chat with my hormones, 'cause my body definitely favored exploring more than just Erick's mouth.

We climbed the stairs and I waited at the top, not sure which door to head toward. He stepped past and opened the double doors directly in front of us, displaying a beautiful room with a high, coffered ceiling.

The white carpets continued and I swallowed as my eyes fell on an ornately carved, king-sized, mahogany, four-poster bed. It was draped in a black crushed velvet comforter and had at least a half-dozen pillows stacked against the headboard. It looked so terribly comfortable and inviting.

The rest of the room was decorated sparsely, but the furniture matched the bed. Dark mahogany that had been polished until it shined with a mirror-like reflection.

I turned toward a noise that came from across the

room. He'd opened another door and gestured me to enter. I stepped past him and into the palatial bathroom. The gorgeous, black slate tile reappeared, accented by natural stone and white marble on the walls. A whirlpool tub the size of my old apartment bathroom was centered in the middle. A large shower with glass walls was positioned in the far corner. There was one set of sinks to my left and another diagonally across from me. The toilet was most likely hidden behind the closed single door to my right.

There was a set of double doors beyond the sinks to the left. I drooled at the thought of having a closet big enough to need such a grand opening.

"It's like a dream."

A chuckle rolled from his chest. "That's what my sister says, too. She helped design the master suite and bathroom."

"I've never seen anything so beautiful. I hate to get it dirty."

"Don't worry about it. I have a cleaning service that comes twice a week. They make sure everything stays in perfect order so I don't have to."

"Must be nice."

He shrugged. "It's not a big deal. She just snaps her fingers and the job is done. Do you need help getting undressed?"

I whirled to face him and opened my mouth to snap, but the broad smile and twinkle in his eye melted my offense instantly. "I think I can manage, thank you," I drawled out and rolled my eyes.

"Just wanted to make sure," he answered. "I'll take your

clothes and toss them, I don't think they are worth trying to salvage."

"I don't have any other clothes!"

His grin widened. "*Kjaere*, I'm going to get you something new. Calliope will have something in her shop around the corner."

"I can't ... I ..." Didn't he understand I had nothing? I couldn't buy anything. Being indebted to a man was not smart. But, he'd already saved my life on a couple of occasions.

Still, I had no intention of stripping down in front of him and handing over my clothes.

He shook his head. "It's not just me. Calliope will insist when she meets you, anyway."

"Is she ... a vampire?"

"No, she's a siren and our local stylist." He chuckled. "She makes all the clothes for everyone in the town. It helps keep her busy and out of trouble. Plus, she makes *really* nice clothes."

"Out of trouble?" I asked, studying the clothes he wore. I didn't notice anything special about them. They fit well and surprisingly still smelled nice, even though he'd been sitting next to me most of the evening. "And what's a siren?"

He shrugged his shoulders and stepped back to the door. "She's a little obsessive sometimes. It can become destructive. When Rose alighted on the idea of a clothing shop, Calliope fell in love with it."

An obsessive-destructive siren that made clothes for a whole town? What wormhole had I fallen into? I'd never heard of a siren. In school we learned about vampires, werewolves, witches, and Djinn. That about covered it.

"What does a siren do? Is she dangerous?"

"She can be." He winked. "Don't worry about her. Just holler if you need me. There are fresh towels on the edge of the bathtub and robes just inside the closet." With one more of his heart-melting smiles, he closed the bathroom door and left me alone.

I turned and glanced first at the shower and then the spa tub. "I might need a shower *and* a bath." My voice echoed around the bathroom and I grinned. Might as well take advantage while I'm here. Who knows how long before I have to run again?

Kicking off my tennis shoes, I sat on the edge of the tub and peeled off my grimy socks. The smell was putrid. How had he managed to stand being near me? My shoes were ruined, too.

I pulled off everything and piled it in the corner with my hobo-style purse then tiptoed across the bathroom to the shower. Once the door closed behind me, I turned on the water and squealed when it shot out, not only from the rainwater showerhead above me, but from spigots in the wall as well. It was like being attacked by garden sprayers.

"Are you okay?" Erick's voice rumbled from just outside the shower.

"Holy shit!" I scrambled to cover myself, but no amount of finagling would hide all of my naked body. I finally settled for crossing my arms over both of the girls. "What are you doing in here? Get out!"

"I'm sorry." He backed away quickly. "I heard you scream and thought you'd slipped."

"I'm fine. Please leave."

He stooped and grabbed up my pile of dirty clothes before disappearing from the bathroom. I almost hollered when I realized he'd taken my purse too, but he didn't need anything I had. From the looks of this townhome, he had more money than he could ever spend. The purse was nothing special. He could get rid of all my stuff as long as he replaced it with something else. But if he thought I would walk around naked and be his slave, he could just keep dreaming. It didn't matter how attracted to him I was.

I wouldn't be anyone's slave ever again.

⚜

AFTER SHAMPOOING MY HAIR TWICE AND USING CRAZY amounts of soap and shower gel, I finally felt—and smelled—clean again. My body was still tense from the stress of the previous day. Hell, I'd probably be tense for the next few weeks. I shut off the water and stepped out of the shower onto a fluffy, white rug.

The beautiful tub lay glistening in the middle of the bathroom. Sunlight from a skylight bathed the tub in a warm light. It couldn't hurt ... right? I couldn't even remember the last time I'd taken a bath.

Turning the handle, I started the hot water and glanced around for something to add. Nothing was in sight, but after perusing through the cabinets, I stumbled on several types of bath salts and bubble bath—probably his sister's stash. Women knew the essentials for a good bath.

I poured in a healthy handful of the salts and several

capfuls of the vanilla sugar bubble bath. The steam from the hot water filled the space with the scent of vanilla. It was perfect.

Without a care in my mind, I stepped into tub and sank down to the bottom, allowing the scalding hot water to cover me inch by savory inch. Tension flowed from my muscles and even my anxiety about being in a strange vampire's house floated away on the scented steam. I could die a happy, clean woman in this bathtub.

"Bailey?" Erick's velvety voice pulled me from my state of bliss.

"Yes?"

"I brought you some things. May I enter?"

"I'm ..." I looked down. The bubbles completely covered my body. It's not like he would yank me out of the bathtub and eat me for breakfast. At least I didn't think he would. "Sure," I whispered.

The door creaked and he stepped inside carrying an overflowing plastic drugstore bag. "I thought you might need the basics." He paused and stared at the floor. "Well, Calliope thought it and gave me a list. I hope these are acceptable." He proceeded to pull out one toiletry product after another—deodorant, feminine pads, toothbrush, toothpaste, hair brush, comb, nail set, shaving cream, and a razor.

Oh I needed that. My legs felt like they were covered with the bristles from a sink scrubber. It'd been over a week since my last razor had officially gone dull.

He glanced at me and raised a quizzical eyebrow. Then held up the can of shaving cream and razor.

"Yes, please."

A few steps put him beside the tub. He knelt down and handed me the desired items. Then he just sat there, staring. His eyes darkened with sexual hunger that even a blind woman could have sensed.

My heart sped up in my chest and I dropped the can of shaving cream. He caught it before it hit the water and I gasped. I'd seen him move fast several times already, but it still surprised me.

"Let me help you," he said, dipping his other arm into the bathwater and catching one of my ankles and pulling it up.

I squeaked a little, but couldn't find the words to protest after he began kneading my sore calves with his strong fingers. He squirted a little gel onto my left leg and began smoothing the foaming cream over my skin. Each time he ventured past my knee, I held my breath. His fingers teased my skin until he'd coated my entire leg from ankle up to mid-thigh.

Heat curled in my belly and I knew my traitorous pheromones were screaming loudly and clearly. I was aroused. And the only thing between his fingers and my throbbing pussy was a few inches of water and bath bubbles.

He held out his lathered hand for the razor and I placed it in his palm. Within minutes he'd finished my entire leg. He pressed a soft kiss to my now satiny smooth knee.

I peered down my leg and saw a tiny drop of red forming at my ankle. Pretty good for a guy. I usually nicked myself at least four or five times on each leg.

When I looked back up, his nostrils flared and a ring of red had formed around his ocean blue irises.

I yanked my foot backward, but he held it in place like it was locked in a vice.

"Trust me, *kjaere*."

"No! Don't influence me. I refuse to be a slave again." I struggled again, nearly sloshing water over the side, but I might as well have been kicking at a two-ton elephant.

"You will never be a slave again, Bailey. I promise you." He raised my ankle to his lips and I trembled.

This was it. He would drain me right here and now. All because of one drop of blood. After everything he'd done to protect me. Maybe Garrett had been right when he'd callously griped at Erick about washing what he planned to eat. Maybe that'd been his plan the whole time.

He kissed the cut and then I felt his tongue sweep across my skin. Something like a cat's purr rumbled in his chest as he licked it once more before releasing my foot from his hold.

That was it?

"There. Was that so bad? I merely sealed your cut."

"Bad? No, but I thought ..."

He reached out and caught my chin gently in his palm. "My eyes will change no matter what. It's instinctual. But it doesn't mean I've lost control. I will never bite you unless I'm invited to do so."

There was so much about these people, these Others, that humans didn't know. At least the average human didn't. I'd learned more in the span of one night than I'd ever learned in school.

"Let's do your other leg, yes?"

I nodded and his hand slipped from my chin and back into the water. My breath hitched, waiting for him to touch other parts of me, but he didn't. He caught my other leg and lifted it just high enough to lather with shaving cream, but not enough to expose me. The bubbles were still in full force.

Attraction simmered between us, but I just couldn't go there. Not yet, anyway.

I was able to relax a little. His hands were gentle, but firm. He worked his hands up and down my other leg until it was completely covered and then picked up the razor again. A few minutes later he had finished without so much as one little knick.

I rubbed my legs together under the water, enjoying the silky sensation. Nothing like smooth legs to make a girl feel good.

"Thank you." I was surprised how easily the words came out. "I ..." What should I say? I didn't know what to tell him and what to keep back.

"You're welcome," he answered, flashing me a soft grin. "Why don't you finish here, then try on some of the things Calliope sent over? Rose is expecting us soon." He stood and took a few steps toward the sink behind him. He patted a stack of clothes on the counter. "I'll be just outside if you need me."

He slipped out of the bathroom, closing the door behind him.

I moved to the edge of the tub and shaved carefully between my legs, thankful to have a nice razor that wouldn't scrape and scratch my tender bits. It was amazing to feel smooth all over again. Rinsing the razor, I pushed the lever to drain the tub, grabbed the plush, white towel to my left, and stood. Cool air made me shiver and I wrapped the towel around my body, tucking the end between my breasts.

When I stepped out onto the black tile floor, I was surprised. Heated floors. How amazing was that? Even in a Texas summer, it was nice not to get chilled in the bathroom. The floor was perfectly warm and the air was a nice balmy temperature.

I pulled the big towel loose and squeezed as much water from my hair as I could, then wove it into a loose braid and knotted it on itself. It would hold for a while. At least until it was halfway dry.

A pretty, purple lace bra and panty set lay across a pair of dark jeans and a sparkly silver, short-sleeved tee. The bra looked huge, compared to my old one. Couldn't the man have read the tags in my old one before just taking a wild guess? Not every woman on the planet had jugs like Darlene the bartender.

Oh, well. Beggars couldn't be choosers. I didn't have a choice really. My girls were too big to go au natural. I'd have to make do until it could be swapped out for something closer to my size.

As I snapped it in place, the strangest sensation tickled my skin. The fabric was shrinking, conforming to my body. The cups were shrinking, too, clinging and changing, pushing my breasts up just the right amount. I wouldn't have been able to find a more perfect fit.

Snatching the panties, I pulled them on. They were so loose, the elastic in the waist barely held them over my hips. It only lasted a second. They too shrunk and formed into cute low-waisted hipsters, exactly my favorite style.

I squealed with delight. There were no sizes on the clothes, because the clothes changed to fit me— *Unbelievable!*

The jeans were next. They were formless and loose for about two seconds before they lengthened to my height and conformed to my body as if they'd been cut just for me. I couldn't help but turn and admire my ass in the mirror. The pants were nicer than anything I'd ever been able to afford. The underwear, too. Usually I made do with stuff off the clearance rack at the cheap general stores.

After admiring my reflection one last time, I pulled on the silver metallic tee and watched in fascination as it, too, changed and conformed into something that fit perfectly and highlighted the lovely bit of cleavage the magickal bra had produced.

The woman looking back at me was someone I didn't recognize. She was clean and well dressed. Maybe even pretty enough to be called beautiful.

Who was I kidding? Being pretty had never helped me in life. It'd only gotten me trapped and harassed by men. Why would it be any different this time around?

Erick Thorson was still a man. And men liked to have their needs fulfilled. I wouldn't fool myself into thinking he just wanted to help me out of the goodness of his cold, dead, vampire heart. All men wanted something. My short years on this earth had taught me that was a constant.

Single women in this day and age were hunted like big game. Women my age were targets for slavers, whorehouses, labor camps, baby factories. The cruelty of the world knew no bounds.

I could only dream of a world I'd read about in secret – a world where freedom and choice were important and protected. Where men and women were equal and found happiness together. When the truth of the Others came to light in 2046, those things disappeared. The government taught women that they had to do what the men in their life dictated—no exceptions. Even Texas, with it's more liberal views, still made sure women knew their place. But even the men were only free if they followed the letter of the law. Anyone who deviated from the expectations was considered an outlaw and was hunted, imprisoned or worse.

The vast majority of the female population was married off early in life, usually by age seventeen or eighteen. I'd escaped that particular fate because I was an orphan. Unfortunately, that meant I was tossed out on my ass when I turned eighteen. Because I had no family to speak for me and protect me, I was considered part of the lowest class. Even though I waited tables at restaurants, most people assumed I whored as well.

I didn't, but I'd come close several times. Hunger could make you consider just about anything. Hunger and fear had driven me to take a chance with Kevin and he'd almost killed me. Now I was in another man's house, starving and afraid.

CHAPTER 4

I took a deep breath and opened the bathroom door. My heart leapt into my throat. There he was, standing only a few steps away. His hands were clasped behind his back.

"Thank you for the clothes." My breathing quickened and I bit my bottom lip.

"They look perfect on you." His gaze locked with mine and a smile slowly curved his lips. "I'd like to take them all off again, but Rose is waiting for us."

That's good. I wasn't ready for that just yet.

I rubbed my damp palms across my thighs and gulped. Heat burned my cheeks and I looked away. It didn't matter. He knew what he did to me. My heart raced and liquid pooled between my legs again. His extra senses would never miss either of those things.

"*Kjaere*, tell me you aren't interested and I won't pursue a relationship with you."

A relationship?

Meaning, I wasn't just a pretty meal in his eyes? Could I have a relationship, intimate or otherwise, with a vampire? Who did that? Why did he want me?

My survival instincts said he wasn't the only unattached male in the town who might choose to pursue me. Better him than someone worse, but that wasn't a reason to lead him on. He deserved better than to be used. He'd been a gentleman so far ... and he was kind. Plus, telling him I wasn't interested in him sexually would be an outright lie. I was a woman, and he'd awakened something that I thought had long ago been beaten out of me.

Desire.

"I ..." I opened my mouth but choked on my words. Rubbing my sweaty palms on my pants again, I looked up into his perfectly blue eyes and relaxed. There were no cages in Erick's house. That I could see. No chains on the walls. He didn't even have bars over the windows.

He wasn't Kevin.

Even with all my doubts, something deep down said it was okay to give it a shot. "I want to try," slipped from between my lips. "Trust has cost me a lot in the past, though. I'm afraid."

"I'm glad you are giving me a chance." Erick stepped closer, each movement calculated and confident. He reached out and touched my cheek, then followed the line of my face down until he cupped my chin. His fingertips brushed over my ears and slipped into the wet hair at the base of my neck.

A shiver flitted across the surface of my skin. Energy charged between his hand and my cheek. Even though my first instinct was to pull away, I somehow found the courage to look up and meet his gaze instead.

"Bailey. I've never brought a human to Sanctuary before. I've never interfered on behalf of a human to save their life before. Darius and I have been at each other's throats for longer than I can remember. But you ... there's something about you."

He rubbed my cheek with his thumb and I leaned into the caress. I craved the affection he offered. He wasn't a drunk customer feeling me up or catcalling to me from across the room.

Erick said he meant me no harm. My ex had said the same thing. He said he would protect me from the monsters. He said he loved me.

I'd been young and foolish, maybe in love. Looking back, it was hard to remember a time when Kevin was kind. After our first couple of weeks together, things changed radically. One day I woke up in our bed with cuffs on my wrists and ankles and a collar around my neck. From that point, he never showed me affection again. I was a prisoner, and I didn't see the outside of his apartment again until I managed to escape.

"I want this." The words surprised me, but they were the truth. I *did* want this. And I wanted him ... completely and totally, but I needed to make sure we took things slowly.

He pulled me close, tucking me against his chest and wrapping his other arm around my waist in an embrace. Firm, but gentle. He kissed the top of my head and then released me.

I missed his touch immediately. No one had kissed me

like that since my parents. Not one of my foster parents had ever hugged me, and my high school boyfriends had only wanted to get in my pants. I was a castoff, like so many others in the masses of working class citizens.

"You have my protection, Bailey. Beyond anything that may or may not happen between us, you are safe in this town. Sanctuary can be your home if you choose."

No pressure. No guilt. Just a haven from all my worries and the nightmares that plagued me ... at least for a while, but nothing was forever. Eventually I would have to leave Sanctuary and Erick, too. But for now, his promise allowed me to relax ... just a little.

"Calliope sent a few pairs of shoes and two bags." He gestured toward the bed.

A pair of white ballerina flats, black tennis shoes, and some brown cowboy boots sat on the floor in a neatly arranged row. On the black comforter of his bed lay a white, crocheted hobo bag and a black leather cross-body purse. They were nicer than anything I'd ever owned.

"She said she had others to choose from if you don't like these."

Tears threatened to spill from my eyes. He was a perfect stranger and considered to be a dangerous Other. And he'd been kinder to me than any human being I'd come in contact with since my parents died.

"Why?" I choked out, wiping my cheeks. "I'm a nobody to you. Why are you helping me? I won't be a whore." It slipped out. My anxiety built. Maybe this was all for show. Maybe he just planned to use me like every other man I'd met in the last five years.

"Bailey," he growled. "Am I dressing you like a whore?"

"No, but ... nobody is this nice to someone without wanting something in return."

"You're right."

There it was. He *did* want something. I knew it was all too good to be true.

"I want a chance to win your affections, but honestly, everything else is just to help you find a place to be safe. If you don't want to stay with me, I'll find you an apartment of your own. If you don't want to see me, I'll find someone else to show you around town."

Affections? Who says that? It sounded like something out of one of those old historical novels I'd found, but then ... he could be very old. My mind ran through everything he'd just said. He sounded so sincere and I wanted to believe him.

I knew in my heart he meant me no harm. I trusted him when he said he was interested in me, though after seeing me the way I'd been before I showered ... it still baffled me. Maybe vampires didn't smell unless they wanted to.

Stranger still, I wanted to be with him. I wanted to stay near him. I wouldn't feel safe alone in an apartment with both a Djinn and Kevin hunting for me.

"I'm indebted to you already for helping me. Now the clothes and everything you've bought. I'll pay you back. It'll take me a little while, but I will."

He smiled and rubbed his hands up and down my arms. "You cannot repay gifts."

I took a step forward and leaned into his chest, needing to feel the strength he possessed, needing to feel secure with my choice. Relief filled me when he wrapped his arms around my back and squeezed. He tucked my head beneath his chin.

"Thank you for your trust, *min kjaereste*."

I didn't need to speak his native tongue to know he'd just called me his. Hope began to fill that empty place in my heart and I prayed to whatever gods might be listening to let me remain in Sanctuary a while. For once, I felt like I might've found a home—somewhere worth fighting to stay.

"I hate to let go of you, but I'm starving and you smell like freshly baked donuts. Did you bring some of those back with you, too?"

A deep laugh shook his chest as he leaned down and gave me a firm but quick kiss on the lips. "Calliope had a box of them in her store from Rose. She's quite the little sugar fiend. Most sirens are." He moved toward the bed and grabbed the white flats, then threw me a questioning glance over his shoulder.

I nodded.

"I didn't bring you any, but you can have as many as you like when we get to the café."

He lay the flats at my feet. I slid them on and then giggled as the shoes shrunk and conformed. I'd never had shoes that fit so well or were so comfortable. They were tiny little flat shoes with barely any sole, but they felt like I was walking on air.

"Good?" He grinned down at me.

"Will they go back if I take them off?"

He took my hand and led me out of the bedroom and down the stairs. "No, the clothing conforms to the first body it touches. The spell is a mixture of appeal and comfort. Everything you wear is personalized to you. But, if your body changes, so will the clothes."

We walked out the front door and he paused to lock the deadbolt. "So, for children, the clothes grow with them?"

"Yes. And they are self-cleaning—one of my favorite updates. She only added that bit of magick last year," he continued, leading her along the sidewalk back the way they'd come earlier. Back to what was obviously the center of the town.

"That's why your clothes don't smell from being next to my dirty ones?"

"Yes."

"She could make a fortune. Why doesn't she sell them everywhere?"

"Think about it. Most people try clothing on before they buy it."

"Oh, I see how that would be a problem."

"Calliope does sell things to tourists who stop in, and she has quite a list of very wealthy clients who travel to Sanctuary just for her designs. Her business singlehandedly funds about half of the town's expenses, so we are very protective of her trade secrets."

"Town expenses? She doesn't own the shop?"

"She does, but all businesses in the town take only a small percentage for personal use. The majority of the profits go to the Castle."

"The sex club?"

"It's a little more complicated than that."

"Doesn't she resent having to give away so much of her money?"

He paused and turned to face me. "Most of the residents of this town were independently wealthy long before they got here. None of us needs money. Calliope is no different. She doesn't care about the money. She cares about Sanctuary. We all do."

"Is this whole town a cult of some sort? Are you going to fatten me up on fresh donuts and then slaughter me on that alter-looking thing in the center of the town circle?" I tried to sound nonchalant about it, but my anxiety quickly returned, roaring to life like a hornet's nest.

A bellowing laugh rolled up from his chest and echoed across the nearly empty street. I noticed a couple of passersby glance in our direction and then continue on without pause. "You are the toughest little human female I've ever met. Scared to your wit's end and just spewing honesty for honesty's sake. Rose will adore you."

I took a step back and tapped my foot on the pavement. His laughter gave me a little more confidence. "You didn't answer my question."

A wide grin split his face. "I apologize. No, we are not a cult. The town functions more like a family or army."

That must be why they had titles, like Protector and Sentinel. It was an hierarchy within the town. They each had their role to play. "Will I need to learn to fight?" I wondered what or who they usually fought. If it was Others like Darius, I wasn't going to be much help.

Erick grabbed my hand again and pulled me along the sidewalk. "Absolutely not. You are a guest."

I dragged my feet and barely managed to pull him to a stop before we reached the café doors. "Erick, if I stay here in this town, I don't want to be a guest. I want to have a purpose, too. Surely there's something I can do to contribute."

"*Kjaere*, you are worrying too much. Please let me get you some breakfast and introduce you to Rose. She can answer more of your questions."

A sigh slipped from between my lips. I really did need to eat.

I didn't want to leave Sanctuary. I would, but I didn't want to. I wanted to stay, be with Erick, and pretend Kevin and the Djinn weren't hunting me down to kill me.

He knew he'd won me over. Again.

The corners of his mouth turned up into a pleasant smile. I mentally fortified myself and nodded. I could do this. They were his friends. Garrett hadn't turned out to be so bad, and neither had the witch who'd helped send Darius packing.

The door swung open and a petite woman stepped in front of it. Her long, black hair was streaked with bold shades of pink, blue, and white highlights. She had it fixed in a high ponytail on top of her head. "Are y'all coming in any time soon, or should we bring the poor girl's breakfast out to the sidewalk?"

"Maven, this is Bailey," Erick said, pushing me closer to the tiny woman.

The woman held out her hand, and I smiled down at her. She couldn't have been more than five feet tall, but her energy made her seem much taller. Something else was a little different, too. Her skin glistened in the sunlight, like she'd bathed in something metallic.

I shook her hand and she grinned before yanking me inside. Erick hurried in after me. She dragged me behind her with surprising strength toward the front counter of the café.

"Rose, Erick finally showed up with his fair maiden. He's completely smitten! I can see it in his eyes."

"Maven," he growled from behind us.

But the little sprite didn't care at all. She pushed me onto an empty stool just as another woman came through the kitchen door. She had beautiful, creamy white skin and silky, black hair. Her soft brown eyes were kind and I instantly felt safe in her presence.

"Hush, Viking. You know that growly stuff doesn't scare me," Maven answered, giggling. "Raven! Come out here!"

I glanced back and saw him roll his eyes. For a few moments he was just a man being teased. Irritated, but entertained at the same time. He wasn't upset with her, more like annoyed the way you would be annoyed by a sibling or a friend.

"Maven, stop shouting. You're scaring the poor dear," the other woman spoke calmly. She made her way around the counter and embraced me. "It is good to meet you, Bailey. We were fortunate that you met Erick when you did. Darius was an unforeseen complication. But, where are my manners? I am Rose. Welcome to Sanctuary."

"Th-thank you." I took a step back and bumped into Erick's large chest. Relief flowed through my body at his touch.

"OMG! Maven, she's so pretty!" A voice very similar to Raven's cut through the noise of the café.

I glanced over Rose's shoulder, shocked to see another tiny woman, identical to Maven in every way except her hair. Instead of white, pink, and blue streaks, she sported a black ponytail with shades of red, orange, and white.

What was with the crazy hair colors?

"I told you!" Maven squealed.

"Girls, please go tend to the kitchen. Corinne is in there all by herself."

"Yes, ma'am." The sprites echoed together and darted away, disappearing around the counter and through the kitchen door, their streaked ponytails flowing behind them like living rainbows.

Rose turned back to me and I met her gaze. "Please forgive the girls' lack of decorum. They have an overabundance of energy, but are two of the best cooks I've ever met. They are sweet and they do mean well. Even though they are about two-hundred years old, they still act like hormonal teenagers." She smiled.

Two-hundred? "It's fine. Really," I answered, trying to wrap my brain around even more new information. They were Others as well, but what?

"Good." She gestured to the empty barstool on my right. "Erick, why don't you have a seat. I'll be right back with some pastries and something to drink."

"Are the two small women twins?" I asked, turning toward him.

He nodded. "Twin sisters. Pixies. They are a touch of crazy mixed with a little bit of everything else, but Rose is right. They mean well. They can't help themselves. Anything new or shiny gets them all worked up. And they are fabulous cooks ... so I've been told."

"He has eaten Corinne's donuts, though. No one has been able to resist those. Not even a vampire," Rose added, walking in from the kitchen with a tray. She placed a plate of several different donuts in front of me and Erick, a glass of orange juice, and one empty tumbler. "When was the last time you fed, Erick?"

He shook his head. "I'm fine, Rose."

She snorted. "You don't look fine. You look hungry."

My heart skipped a beat. I picked up the juice and took a quick sip. Both of them stared at me as I swallowed.

Erick finally broke the silence. "Are you unwell, *kjaere*?"

"I'm fine. She ... she said you looked hungry. How can she tell?" I studied his face, but couldn't discern any noticeable change in appearance.

Out of the corner of my eye, I saw a frown tug at Rose's smile. "You've already tasted her blood, haven't you? What were you thinking?" She laid a knife on the counter and heaved a sigh. "I can feed him, but he'd rather have yours now."

Mine? "Feed him ... what? I ..." So he did want to make a meal of me after all?

"Rose," he growled under his breath.

"You drank from her. You started it, not me. When were you planning on telling her you're psychologically bonding to her as we speak?"

"It happened so quickly, I was distracted and I didn't think," he snarled.

"You're over a thousand years old, Thorson. You knew exactly what you were doing."

"Hey, guys. I'm sitting right here. It was a tiny cut. More of a lick, if you could even call it that."

Neither acknowledged me and their argument got

nastier by the second, making me more and more uncomfortable. I took another gulp of my orange juice and then snatched a donut from the plate. If they weren't going to talk to me, I could at least eat.

After one bite, I had to hold back a moan of pleasure. The sweet buttery bread melted in my mouth, revealing just a hint of cinnamon and vanilla. The frosting tasted a little like a mix between maple syrup and honey. Simply divine. I shoved the rest of it into my mouth, ignoring their quarrel.

Food was now my only concern. I was starving. The last thing I'd eaten was that tiny pack of animal crackers. And that's all I'd had yesterday. I grabbed another donut and bit into the sticky, sweet bliss. A few moments later, I'd polished off all four and had gulped down the rest of the orange juice.

Honestly, I was still hungry. The alluring smell of bacon and eggs wafted from the kitchen. At home, my breakfast usually consisted of a piece of toast. An actual breakfast was a luxury I rarely afforded. Peanut butter and day-old bread made up eighty percent of my diet. The restaurant leftovers usually accounted for the other twenty.

"Let me get you a plate, Bailey. I'll be right back."

I glanced up from the countertop, surprised that Rose was talking to me. Her voice was calm and friendly, unlike the cold biting tone she'd been using with Erick.

I twisted in my seat and met his gaze. "Why is she upset with you?" I asked, once she'd gone through the door into the kitchen.

"She is right. I took without asking."

"I'm fine. Really."

"You are right now," he sighed, resting his elbows on the counter. "I'm the one who is feeling the bond already. I will always desire your blood now."

"Why?"

"If we heal those we drink from, our blood links us together. Some vampires choose to feed only from other supernatural beings. Their blood is different and doesn't create a connection. Not only did I taste your blood, but I used the smallest amount of mine to heal your cut."

"Meaning?"

"Meaning ... my blood is inside you now. I am linked to you."

"What does that do to me?"

"I can sense where you are. If you are in pain or need help, I will know. I will protect you with my life, *kjaere.* You are part of me."

I looked down at the counter, taking a moment to absorb. He'd bonded to me?

The door from the kitchen swung open, distracting me, and Rose returned, setting a plate full of scrambled eggs, bacon, and buttered toast down in front of me. I considered how easily I could scarf down the entire plate. I knew I shouldn't, but over the years, I'd taught myself to eat when I could. Survival was everything.

"Thank you for the food." I glanced up and met Rose's gaze.

"When was the last time you had a full meal, dear?"

I stopped, the fork midway to my mouth. "A couple of days."

She nodded. "We have plenty and you are welcome to

come back for more anytime of the day. One of us is always up cooking."

I thanked her again before I continued eating.

"Erick, we'll talk more later. Do you want a drink, or ..." Her voice trailed off as her weighted gaze fell back on me.

She seemed really concerned about the fact that he hadn't fed in a while. It started to bother me, too.

"What happens if he doesn't eat?"

"He gets cranky," Rose answered, a smile returning to her face. "Staying sated gives a vampire good control. If they are hungry, they turn into a one-track record, only able to think about the thing they need."

I glanced at the blade she'd laid on the countertop. "How does he normally eat?"

Erick interrupted. "I drink Rose's blood or blood from one of the pixies. They cut their hand and fill a glass." His voice was clipped and sharp, like he was disgusted at the very thought. How could one drop of *my* blood throw him off his norm?

"Because it was a really good drop," a familiar male voice called out. The bell on the door rang as it closed behind Garrett. He walked in with a swagger that announced he was quite pleased with himself.

Stop reading my mind!

"You were the one asking the question," Garrett answered, chuckling.

He and Erick exchanged a look I couldn't decipher, but it didn't enhance Erick's mood at all. In fact, it made him even more agitated. So much so, I thought he would get up and leave the café without me.

I placed a hand on his thigh. He instantly turned his gaze on me and it softened. The sweet, sexy man who'd taken care of me in his bathroom this morning returned and some of the tension in his shoulders melted away. "The thought of cutting myself really makes me ill, but maybe ... if it doesn't hurt too much, you could just bite me and drink from my arm or something."

His eyes widened at the suggestion and the entire café silenced. Even Rose stopped walking across the dining room with a tray full of food.

"Bailey, I can't. Drinking from your vein is not something to take lightly. You can't come back from it. Your people would label you a blood whore if I left the marks. If I heal the marks, that means you continue to be exposed to my blood, which will only strengthen the bond between us."

The words stung. I'd always sworn I'd never let a vampire drink me for money. Erick had saved my life several times. It only seemed fair that I repay his kindness in the only way I could—with blood.

But now they were reacting to my words like the very act was something much more than just me providing a man with a meal. Why would being exposed to more of his blood be a bad thing? Bond or no bond, it was still just food to him.

Garrett rose from his table and crossed the room.

Erick's leg twitched beneath my palm, but he didn't speak.

Garrett leaned against the counter to my left. "It is more. By agreeing to do this, you agree to be his. The more of his blood in your veins, the stronger his claim to you in our world. You shouldn't make a decision like this without knowing the facts. No one will think less of you if you turn him down and consider other options."

A low growl rumbled in Erick's throat and his muscles tensed beneath my hand. I knew what Erick held back. Garrett did, too. He took a step back, but didn't leave.

He was interested in me. I could see the heat in his eyes. Garrett's nostrils flared and he stared back with an intensity I couldn't match. Dropping my gaze to the floor, I shook my head. I wasn't interested in him that way. No argument, he was more than handsome, but his touch and gaze didn't light my body on fire the way Erick's did.

I've made my choice, Garrett.

Looking back up, he held my gaze for a moment before muttering something unintelligible beneath his breath. Apparently, it hadn't been difficult for Erick to understand. He leapt from his seat with a terrifying snarl and his fangs bared.

My heart stopped in my chest and I held my breath. *No. No. No.*

"Stop." Rose's voice cut through the noise and I tried to turn to look at her, but found I couldn't move.

What the hell? I was frozen as if someone had paralyzed every muscle in my body. Erick and Garrett were the same, stuck in mid-air, just about to try and choke the life out of each other.

What had happened? What had such power over everything?

My question was answered when Rose walked up to the three of us and lowered the tray to her waist. If she was the only one moving, she was the one doing the holding.

"You will leave her alone, Garrett. Bailey belongs to Erick until she states otherwise. Blood or no blood."

Belongs? Hell, I didn't belong to anyone. I tried to speak, but whatever was holding us prevented that as well.

Garrett turned his gaze to mine.

I noticed the movement out of the corner of my eye. He'd heard my thought. Damn mind reader. The amusement in his eyes was infuriating.

Who the hell was he to think he could lay any claim to me? I hadn't belonged to a man since my ex beat the shit out of me, and that wasn't about to change. I might stay with Erick and grow closer to him, but I wasn't "his."

I turned my gaze toward Garrett, as far as my paralyzed head would allow.

And I'm sure as hell not yours to worry about!

He looked away. The amusement was gone from his sparkling eyes. He'd gotten the message.

Stay out of my fucking head, too!

As quickly as it'd washed over the café, the energy that locked us into place faded away. Garrett stomped out, slamming the door behind him. Erick stood and glared at Rose.

"I wouldn't have hurt him," he muttered. "Not much."

"Not in my café," she quipped back. "If you want to act like a barbarian from the tenth century, do it outside, away from the buildings."

Tenth century? I'd heard Rose call him a Viking, whatever that was. How old were the rest of the people around here?

"Please d-don't," I faltered. "I'll leave if it's going to

69

cause problems. I've been running for years. I'm used to being alone."

"No, dear. You're not leaving. Travis and his brother Garrett are rough around the edges, but it was just his way of making sure you really wanted to be with Erick. Wolves are like that. They develop attachments quickly and are very protective. When he realized you would be staying in town, you became part of the pack, so to speak."

Erick rolled his neck and narrowed his gaze at Rose. "You should have warned me he was coming. I didn't even know Travis had a brother. Is he staying in Sanctuary or just passing through?"

"I wasn't sure when he would arrive, so there was nothing to tell. He is joining his brother at the tattoo shop. Travis lost touch with Garrett until just recently. They both thought the other had died in a firefight in the Middle East."

"Army like Travis, huh?"

"Special forces." She nodded.

He slipped an arm around my waist and pulled me close to his chest. "Sorry about the show of testosterone. We get a little territorial when it comes to women, and vampires and werewolves especially aren't fond of each other."

"But, everything is okay? You aren't going to fight? I can't stay if I'm going to cause problems."

"There will be no more problems with Garrett. I promise. I do need to introduce you to the Blackmoor brothers, but we can tackle that later."

"More brothers? What are they, cats?"

Erick snorted. "There *might* be more problems if they ever hear you call them that."

"What did Rose do?" I asked, after she disappeared into the back of the restaurant. "What kind of Other can do what she did?"

Erick sighed and leaned his elbows on the café countertop. "She is something very ancient and very powerful. If and when she wishes to share, she will. Just know you are safe here, Bailey. She promised to protect you like one of her own."

I nodded. Their desire for secrecy was understandable. I could only imagine what might happen if people found out about her. About this town.

"Maven, would you bring me a box of the donuts to go?" he hollered at the back wall.

The little pixie came scampering out a few moments later and slid a box down the counter. He caught it and tipped his head in her direction.

"Corinne says to enjoy."

"Tell her thank you."

"Will do." Maven's smile widened, and I couldn't help but smile back.

They all seemed fine. No one was still nervous about what'd just gone down. The other people eating in the dining room were laughing and carrying on as if nothing had happened at all.

Erick scooped up the box in one hand and looped his other through my right arm. "We have a few things to talk about. Would you please walk with me?"

CHAPTER 5

My body came to life the second his hand slipped around my arm and he led me out of the café. Nerve endings sparked all over my skin, and I struggled to nod. Excitement fizzed inside my body like bubbles dancing in a champagne glass.

This whole place ... it was filled with amazing people ... Others. Supernaturals that no one knew about or had ever heard of. A little scary, but even more intriguing. They knew things about the world. History. Customs. The way life was hundreds of years ago. Maybe even longer.

Erick was right. It was a textbook fact taught in school that vampires and werewolves didn't get along. So why were they living together in Sanctuary? Were there more wolves than just the two brothers they'd mentioned? Were there more vampires? Who or more appropriately *what* else made its home in this little weather-beaten town.

I stared up at the Castle across the circle as we walked the sidewalk. It looked scary—and probably was. Even though I was curious about its inhabitants, when Erick said it was a fetish club, I'd wanted to vomit. Kevin had tortured me for years. The last thing I ever wanted to see again was cuffs, collars, whips, and chains. I shuddered and looked away, refocusing my gaze on the upcoming shops.

"What scares you about the club? You don't seem like the type of person to let things rattle you."

"Why would you think that?"

"Because you kept your cool in the park, even after you realized what was stalking you. You didn't panic when the vampire tried to get you into his car. And when everything went to hell in the bus on the way here, not once did you scream or try to run off."

We turned the corner and I recognized that we were headed back to his place. "My ex taught me that panic equals more pain. It was a painful lesson, but it's helped me keep away from him for a long time."

"He taught you ... how?"

"He tortured me." I said it so easily. So matter-of-factly, like it wasn't a big deal. Like it hadn't ruined my life and made me withdraw from most all human contact.

Until I met Erick last night, I hadn't been interested in a man in almost five years. The girls at the restaurant called me the ice queen. I'd been called worse. That particular epithet was almost a compliment.

I couldn't figure out why I had warmed to Erick so quickly. Maybe it was the blood thing he and Rose had been arguing about. Maybe there were some pheromones influencing my hormones. Regardless of why, my thoughts kept drifting and imagining us in bed together, wrapped in each other's arms. Images and sensations of pleasure developed in my mind and my body shook with anticipation. Moisture dampened the skin between my thighs and I felt an unfamiliar thrum in my sex. A desire I wouldn't be able to ignore for long.

We climbed the stairs to his front door in silence. I wondered what he thought of my statement. Had it turned him off? Would he ignore me and not pursue me any longer?

He opened the door. A flash of blue crossed the open doorway for a second. Static electricity? But then it disappeared and he gestured for me to walk in first. I did.

I slipped off my flats in the foyer and went straight for his comfy sofa in the front room. The door closed with a click and I heard him turn the deadbolt. A second later, the outside wall of the living room glowed a bright blue, just like the door had a few moments ago.

It was just for a second, but maybe a little bit of panic was called for?

"Bailey?" Stepping into the living room, he set the donuts on the coffee table in front of me and sat next to them. "Are you okay?"

I could only imagine how white my face was. "What did you do? The walls. They were..."

He narrowed his gaze and cocked his head. A second later, he relaxed and smiled. "The blue?"

I nodded, licking my dry lips and wondering what would happen next. Why had he smiled? Maybe I shouldn't have trusted him so completely. Maybe I should have asked to stay somewhere else. The feeling of being caged haunted me, reaching up from the depths of my soul and clouding out every rational thought.

"It's a spell. All the buildings in town have an enchantment that prevents Djinn from being able to teleport inside. The door is the trigger. Like an on-off switch. The spell turns off if the door opens and turns back on the second the door closes. I'm surprised you didn't notice it at the café."

He reached forward and laid a hand on my knee. Some of my anxiety ebbed at the reassurance, but I couldn't shake the feeling of being trapped.

"There's nothing to fear from it. The spell doesn't keep you in. It doesn't keep the Djinn out either, but it does slow them down ... a little."

"So I could go open the door right now and walk outside?"

"Yes."

I needed to know. I had to know. Even though my heart told me he was being honest, my head needed to know I wasn't in a cage. I stood abruptly from the couch and hurried to the door.

Slowly reaching out, I touched the handle of the deadbolt. It didn't zap me or burn me. I turned it and then pushed the lever down on the door handle. It swung open without a hitch. A quick flash of blue showed and then disappeared. I let go of the door and stepped across the threshold onto the front landing.

Nothing.

I was fine. He hadn't been lying.

Relief surged through my body as the warm, summer breeze fluttered through my hair.

Stepping back inside, I closed the door and watched for the flash of blue. It was almost instantaneous with the door touching its frame. It was incredible to think that magick like this existed and still no one knew about it. Although, not many had known Others existed until fifty years ago.

The world was full of secrets. Apparently a great deal more than most people knew.

I turned the deadbolt and made my way back to the couch. Erick hadn't moved from the huge, wooden coffee table. Sinking onto the white leather cushions, I released a long sigh. "There's so much."

He nodded and moved his body from the table to the cushion next to me. The weight of his body tipped me closer to him and he slid an arm around my shoulders, pulling me onto his chest.

His hold was firm, but gentle. I knew if I resisted, he'd release me instantly, but I wanted to be near him. The closeness offered a comfort I desperately craved.

"Rose said you needed to eat," I murmured against his shirt.

He sighed. "I'll find something later. You need to rest."

The thought of him feeding on anyone but me struck a chord. I didn't want his mouth on anyone else. As much as Rose had declared I "belonged" to him, I had begun to feel quite strongly about him "belonging" to me.

"Why did you hesitate when I offered at the café?"

"Because you were scared. Then when Garrett reacted the way he did to whatever he overheard in your thoughts, I knew we needed to talk before anything else happened."

He stroked my hair, rubbing my scalp in small circles with his fingertips. If I hadn't been so intent on listening, it would have put me to sleep for sure.

"I need to know your past, *min kjaereste*. I refuse to make a mistake with you because I don't know what you fear. I sense your attraction to me, but I feel you holding back. You tell me you want this ... me ... but then fear that I would trap you in my home. Your mind and your heart are at war."

It was like he could see straight into my bloodied and battered soul. Was I ready to bare it all, though? Part of me worried he would abandon me if he knew. What Kevin had done to me was monstrous. I didn't want to lose the comfort I found in Erick's presence. His arms holding me tightly, making me forget the troubles that followed me was enough for me for now.

I knew he would want everything. More than I could give him so soon. Maybe ever. I had to hold on to this comfort a little longer. I just needed a few days of eating real food and sleeping with both eyes closed.

I wondered if I would ever be free of my demons.

A single tear ran down my cheek.

"Don't cry," he whispered in my ear. "We don't have to talk about it now." He nuzzled my hair and he kissed my temple, letting his lips linger just a few moments on my skin. The tenderness undid me. I couldn't help the stream of tears that fell, nor the sobs that followed.

Erick held me tighter. Without judgment, without words. My body heaved with each sob I'd forbidden myself to release for so many torturous years. I needed to cleanse myself of the emotional pain I had suffered, and he let me.

A deep hum rumbled from his chest, and I slowed my sobs as the hum changed to words. It was nothing I could understand. The words were in the same foreign language he'd used off and on before, but the melody was calming, ebbing and flowing like waves on a beach, and I felt myself fading.

He was singing me a lullaby.

※

I INHALED A DEEP BREATH AND STRETCHED MY LEGS, startled to find an extra pair beneath mine. My lips turned up into a smile. He'd sung me a lullaby and I'd slept the whole time on top of him. I opened my eyes and rotated my head to look at him.

He smiled and rubbed the small of my back with one of his hands.

"How long did I sleep?"

"About two hours," he answered.

I shifted, trying to find the best way to peel my body off of his. After a few attempts, I realized he would have to make the first move.

He moved his hands to my waist and lifted me, slipping out from under my body with the grace only a supernatural being could possess. I barely felt the move and then I was seated next to him once more.

"Are you hungry?"

As he waited for me to answer, I noticed him lick his lips and then frown. I wasn't really that hungry, but I knew he still was. He hadn't left my side this whole time.

"I'm fine, but you ..."

He shook his head. "You aren't ready for that."

"Why not?"

"It will complete the link between us. I will be able to

feel where you are always. And by allowing me to drink directly from your body, you acknowledge and accept my claim on you. Each time I feed, the bond will grow stronger."

"If I left, would the bond fade?"

He frowned and narrowed his gaze. Apparently the thought of my leaving was already unpleasant to him.

That feeling was mutual.

"It would fade some, but it would never completely be gone. I would always be able to find you ... your blood would be like a homing beacon."

"Where do you prefer? Neck? Wrist?"

"Bailey." His tone questioned. I knew he was trying to give me another chance to back out.

"I agree to your terms, but I don't know how long I can stay. I certainly can't promise you forever, but I agree for as long as I am here." A shiver ran down my spine as I watched his bright blue eyes darken and a thin line of red circle the edge of the irises.

"Straddle me."

I gulped. It wasn't a question and I didn't hesitate. I twisted my body and lifted my leg over his lap, situating myself across his thighs. I wiggled a little to get comfortable.

He grabbed my hips and pulled me closer, grinding my sex against his hard length. My body throbbed and my panties were soaked in seconds. Taking a deep breath, I focused on slowing my racing heart and trembling body. What I thought would be an uncomfortable bite and awkward aftermath had turned into something completely different.

Fire licked at my belly and I swayed my hips, allowing his hands to guide the movement. Another growl rumbled from his chest. His hands abandoned my waist and slid upward, grazing my breasts and then over my shoulders. He cupped each side of my face and pulled me closer, kissing me slowly. His tongue grazed first my top lip then my bottom, then plunged between them, sweeping inside. It was euphoric. He tasted sweet and I opened further for him.

My gesture did not go unnoticed and I received an encouraging gravelly moan as a reward. He sucked and nipped at my lips again before trailing his kisses slowly across my jaw and down the side of my neck below my ear. His right hand caressed the nape of my neck and grasped the base of the loose braid of my hair. He pulled my head gently to the side, further exposing my neck and collarbone to his hungry mouth.

My heart raced again. The bite had to be coming soon. I leaned into his kisses, pushing my neck closer. Something had changed in my mind. I no longer feared the bite. Instead, I desperately wanted it.

A slight pinch just above my collarbone startled me, then pain flared from that point on my neck for a brief moment before morphing into pleasure that coursed through my nerves, touching and awakening even more of my hibernating libido. My breasts swelled uncomfortably in their lacy confines and my clit throbbed beneath the layers of damp lace and denim.

He drank deeply, but the pain changed into something rapturous as our bodies continued to grind against each other. I knew I wasn't the only one silently cursing the barriers of clothing.

I arched my back as his hand slid down the back of my jeans and slipped beneath the waistband. He squeezed my ass and then pulled me even closer, crushing me against his straining cock.

What was quite frustrating and unfulfilling for me had to be excruciating torture for him, but I knew he wouldn't take it that far. I trusted him to wait for me to be ready.

I wasn't. Not yet. My body was just reacting to the moment. To him.

The pain heightened for a split second before receding to a dull throb as he pulled away. His tongue laved over the bite and I shivered as a tingle of something swept over me, similar to what I'd felt in the bath earlier this morning when he'd licked the cut on my ankle.

Then it was gone.

No pain.

Only the throbbing in my sex still remained, and possibly the frustration from four years of sexual abstinence. I wasn't ready yet, but it wouldn't take me long to get there. He'd woven a spell around me and I was intoxicated on it. On him.

"*Min kjaereste*, I cannot wait to taste the rest of you. On my honor, I vow to protect and keep you safe as long as I walk this earth."

Perhaps it wouldn't be such a bad thing to belong to Erick Thorson. I curled into his chest and breathed in his light peppermint scent, loving that he smelled like the candy. Over the years, I'd developed quite an addiction to them. They were inexpensive and lasted forever. Now my suddenly naughty mind wondered if the rest of him tasted like my favorite candy, too.

"Thank you," I murmured against his chest.

"You are the one who has bestowed the gift, *kjaere*. It is I who should thank you."

Thanking me ... A man had never thanked me for anything. Men took what they wanted and women did the best with what they could get. Even though there were more freedoms in the Texas Republic, most women still were forced into choosing a partner at the ripe old age of eighteen.

The fact that I was in my twenties and unmarried automatically threw me into the prostitute population pool. I would eventually be caught and sold into a brothel, it was just a matter of letting down my guard.

There had been several times someone, probably sex traffickers, had followed me and I ended up riding around on a city bus most of the night until they gave up and left.

The thought of being locked up and used by strangers terrified me nearly as much as the idea of Kevin finding me. Though I knew in the brothel, at least they would keep the men from beating me.

"There's no brothel in town, is there?" My voice was so soft, I wondered if he'd hear me.

His body stiffened immediately. "No," he replied sharply. "There used to be more human inhabitants of Sanctuary, but things changed after the riots in Los Angeles. We convinced them all to leave."

"You influenced a whole town?"

"No, just a few of the men. The rest followed easily once the leaders were convinced. We already owned most of the town. Rose founded it in 1920. Cohabiting with humans wasn't ever an issue until that stupid drug surprised us all. No one knew it would affect supernaturals the way it did. Our bodies usually metabolize drugs so quickly they don't matter. But this one exposed an entire pack of wolves. There were public sightings, maulings, even a few deaths." His voice faded away for a moment. "It's so sad when the mistakes of a few can completely alter the course of history for the entire planet."

I'd read about the laws changing when I was in high school. The general population rose up in outrage that Others might be mixing with humans. Martial law was declared in 2047, one year after the Los Angeles riots Everything in the country changed overnight. Soldiers patrolled the streets and the country broke into pieces. We were taught that it was for the better. Better for whom? What they failed to teach was anything about life before 2047.

The U.S. had been drastically different. I knew, because I'd found that precious stash of contraband books in an abandoned barn in Tennessee. Some were fiction— fantastic stories of love and devotion that I couldn't imagine existing nowadays. Some had been textbooks of American history going back two centuries.

Taking the books with me hadn't been an option, but I had camped there almost a week, reading and absorbing everything I could before I ran out of food. I'd been fascinated and disgusted by the turn the country had taken. Lots of people said Europe hadn't changed as much, but America had become a closed country. International flights had been banned since 2050. In 2052, the Mexican and Canadian borders were closed.

The knowledge eventually propelled me toward the tolerant states of the Texas Republic where politicians support Others' rights instead of eliminate them. They encourage acceptance of and cohabitation with Others, and that citizens shouldn't fear them but accept them as our friends and neighbors. They viewed Others as an asset to the country. Of course that probably wasn't the whole story. Governments never shared everything.

Now I was curled up on the lap of a Vampire—a man who had seen centuries of change and still lived. What stories he could tell. And I wanted to hear all of them.

"Will you tell me about what it was like before the riots?"

He leaned down and kissed my forehead. "You wouldn't have been running from a jerk of an ex. The police would have arrested him. You could work in any type of field you wanted and go to college and study any subject your heart desired."

"Is it true that Europe didn't change much?"

He chuckled. "Much of Europe is the same, yes. Though some countries did adopt some of the same intolerant policies you find in the other U.S. republics. Supernaturals were more established there and had a better foothold in most of the governments. And, once we knew about the drug, we prepared our people and they knew to avoid it."

"So no riots."

"Exactly." He rubbed her back, tracing his thumb around and around her shoulder blade. "People don't like change. Because there had been no obvious direct threat in their own countries, it was much easier to convince citizens of their safety. Life goes on."

"But you are stuck *here*."

Another chuckle rumbled in his chest. "We are not stuck, *kjaere*. We are in Sanctuary for a reason. It is our home and we will not leave it." He slid his hands under my arms and pushed me back, meeting my gaze with his beautiful blue eyes. "You know a lot for a human born after the riots."

"Knowledge is power."

He nodded. "Very true."

"I listen and I read a lot. When I got away from Kevin at the beginning, I ran to Tennessee. People there saved a lot of old books from the government burnings. Then I went to Florida. There are a lot of old people there who like to talk."

A laugh resonated from deep in his belly, shaking me a little. "The land of sunshine has long been a destination for retirees."

"I got a job at one of the few retirement centers still operating. They gave me an apartment on the property. I was there almost a year before SECR investigators came sniffing around.

There was one sweet, old lady who always told me stories, and she let me know there was a detective looking for me. I kissed her and told her I had to go. That was the first time I ran with nothing but the clothes on my back ... but not the last."

"Your ex is part of the police force? Where?"

"Montgomery, Alabama."

A grimace turned his lips downward. "What is his name?"

"Kevin Holt. After I ran from him in Florida, I knew I'd never be safe. What kind of man continues to hunt a woman years after she disappears?"

"A sick one," he replied, his voice cold and angry. "Why does he want you back so badly? Why didn't he just find another woman?"

"He told me the first time I tried to escape that no one leaves him. I know too much. Even though the police wouldn't listen to me, I suppose he fears some sort of public exposure."

"How often did you try to get away?"

"Twice." I sighed, rubbing my shoulder. "The first time I made a timing mistake and paid dearly for it. He at least had a doctor come set my broken bones. The doctor told him I should rest in bed for four to six weeks." Scorn and bitterness flowed through my voice, darkening it to something I barely recognized. I rarely let myself dwell on these memories and hated that he dredged them up. "I really don't want to talk about this." I pushed away from his chest and tried to move off his lap.

"Bailey, please. If I'm going to protect you, I need to know." He held my hips tightly, refusing to let me go.

"Don't beat me, chain me, or cage me and I'll be fine," I spat out. Anger welled inside my chest like a pool of molten lava. "I'll die before letting him touch me again."

If a vampire's face could pale. His did.

He released his grip on my hips immediately and I got off his lap and walked to the other side of the room. I didn't know where to go. I didn't have a place of my own. I couldn't very well go hide in his bed. It was his.

Even as my emotions warred inside me, I knew his scent would be the only thing on the planet that could calm me.

A knock on the door jarred me from my thoughts and a small squeak of surprise slipped from between my lips. Erick took a deep breath and his eyes widened ever so slightly. I was good at watching people. Year of running had taught me to watch everyone. The knock had surprised him.

Another heavy knock sent vibrations shuddering through the house. "If you don't want to meet anyone else right now, you should go upstairs, *kjaere*."

I sucked in a breath and fled across the foyer and up the staircase, two steps at a time. His door was still ajar and I went inside and closed it not quite all the way, leaving enough of a crack to allow me to hear some of what was said downstairs.

The front door swung open and two male voices entered the foyer mixing with Erick's. Curious, I opened the door farther and crawled on the floor to the edge of the banister, peering between the rails at the scene below. What I saw stole my breath. I'd thought Erick a large man, but the two standing across from him were at least half a foot taller.

"Rose said you brought in a human woman this morning," one of the men spoke. His skin was tan and his hair was as black as night. "She also said Darius was tracking you again."

"She's upstairs. As far as the Djinn, Darius has made

trouble before. Nothing has changed because of her."

"She's a distraction, Thorson." The first black-haired man glanced around and I ducked back, hoping he hadn't caught sight of me. "I can smell her all over you. Look, just have your fun and send her on her way tomorrow when the next bus runs through town. We don't allow humans to live in Sanctuary for a reason."

Tomorrow? That barely gave me time to catch my breath, but Kevin would be searching every travel route out of Fort Worth. It was only a matter of time before he found the footage of me in that bus station. Maybe it would be better if I did leave. Even thinking about it made my heart hurt. How had I fallen for him so hard, so fast?

"Human or not, Bailey is mine and she is welcome in this town and my home as long as she desires."

"Last time you hooked up with a human woman and things went south, you went off the deep end, Erick."

"Is that how you feel too, Eli? Do you think I'm going to go off the deep end? Should I mention Diana? Or am I the only one to be guilt-tripped over the loss of a woman I loved."

I leaned forward again. Who was Diana?

He was focused on the two identical giants. Both had shoulder-length black hair, tan skin, and honey-brown eyes, like liquid gold.

"Diana was our kind." The dark giant on the left pointed straight at me. "She is a human. She has already been told too much."

My chest tightened painfully and I gasped for a breath. The vehemence in his voice burned. The air around me seemed warmer than usual and I gasped again, drawing in another scalding breath. I backed toward the bedroom door, but froze when I heard a scuffle downstairs.

A flash of bodies and growling moved up the stairs at the speed of light. Suddenly Erick stood in front of me, blocking their advance and the two men from downstairs were staring angrily down at me from the top of the landing. More growls were exchanged back and forth. The twins' golden eyes were glowing almost orange like a fire burned within their very beings.

"She is a guest of Sanctuary and she is mine," Erick snarled. "Stop."

"You haven't taken a mate in three centuries. Why her?" The giant on the right spoke again, reining in his anger, his eyes changing back to a light brown.

I couldn't see Erick's face, but his shoulders were pushed forward and his stance was solid, ready to lunge at the other men. He stood between them and me, protecting me from people he knew. Perhaps even men he called friends.

Standing slowly, I approached Erick's side and the men's gazes softened. One twin cocked his head to the side. His nostrils flared as he took a deep breath and I noticed his eyes narrow in on my neck. I brushed my hand across the place where Erick had bitten me, but couldn't feel anything. He'd healed it completely. Did something still show?

"The bite is gone, but the smell of your blood remains fresh, little one." His voice was deeper than Erick's, darker and kind of scary.

"You both need to go. Now." Erick's chest rumbled.

I touched his arm and felt the rigid tension in his muscles.

"I'm okay." I glanced back at the two men, poised, breathing like bulls about to charge. They were only trying to protect their own. Protect their town. "If Rose didn't want me here, wouldn't she have said? She welcomed me to the town and I promise I will do nothing to endanger anyone here."

Their eyebrows rose ever so slightly. It was almost comical.

"Brave little thing, Viking." The giant on the left spoke again.

The last thing I wanted was Erick having to fight his comrades, but I really didn't want to pack up and leave tomorrow, either.

"If Rose didn't ask her to leave, then she stays," the other man rumbled. "We shouldn't have tried to interfere. It's obvious the woman means more to you than a passing whim. We should have spoken with Rose before jumping to conclusions." His gaze refocused on Erick, whose shoulders had relaxed slightly.

Tension released from the muscles in Erick's arms and he relaxed his stance. He wrapped his right arm around my waist and pulled me in tight. It was an embrace more than a restriction and I allowed my body to melt into his.

This man, this supernatural being, wanted me with him enough to fight two giant, probably ferocious men ... supernaturals of some sort. Their eyes didn't speak to any species of Other I'd learned about in school, but that didn't mean anything. I'd already learned about sirens and pixies today—two species that had obviously remained hidden after the riots. More unknowns weren't surprising. I still didn't know what Rose was.

"You guys really need to work on your tact," Erick snorted. "No wonder Rose sends me out to do the sensitive work."

One of the twins snarled and I couldn't help a squeak slipping out. Though the sound was terrifying, I was shocked to see his face split into a wide grin.

"Quit scaring her," Erick snapped.

"Sorry." The other man frowned and stretched his neck from side to side.

"Bailey. These assholes are men I've called friends for a very long time." Erick gestured to one and then the other. "The Blackmoor brothers, Miles and Eli."

I stared, trying to find some point of reference to tell them apart. Finally, I noticed a thin scar above the right eye of the man on the left.

The first one who'd spoken—the one who'd been angry when Erick brought up the woman named Diana—smirked at me as if he knew I was trying to figure out which brother he was. He was the one with the scar.

"I'm Miles," he spoke again. His deep voice made me shiver. I wanted to run and hide under Erick's bed. The air seemed warmer again, stifling, almost as if the heat were coming off their bodies in waves. "My brother Eli is the polite one, apologizing for our shit-storm and all."

The one he called Eli laughed. His voice wasn't quite as deep as his brother's and his jovial mood set me more at ease, but his eyes were still the color of molten steel—bright yellow, swirling with red. "My words might be more polite than his, but my hands would find hours of pleasure torturing you until you screamed in ecstasy."

Erick's arm tightened again. I gulped at the visual. These were the men who ran the club. The Castle.

"With your permission, of course." He grinned at Erick and then at me again.

"I don't like to share," Erick's softer, velvety reply rumbled back at them.

"It never hurts to offer," Eli replied.

The two men turned and moved down the stairs with the same speed they'd ascended. Erick followed with me in tow. My feet were lifted from the floor and air rushed past my face. When he stopped we were sitting on the couch in his living room again.

Miles and Eli were lounging in chairs opposite us. The furniture was large, but their size made it seem small. In fact, with all three of them in the room, I suddenly felt cornered. I took a deep breath and tried to focus on slowing my racing heartbeat. It wasn't working. Instead, my breathing sped up, too.

"Step outside, *kjaere*. Get a breath and then come back." Erick pushed me up from the cushion and I looked back at him and the other two. It crossed my mind that they could attack me now. They were closer to me than he was. I shook it off and continued to the front door, opening it and stepping onto the porch.

Erick trusted them. Eli had apologized for their behavior. I was fine. Safe. Right?

I stood in the open doorway, drinking in the fresh air and sunlight. It helped. He'd somehow known exactly what I needed. I smiled. Was there a pheromone for everything?

CHAPTER 6

I turned back to the door.

Erick was standing there. He hadn't made a sound.

My hands flew to my chest as I sucked in a quick gasp. The man certainly knew how to sneak up on a girl. "You all need to slow down a little."

"Are you all right? I know Miles and Eli can be overwhelming, but they usually growl before they think. I promise you will like them after you get to know them."

I nodded and he slipped an arm around me, guiding me gently back to my seat on the couch. The other men had beers in their hands now and smiled at me. They didn't seem quite as scary as they had only a few minutes before. Granted, they weren't growling and standing over me aggressively. Now they just looked like regular, albeit oversized, guys throwing back a couple of drinks. Friendly even.

They looked completely human. No wonder they'd

been able to hide their kind so easily. Whatever their kind was ...

"You know, I haven't heard Erick call a woman *kjaere* since the Middle Ages," Eli started, taking a swig from his longneck.

Miles growled, sending his brother a look that would've frozen the blood in my veins.

Erick waved his hand. "Elinor was very special to me. He does no disrespect by bringing that to light."

Miles relaxed back into his chair and nodded. I made a mental note of their ability to shift moods very quickly. And that they growled when a human man would have raised his voice and shouted.

"Who was Elinor?" I asked softly—very curious about a woman who had lived more than a millennium ago. I didn't know much about the time period. The concept that Erick and these two men sitting in his living room had lived for so many years was overwhelming. How does a person cope with so much change? So much loss.

"She was my wife for a brief ten years. I loved her dearly and treasured every moment I had with her. Your strong spirit reminds me of her."

"Did she die?"

"Yes," he answered. His eyes held sadness, but so much love. "She was human and made me promise never to use my blood on her. Even when she lay dying in my arms, bleeding out, she reminded me of my promise. Losing her was the hardest thing that's ever happened to me. Even harder than watching my family grow old and die until there was no one left who remembered me."

"You said you had a sister."

"We call each other family, but she's not from my human life."

I'd lost my parents years ago, but that pain still resonated inside me. I knew what it was to feel loss. But to lose a wife, too? I'd never loved a man before. I thought when I first met Kevin he would be a man I could love. Yeah, that didn't work out as planned.

"I'm so sorry."

He nodded.

I glanced at the men across the room. Both zeroed their gaze on me in an instant, curiosity in their eyes. An uncomfortable silence fell on the room. Squirming in my seat, I said the first question that came to mind.

"What are you?" I didn't direct the question at any one of them particularly. "Your eyes ... they look normal now."

Eli straightened in his chair and set his beer on the coffee table. "My brother and I are Drakonae. We run the Castle."

"Drakonae... like dragons? Like King Arthur and the round table? Knights fighting fire-breathing dragons kind of dragons?" I remembered reading tales of knights and ladies from a castle called Camelot. It'd been one of my favorite books from the stash in that old ramshackle barn. "Erick said the name of the club is the Castle? But why is it called the House of Lama-dis or Lamidae?"

"Did you tell her everything already, Viking? Damn. You could leave a little mystery for us to share." Eli tried to sound peeved, but the twinkle in his eyes said otherwise. His amusement was comforting. As secretive as they all were about themselves, they seemed willing to share with me.

"We are very old. Older than King Arthur. Our race is called Drakonae. The Castle, or club as you said, is the home of the Sisters of Lamidae."

"So the club is a front?"

Eli shook his head. "The club is very real."

I turned to Erick. "You're not going to influence me and make me forget everything, are you?"

"No. If you choose to remain in Sanctuary, you need to know everything about it to help protect it. In our world, ignorance is not bliss. It's a death sentence."

He brushed his fingertips along my jaw and leaned toward me. His fingers threaded into my hair, cradling my chin in his large palm. He brushed his lips over mine and sucked my bottom lip into his mouth.

His statement worried me, but my fears fled for a moment when his lips were on mine before embarrassment reared its head in their place. I pulled away. Heat rushed to my cheeks. I wasn't used to displays of affection in front of anyone, much less two very intimidating dragon men.

Erick smiled and placed a gentle kiss on my forehead before releasing me and dropping his hand from my neck.

I spoke again, with more confidence this time. "I knew the castle had to be protecting something or someone. What or who are the Sisters?" The two men both snapped their mouths closed and frowned.

Not quite the response I expected.

"That is a story for another day." Miles stood from his chair, his jaw set firmly. "We should head out," Eli stated, rising to stand next to his brother.

My knee bounced, a nervous habit I'd had since I was a

kid. Erick ran his palm over my thigh to settle me. Not even a single twitch dared to go against his soothing touch.

The way he could calm my body or settle my nerves with a touch or a word baffled my mind. The idea that a man would be thoughtful to my needs was foreign. The world I'd grown up in didn't cater to women. It used them.

The twin brothers ambled to the door. Erick pressed down gently on my leg before rising and following them out to the front. I stayed exactly where he left me. Exactly where he wanted me.

It was rapidly becoming exactly where I wanted to be. The thought of leaving him, of leaving this town full of its amazing and unique people, grew more difficult by the minute.

I could hear them talking outside, but couldn't make out the conversation. Only a few moments passed before the door clicked shut and the wall in front of me shimmered blue for just a moment, reminding me why I'd been running in the first place.

Sanctuary might have welcomed me. Rose might not mind my being here now. But when Kevin found me, hell would break loose and they wouldn't want me anymore. Erick wouldn't want me if he really knew what that monster had done to me. And Kevin was a monster. He might not have fangs or claws, but he could tear apart a person's soul. He was still trying to finish off mine.

Staying in Sanctuary for very long wasn't an option. No matter how much I wanted to stay with Erick, I couldn't risk exposing his friends to my ex. Whatever they were protecting was important. A lot more important than little ol' me.

"I leave your side for but a moment and you're upset again." Erick leaned against the doorframe, his tall lean body called to mine, banishing my previous thoughts. "I assure you my friends mean you no harm ... they were merely concerned about me."

"Why?" I asked, glad to focus his attention away from my thoughts.

"When Elinor died ..." He paused, staring a hole in the floor for a moment before meeting my gaze again. "I left them for over a century. I wallowed in my sorrows and did many things I'm not proud of. Things that would have broken my sweet Elinor's heart."

"Grief and anger are difficult beasts to conquer," I whispered, remembering the rage I felt after my parents' accident. When the social worker and police took me to the foster house, I wanted to hurt anyone and everyone around me.

"Did you conquer them, *min kjaereste?*" He beckoned me toward him with outstretched arms. I stood and walked across the room to him, allowing my body to be tucked tightly against his, shocked by how much I wanted to be near him. Shocked more that I allowed myself that pleasure.

"I learned how to bury them." My words were muffled by his shirt, but it didn't matter. He'd heard me.

"The thing about burying beasts is that they keep coming back."

"Mine keep me alive. I learned to survive on my own because of my demons." I pushed away from him. I couldn't let myself become dependent on his strength, no matter how comfortable he was. My battles were just that—mine.

"I will let you go ... if that is what you really want. But if you want a home, you've found one. You were right earlier. If Rose didn't want you here, she would have made it very clear. Instead, she almost seemed to be expecting you," he paused, his gaze drifting away from me.

I saw the light in his eyes and the determination. Like he'd just had an epiphany. Why would Rose have been expecting me? We'd never met. I'd only been in Texas for three months.

Leaving wasn't what I wanted, but it was inevitable. Kevin always made sure of it. The friends I made in Florida had paid dearly for their association with me. I read in the news that not two days after he'd tracked me there, the nursing home where I'd lived and worked had been burned to the ground, claiming over forty souls. After that, I stayed away from people. I never socialized and worked as many shifts as I could find. I'd learned over time, the more I worked, the less likely I was to be hassled by male staff. I never took breaks. Never smoked. Never spoke unless spoken to.

"I will only bring pain to this town. It follows me wherever I go. I can't stay ... even though I want to."

"Try."

It was just one word, but it said everything. He was right. I'd already given up. I didn't try anymore. It wasn't worth it. I never stayed anywhere long enough to care. My thoughts were getting all jumbled.

He stepped toward me, but I backed up, keeping the distance between us the same. "I do want to try, but then I think about you and Rose, Maven and Raven, and Calliope, and everyone else I haven't met yet. I know what's coming." Tears burned down my cheeks now in a waterfall of pain.

"I want you to stay with me," he stated slowly.

"Why?" A whimper slipped out. "Didn't you hear me? He'll kill you. He'll kill anyone who won't help him find me. He killed Matilda and Joe, and George, and the others. I know he did."

My body shook from sobs. I'd never admitted it out loud before, but I knew the fire had been his fault. The news reported it as an accident. They said it started in the room of an elderly resident named Matilda Jones.

It hadn't been an accident. It had been my punishment. He'd found out they were my friends.

I crumbled, my legs gave way, but my knees never hit the floor. Erick's arms encircled me, lifting me away from the hardwood, and he whisked me up the stairs to his room.

"Things are different here," he murmured, laying me gently on the satin covers.

The bed dipped under his weight as he crawled next to me and tugged me firmly against his hard chest. I tucked my arms between us and accepted the comfort he was providing.

It wouldn't last. It couldn't. Nothing good in my life ever did.

"I will protect you."

My mind raced, struggling to process what he'd just said. Maybe he was right. Maybe this town could protect itself. But, maybe not. I sucked in a gasp between sobs.

Just being supernatural didn't make you immortal. Even vampires could be killed.

"I can't just hide here in your house for the rest of my life. I thought staying here might be a good thing. But, I can't hide in a small town. There's no way to blend in. No crowds to disappear into. I'm vulnerable here." The pros and cons list in my head started to appear. My usual habits and ways of avoiding detection wouldn't work in Sanctuary.

There was one main street. One restaurant, as far as I could tell. A castle with dragons, whips, chains, and who knew what else.

"I will keep you safe."

"What if you aren't around? I heard you tell your friends you go out of town for business. What if Rose needs you to do something?"

"They will watch you if I'm gone."

"The dragons?"

A soft chuckle rumbled in his chest. "In all honesty, you would be safest in the Castle but probably very uncomfortable."

"Because of the whips and chains and stuff?"

He laughed aloud. "Yes, *kjaere*. But, everything that happens in the Castle is consensual. Nothing is done between two people that isn't agreed upon in some form beforehand."

"I can't imagine *wanting* to be beaten," I hissed back, my emotions seesawing back and forth between wanting to trust him and hating myself for even thinking I could. Kevin had used many things on me, including a whip, but his belt had created most of my scars. That, and his baseball bat.

"No one is beaten the way you are describing. A whip is used to heighten pleasure, not to torture and disfigure." He spoke slowly, melodically.

I knew he wasn't lying to me about the club, but even the idea of a whip or a chain made me want to vomit.

Most of my scars had lightened as the years passed. I was so used to them, I didn't notice them much anymore, but one of the waitresses at the Seafood Shack saw one of my larger ones one day when my shirt came un-tucked. She never asked me about it, but her slight gasp of horror was enough to remind me how ugly Kevin had made my body.

I never dated. Never flirted. I refused any man who showed even the smallest interest in me. It was better to be labeled a cold-hearted bitch than to end up with another man like Kevin. Once or twice when I'd admired a handsome man from afar, I always reminded myself that I wasn't good enough. I wasn't a young eighteen-year-old with a perfect body. Society labeled me a whore because I lived alone, unprotected by family. Most of the male staff thought I turned tricks on the side and had asked for my number on several occasions.

Erick was the first man I'd let embrace or touch me since Kevin.

"You'll never ask me to do those things. Promise me." I turned my head and strained to look up at him.

He loosed his grip, as if sensing I needed a visual connection with him.

I did.

His ocean blue eyes were soft. Kind. Tender. And then

... there was something else in his gaze I didn't recognize. Something unfamiliar that reminded me of those romantic books back in that Tennessee barn. He pressed another kiss to my forehead and shook his head. "I would never do anything you didn't enjoy, *min kjaereste*."

His endearment brought tears to my eyes again. He'd called me beautiful, when I'd smelled like a sewer, but would he still think of me that way when he saw the damaged parts of me? Even faded, I knew the scars were ghastly to look at.

"Why me?"

He looked away for a moment and sighed. Then back at me. "I've been hunting Darius since Elinor died."

I gasped, biting back a sob. The Djinn had killed his wife.

He nodded. "Darius is a bloody menace who needs to be wiped from the face of the planet." Erick laid me on my back and then stretched out on his side next to me, propping his head up with his arm. "When I saw you ... your eyes were so determined. You knew he was out there. You knew what he was and yet you stubbornly fought to get to a place where you thought you'd be safe."

I closed my eyes as he traced the line of my jaw to my chin with his free hand. Then he let his hand travel back up my face and his fingers sank into my hair. He rubbed my scalp, massaging ever so gently.

"I wasn't safe in the bus station, was I?"

"No."

"Would he have killed me?"

"Eventually."

I had run from one lunatic straight into another. It

wasn't fair. I deserved a break. A little bit of happiness in this screwed up world. Was that too much to hope for?

"I want to give you new memories, Bailey. Something to help drown out the pain and self-blame. I don't know what your ex did, but I want to help you find a way past it."

I relaxed into his touch and felt tears well up in my eyes, I closed them to hide the pain.

"You've been running from him for so long to avoid physical pain, you never had time to forgive yourself for the emotional pain he inflicted. None of it was your fault. He was a predator."

"I'm scared you won't like what you see. He did things to me that ... that I have to carry with me. I'm a fucked-up mess." When I looked in the mirror in the mornings, I saw a broken, battered mess of a woman who had survived by the skin of her teeth. More sobs slipped from my chest. I couldn't hold them back.

"You never gave up, *min kjaereste*. You may feel broken or ugly, but you have the spirit of a warrior. In my homeland, you would have been respected and honored for your scars. My people see wounds as badges of honor. You didn't let your enemy win—you never quit fighting."

"They keep calling you a Viking. Were those your people?"

"Yes. We were seafaring warriors and raiders. Strong. Independent. Fierce. Loyal. Passionate."

It would've been nice to live in a world where more people had those qualities. I opened my eyes and stared into the endless blue of his. He had such a beautiful way with words. I could listen to the ebb and flow of his deep velvety voice for hours.

My sobs had turned to the occasional hiccup, and my heart had slowed to a more normal rhythm.

He moved his hand from my hair slowly down my neck, over the curve of my breast, and along my torso. Stopping at my hip, he caught the hem of my shirt and tugged it up a few inches, revealing half of my stomach and a handful of white jagged scars.

I held my breath. What would he do? Would he say something? I listened for an intake of breath, a gasp, a groan. Nothing. He didn't make a sound.

The bed shifted as he leaned forward and kissed along the length of one scar and then the other, until he'd kissed every inch of the marred flesh he'd uncovered.

Then he looked back at me. Our gazes met and the heated desire in his eyes made me tremble. I wanted him. Not just a little want. I was wet, aching with need. If he couldn't smell my arousal, my pheromones had to have given me away by now.

"Tell me what you want, *kjaere*. This only goes as far as you desire."

Meaning what? If I said no in the middle of stripping, he'd back off? If I started panicking, he'd just quit? I was supposed to trust this vampire, a predator by nature, to leave me be if I so dictated?

But it wasn't his wants and desires that left me confused the most. It was mine. I wanted to taste his lips again. I wanted to feel him against me, skin to skin. I wanted his cock inside me, stretching me, filling me until it was all I could feel.

He said I was a fighter, not a victim.

I hadn't given up. Even though I'd been running, I never gave in. He called me honorable, not shameful. No one had ever called me anything but worthless.

I lifted my arms, put my hands on his neck and pulled him closer. Our lips met and I parted mine, inviting him in. But it wasn't just my mouth I opened. I knew a crack had opened in the walls surrounding my heart, too. I was falling in love with this man who called me beautiful and strong—a warrior.

It was time to fight.

CHAPTER 7

He nuzzled my neck and licked along the pulse point. Then his right leg moved across my abdomen, straddling me, but not putting pressure. He straightened himself, leaving my skin tingling and desperate for more attention. Pushing up my arms, he grabbed the hem of my shirt and tugged, gently pulling until it came over my head.

I closed my eyes, not wanting to see his initial reaction to my scars. I could hear him take a deep breath. "You are exquisite, Bailey. Look at me."

The words surprised me. I opened my eyes slowly. He held my gaze with a look I could only describe as adoration, while his hands slid behind my torso and unsnapped the bra. It slipped off easily and he tossed it, along with my shirt, to the floor.

I heaved a breath in and out. I was completely bare from the waist up. Long jagged streaks crisscrossed my chest and stomach, some were raised and others were just ghostly white shadows.

His hands caressed my breasts, rolling the nipples between his thumbs and forefingers, bringing them to a hard point. He leaned down again, pressing his lips against a scar that crossed over my left breast. "So beautiful, *kjaere*. So brave."

Tears poured from the corners of my eyes, running down my temples and falling to the pillow beneath my head. He didn't stop until he'd kissed and licked every mark. Then he gently rolled me over and began again.

"I will know and see everything. And I will revel in the beauty that is you."

The way his words flowed made my heart full, and my tears slowly subsided. I began to enjoy the way he ran his lips and his hands over my skin. Lines of fire surged from each touch, warming me all over. My breasts felt heavy and my sex wept with need.

He slid his hands down my hips and unsnapped my pants, pulling them off slowly. The waistband dragged across my mound and put delicious pressure on my swelling clit.

A wave of cool air grazed the cheeks of my ass. Worries emerged again, but were dispelled as his mouth planted a kiss on each of my exposed cheeks.

"Perfection."

The word was just a whisper, but it resonated deep inside me.

I knew there were scars on my backside, too. But they didn't seem to be turning him off. In fact, when he leaned down to kiss me again, I felt his arousal prod against the back of my thighs.

He wanted me—scars and all.

A breath later, he turned me onto my back, still gazing down on me as if he'd never seen anything more beautiful in his life. I knew I could never tire of seeing him look at me with such reverence.

I wanted to see him, too. I raised my hands to the hem of his polo shirt and tugged. He obliged and pulled it off, tossing it to the floor where my clothes had landed.

My lips parted at the vision before me. The light tan on his arms continued over the rest of his body. His shoulders were golden, too. Light blond hair dusted his chest and I drew my fingers along the center slope between his pecs. My gaze trailed lower, taking in and appreciating his tapered waist and six-pack abs. A thin trail of hair started again at his navel and led my eyes on a downward path. The waist of his pants hid the rest of him from view, but the bulge beneath spoke to his desire. When I looked back to his face, the intensity in his eyes heated me even more.

I fumbled with the button on his jeans for a second before I got it loose. Then pulled down the zipper and pushed them, along with his boxers down over his hips. His cock sprang free, already hard and glistening with pre-cum.

Instead of being nervous, like I thought I would be, I was excited. My heart raced and my skin tingled in anticipation. Even my mouth watered at the impressive male display. He wriggled the rest of the way out of his clothes and kicked them off the bed, turning back to me with the hungry look of a lion that hadn't eaten in days.

He didn't attack, though. Each move he made was slow and deliberate. His legs were on either side of my thighs, holding me firmly in place. He leaned down, blowing a stream of cool air across my bare nipples. They pebbled in an instant and I wanted nothing more than to feel his lips on them.

A tiny moan slipped from between my lips. Please. I wanted his mouth on me more than anything. "Please." It was a whisper, but I had said it.

My eyes closed when the wisps of cold air returned to my breasts. Then the cool touch of his lips. They were so close. He kissed around the nipple, caressing every part of my breast with his mouth, then moving and doing the same with the other, but never taking either nipple.

"I love how sensitive you are. Your breasts are like heaven—soft, supple, and full."

I was awash with sensations. His mouth made love to my breasts. There was no other way to describe it. He licked and sucked and nipped until I could feel my pulse pounding in my sex. It drove me wild.

When he finally closed his mouth over one of my nipples, I gasped. Each tug sent ribbons of fire coursing through my body straight to my wet, needy core. He switched to the other and used his fingers to roll the wet nipple back and forth, exerting just enough pressure to make me start panting.

My back arched up, thrusting my breasts closer to his luxurious mouth. He nipped and pulled at the other nipple, not giving a second of reprieve. I pushed my head back and fisted handfuls of the satiny comforter, biting back a groan. I couldn't remember the last time I was this turned on.

Warmth flooded across every inch of my skin. Full-on body blush.

He shifted so that his shaft nudged at my mound while his mouth delved up and down the lines of my throat. "Look at me." The command rumbled from deep in his chest.

I couldn't deny him and I opened my eyes again just as he captured my mouth, plunging his tongue deep. He leaned to the side, resting on an elbow and sliding one palm beneath my head. His grip on my skull was firm, and he used the leverage to kiss even harder.

His other hand slid down the left side of my body, sending shivers of exhilaration straight to my nerve endings. I rolled my shoulders, wiggling my arms free, and wrapped my hands around his bulging ones, giving myself the ability to push back into his all-consuming kiss, wanting to give back as much as he was giving me.

His biceps flexed beneath my fingers, distracting me for a moment from his wandering right hand, but I froze when his fingers brushed over my swollen clit. Nerve endings fired, and I sucked in a breath to keep from tumbling down the cliff of the first orgasm I'd had in years.

He pulled back from my mouth and nuzzled my ear. "If you don't want this to go further, just tell me."

"Please don't stop. I'm going to come, but I don't want this to be over." I gasped for a breath. "And you haven't even taken your pleasure yet."

His tongue traced the lobe of my ear. "My precious,

Bailey. I have no intention of stopping after you come. I do not *take* from a woman. Sex is a gift from your body to mine."

"But, everyone ..." I quashed those thoughts. It didn't matter if I understood what he said. It didn't matter if this expression of physical love went against everything I'd been told my whole life.

He slid his forefinger between my slick folds, brushing ever so slightly along my clit as he delved into my vagina. I gasped. The pressure of having his finger inside me was exquisite and worrisome at the same time. I was so tight and it was just one finger. How would I ever take all of him?

"Just feel, stop thinking," he whispered before covering my mouth with his again. The faint scent of peppermint filled my lungs and I relaxed into his touch.

My orgasm built, swirling inside me like the outer winds of a hurricane. I moaned into his mouth and arched my hips, giving him better access to my sex. His finger slid in and out, coated with my juices. He circled my clit with his thumb and thrust inside again, but this time with two fingers. Pushing, stretching, and getting me ready for more. I shuddered. His thumb touched my swollen clit and I moaned again. So close. I was almost there.

As nerves fired throughout my body, I began to writhe between him and the bed. I wanted to come. I needed release. He worked me close again and again and then backed away at the last second. His two fingers were still in my vagina, scissoring open and closed, pumping in and out.

"Please," I begged into his mouth.

He pulled back and I stared into his bright blue eyes. "Come now." He pressed down on my clit and pushed his fingers inside as deep as he could.

My pussy clenched and I screamed as the orgasm ripped through my body. I arched upward, trying to follow the floating feeling. It was as if I had left the gravity of the earth's atmosphere. I'd never known an orgasm could feel as if the entire universe rocked.

Every muscle in my body contracted and squeezed. My toes curled into the covers and I dug my fingers into the muscles of his biceps. He pushed his fingers deeper than I thought possible and another wave of contractions fluttered through me like a swarm of butterflies.

I slowly relaxed, sinking back onto the bed. My arms slipped from his and fell silently to my sides. My legs relaxed and my body felt exhausted and limp.

"Oh my." I stared into his eyes, drinking in his lustful gaze. A twitch against my thigh reminded me we still had a long way to go. His hard cock was cool against my skin. In fact his whole body was cool to the touch, although my body burned with arousal. Each graze of his arm, touch of his lips, brush of his leg was like ice against my flushed skin.

"That was only the beginning, *min kjaereste*. I want to hear you scream in pleasure over and over, until the only thing you worry about is when we will have time to make love again."

I gasped. Make love? No one I knew had ever referred to having sex as making love. Sure, there were some couples who seemed really happy together, but that was not the norm in my world. In my world, people fucked or had sex. Maybe it was because he was from a different time.

"I don't think I can move." A tiny giggle followed my admission. Where had that come from? I couldn't remember the last time I'd laughed at anything. What would he think? "I'm sorry. I wasn't laughing at you. I ... I just ..."

"Bailey," he hushed. "It's perfectly natural to be happy." His face split into a wide grin and he leaned down, sucking first one of my nipples and then the other, each tug reawakening my nerves.

"Ahhhh," I moaned, arching my back, taking pressure off of the nipples he pulled on.

His hand pushed against my thighs and I parted my legs, allowing him to move between them. He lowered his body along mine, tracing his tongue along my abdomen, a hipbone, and then straight across my clit.

He licked me there and I flinched. No man—not even my ex—had ever tasted my sex. It was unlike any sensation I'd ever experienced. Gentle. Soft. Cool against my hot center. It was heavenly.

I watched, fascinated as he took another lick. A twinkle in his eye told me I was in for much more than a few little tastes. He slid off the foot of the bed, grabbed my feet, and tugged me to the edge. I tensed when he sank to his knees on the floor. I couldn't see him or what he did unless I craned my neck. But, I could feel his cool breath as it blew across my wet sex. I trembled, anticipating the touch of his mouth on me there again. I wanted it. I wanted everything he would give.

He slid his arms beneath my thighs and wrapped his

hands around my legs, locking me in place. I tested his hold, but budging my hips wasn't going to be an option.

"Do you want this, Bailey?"

His voice cut through my panting breaths.

"Yes." I did, though I knew I sounded a little tentative. I wanted to feel joy in a man's arms, not terror. I trusted him. That little voice inside my head told me it was okay to let go. It was okay to find happiness. It didn't matter if he was a vampire. I was better off with him than the humans who viewed me as ruined leftovers. "I want you." The words came out more like a plea than an answer. I not only wanted him, I needed him.

His tongue swirled around my throbbing clit, then he closed his lips, pulling it into his mouth. I gasped and my back bowed, the sensation nearly sending me straight to the stratosphere again. Taking a deep breath, I tried to concentrate on him, on his mouth and the divine things he was doing. I couldn't believe my body could regroup that fast and be so close to the edge of coming again.

When he released my clit from his mouth, I sighed in relief. It was short lived. His voice rumbled above the roar of my blood rushing through my head. "Come again, *kjaere*. Now." He captured my clit once more and the pressure exploded inside me like fireworks.

"Erick!" His name tore from my throat in an ear-splitting scream. I sat up, grabbing his head, entwining my fingers in his shoulder-length hair, trying to move his mouth from where it was latched to my body, but it was useless. He wasn't letting up until he'd pulled every last bit of the orgasm from me. I hung on for dear life as contractions continued to spiral from my center out to the tips of my hands and feet.

When he finally released me, I fell backward onto the comforter once more. My body jerked a few times and shivers were still running up and down my spine. My skin had been hot before, but now I felt as if I were truly on fire.

The contrast of his cool skin only excited me further. My body worked overtime to warm his. I wanted more contact, not less. I wanted his body next to mine. Skin on skin. I wanted to give back as much as he'd given to me.

Sex had never been pleasant with Kevin, not even at first. What Erick had just shown me awakened a need I'd forgotten was there—deep inside, just waiting.

Erick lifted me as if I weighed an ounce and gently tossed me back to the center of the bed.

"I like where your head is now, Bailey. Tell me what you are thinking."

He crawled forward, gliding up my body like the lethal predator I knew he was, but it didn't scare me. I loved that he could be so tender and compassionate, yet at the same time, so firm and demanding. He pushed when I needed it and held back when I couldn't handle it. Maybe being with a man who could read my pheromones wasn't such a bad thing after all.

I smiled up at him. "How much I want to feel you inside me." I parted my legs, offering him a clear view of my closely shaved pussy I hoped he couldn't turn down. Not that he hadn't just seen it. He'd practically been worshiping it a few moments ago. But, I wanted more than his mouth on me now. "Do you have a condom?"

"I can't get you pregnant, and I don't carry diseases. I have condoms, but I would much rather feel your heat directly." His icy blue eyes darkened and I knew he wanted the same. As he drew closer I could see a thin rim of red around his irises, but his fangs hadn't descended. He wanted to bite, but held back.

"Me too." I nodded and reached for him, tracing the line of his angular jaw. Just a hint of rough stubble scratched at my fingertips.

"Good." The word was more of a growl. He dipped his head, nuzzled my neck, and then nipped at my ear.

He raised his torso up, abandoning my neck. Then nudged my legs apart with his knees and pulled my hips up until his erection just pressed against the opening of my vagina.

Leaning down for another kiss, he pushed with one fluid movement, splitting me apart with his hard cock. I trembled, waiting for him to make another move, but he just stared down at me and waited, realizing my body needed time to adjust to him. It'd been so long.

My discomfort faded quickly and I moved first, wrapping my legs around his waist and pulling him deeper. It was all the encouragement he needed. He started with slow, steady thrusts, pulling in and out until I took his full length.

"So tight, so perfect," he rumbled. His hands drifted from my legs to my breasts. He kneaded them, switching between rolling my nipples between his fingers and pinching them until I gasped.

The now familiar twinge of a building orgasm fluttered through my belly. I couldn't possibly be able to come again. Just at that moment he grinned and moved one of his hands along my hip and between our rocking bodies.

My breath turned to pants. He knew. The damn vampire knew. He'd probably planned to get another one out of me before we finished.

His fingers grazed my swollen and throbbing clit. My heart skipped a beat, and I moaned. I squeezed my legs, digging my heels into his back, pressing us closer and pushing his hand away from my super-sensitive clit. His cock swelled more, filling and stretching me.

"Up," he groaned. He pulled me toward him and pressed us together, chest to chest. I rode his cock as he lifted me from my hips and then pulled me back down on him.

The friction was too much. Another orgasm came barreling up from my center, exploding inside me with a force I couldn't control. My fingers dug into his back and I let my head drop backward and screamed his name again as he drove into me even deeper. I clung to him, taking everything and finding that euphoric place where my body and my mind floated apart. In that moment, his mouth closed over part of my neck. The sting of his bite sent another wave of pleasure rolling through my body. He came hard, growling against my skin as he both filled and drank from me.

Minutes passed before he slowly released my neck, swiping his tongue across the wound several times. I knew there would be no visible mark. Whatever he did, it healed me completely, leaving no trace of his bite behind. Something I truly appreciated. The last thing I wanted another scar.

He yanked back the covers, pulled me off his lap, and laid me ever so gently on the sheets. The bed dipped and moved as he crawled to the edge and got off.

"Don't leave."

"I'll be right back," he murmured, disappearing into the bathroom. Sure enough, he reappeared with a washcloth a few moments later and attended to me, cleaning traces of our lovemaking from my legs and sex. "Better?" His blue eyes were back to their brilliant shade of tropical blue ocean water.

He might be able to read my pheromones like a book, but his eyes were the windows to his soul. They darkened when he was aroused. A ring of red appeared when he needed to feed. They sparkled when he was amused. Mostly they stared at me, wrapping me in the unseen blanket of comfort and ... love. How could he love me? We'd only just met.

A moment later he disappeared into the bathroom again. I heard water running for a few seconds then he was back, crawling into the bed with me and cuddling up behind. I shivered, still coming down from my high. Contact with him sent sparks through my body, warming parts of me that should've been totally spent.

"Lustful little thing, aren't we, *kjaere?*" He chuckled, tugging a sheet over our naked bodies and then wrapped his arm around my waist.

Heat flooded my cheeks. Damn pheromones. "I don't know what you do to me," I admitted.

"You're mine. This is your home, Bailey. At my side. In my bed. All you have to say is yes."

His. Though it sounded like he was saying he owned

me, my heart now understood that's not what it meant. It wasn't something he'd forced on me. It reminded me of how he'd called sex a gift from me to him.

But it wasn't sex that was the true gift. It was me, giving myself to him. And I had. I was his, body and soul. I'd wandered the country for nearly four years, searching ... running ... wishing for something I didn't believe even existed.

"Yes." Hell yes!

CHAPTER 8

I opened my eyes. The bright, afternoon sun was setting and swaths of oranges and reds were painted across the Texas sky. My gaze flitted from the window to the rest of his bedroom searching for a clock, but I didn't see one. I had to have slept for several hours. It'd only been midday when we made love.

I turned onto my stomach and drank in the faint peppermint scent on the pillow where he'd been sleeping beside me. "Erick?"

He was at the bedside in a second, startling me. I still wasn't used to how quickly he could move.

"Do you feel okay?" he asked.

I stretched and let out a soft moan. "Pleasantly sore." I grinned and sat up, letting the sheet fall away from my breasts.

His eyes darkened, but just for a moment. If I hadn't been watching him, I wouldn't have noticed. It felt good to know that just a glance aroused him, especially after everything we'd done. After he'd seen ... all of me.

"You are beautiful, Bailey. As I have already said, your scars are nothing more than badges of honor. I find them as beautiful as the rest of you."

"I believe you."

"Look up at me," he said.

I did as he said, pulling my gaze from the jagged white line running across my left breast.

He was perfection defined. His sexy, golden mop of hair was sufficiently mussed, so that anyone who saw him would likely know what we'd done for several hours this afternoon. His chest and shoulders were muscular and defined, but not bulky. A tapered waist teased my eyes and a light trail of blond hair drew my gaze downward, where I focused on his groin, hidden once again beneath a pair of perfectly fitting jeans. I traced my lips with my tongue, hungrily wondering when I would get to see him naked again.

"Bailey," he chuckled.

I glanced up, seeing amusement in his smile. He had the most adorable dimples. My heart did a flip-flop. How had I ended up in this man's bed? In his universe at all?

Stripping him naked and coaxing him back into bed crossed my mind, but my thoughts were interrupted by a loud rumble from my stomach that ruined the moment.

"You must be starving. Gods, I fed from you, too. You need to eat—now."

His exasperation tickled me. A thousand-year-old vampire worrying that I needed to eat something.

He moved swiftly across the room and picked up

several things from the large chaise near the window. They were my clothes from earlier—jeans, t-shirt, bra, and panties. Everything looked perfect. Not a wrinkle to be seen ... as if they hadn't been worn at all. Major score for enchanted clothes!

I slipped from beneath the covers, wriggling my toes in the plush carpet. He walked back to my side and handed me one piece of clothing at a time, watching me put it on. If he'd been a dog, his tongue would have been dragging the floor as he panted. A grin spread across my face at the thought. I took the last garment, a t-shirt, and pulled it over my head.

"If my hair looks anything like yours, I need a brush," I said.

He feigned a look of offense and then smiled, running his fingers through his wayward hair. "You don't like my sexy, bed hair?"

"I would rather others not see it." I coughed out a laugh and scurried into the bathroom. Picking through the pile of toiletries he'd brought me, I found a brush and some leave-in conditioner. *Hallelujah!* I would have to thank Calliope later. I spritzed some on and worked the brush through my tangles. He'd followed me into the bathroom, waiting in the doorway until I finished. He took the brush and ran it through his hair a couple of times until it was back in place and sexy as hell.

"Better?" He questioned me with a teasing grin.

I nodded. "Yes."

"Let's head over to Rose's and get you some food."

"Is that where everyone eats ... every meal?" I followed

him through the bedroom, slipping into my shoes on the way.

"No." He glanced over his shoulder. "But, I don't have food in the house, so until I take you to the market, you will."

"Oh." Facepalm. Of course he didn't have food in the house. He did, however, have beer. His friends had been drinking it. "You drink alcohol, though?"

He unlocked the front door and gestured for me to exit first. "I enjoy alcohol. It takes the edge off my hunger and helps me relax a little. I can eat food, but it is unnecessary."

Interesting.

I walked down his front steps and waited for him on the sidewalk as he locked his front door. I looked up and down the street that was lined with brownstone-style apartments on each side. They looked so out of place in this tiny western town, like a whale would look in the middle of the desert.

"Who else lives here?" I waved down the street.

"Vampires live on this street," he answered, and slipped an arm around my waist. "Rose brought together many different types of supernatural beings, but most of us still prefer to live close to our own kind."

"Pack mentality?"

"You could call it that, but the wolves are the only ones who consider themselves a pack."

"How many vampires live here?" I glanced up and down the street, trying to count entryways.

"Four." We turned the corner and were quickly back on

the main circle. "All of us were picked by the House of Lamidae to be Protectors."

"So where does everyone else live?" For some reason, I thought there would be more. But maybe vampires weren't that social. I certainly wasn't an expert.

"There are groups of flats like this in other areas of town and there are also several small neighborhoods. Some of the citizens don't mind being neighbors, but there are some who just prefer their own space."

We turned the corner from his street and walked along behind the apartments until we came out on the main circle again, just down from Rose's Café. The smell of barbecue hung in the air and my mouth watered.

Directly across the circle, the Castle bustled with people moving in and out of the front gates by the dozens. Most were dressed in scraps of leather or skintight costumes. There were a couple of women I would have technically called naked, except for a few strategically placed straps. One of the men standing at the gate waved.

Erick raised his hand in acknowledgement and hurried me toward the door of the café. He pulled the door open and I stepped into a crowd of laughing, happy people. A pink-haired woman grabbed my hand a second later and pulled me away from Erick.

I stiffened and pulled back, but a backward glance at him assured me that I was perfectly safe with the unfamiliar woman.

"Rose wants to talk to you for a moment before you sit down for dinner." She tugged again and I followed compliantly this time.

"I-is something wrong?" We went behind the café counter and through the swinging door into the kitchen.

"Nope."

That was all I got? Just *nope*?

The kitchen was much larger than I thought it would be. Huge, stainless steel prep counters ran the length of the room's center. Glistening stovetops, ovens, a brick pizza oven, refrigerators, and evenly spaced sinks decorated the outside walls. It was something I would have expected to see in a swanky, five-star restaurant, but not in a West Texas café. This town was full of surprises.

Several women were kneading dough on one end of the long prep counter and several others were tending to large pots on the various stovetops. A large, silver door at the end of the room opened and Rose walked out. A white apron was tied around her waist and traces of flour clung to her cheeks. Nothing about her said, 'I run this town.' At the same time, I could feel the respect everyone else in the room had for her. Subtle nods as she walked by. The way they made eye contact. It wasn't fear ... more like adoration.

"Bailey." Rose's voice carried across the clatter of the kitchen as if it was a library. She made her way to my side.

"Your kitchen is amazing."

"Thank you, darling. I can't imagine trying to feed this town with anything else. But, truly, I couldn't do it without the brownies and the pixies. They are the heart of this place."

A brownie? Nobody in the kitchen looked like they were made out of my favorite chocolate dessert. I must've made a face because she laughed right at me.

"The pixies are easy to spot. They like to have bright colors in their hair. Raven and Maven help run the café and their friends cooking the pizzas also run our market." She pointed to the rainbow-haired group by the large pizza oven.

"I'll see you later, hon," the pink-haired pixie who'd stolen me from Erick's side grinned and trotted across the room.

I nodded. I didn't even know her name.

"The ladies cooking on the stoves and kneading the dough for tomorrow are some of the brownies in town. Corinne, do you mind?"

One particularly tall brunette looked up from her work and smiled. Her skin shimmered and glistened, darkening from a natural human ivory color to luminescent sparkling bronze. Her hair turned black and her eyes changed from brown to a bright green. Then the transformation faded as quickly as it had appeared.

I swallowed and turned to meet Rose's gaze. "Why are you showing me all of this?"

"You're more important than you know." She shook her head. "And there's a lot more to this town than you realize."

Yeah. No kidding, but why was I important? As far as I could tell, I was the only human visitor outside of the Castle guests. I shifted on my feet and wiped my sweaty hands on the sides of my jeans. A second later, Erick stood next to me. His big hands rubbed up and down my bare arms and his peppermint scent drifted into my nostrils as he nuzzled my neck. The tension in my muscles eased and I leaned into his caress.

"Are you okay, *kjaere?*"

"I'm fine, really. I just saw a brownie."

Corinne chuckled from across the room.

"I wouldn't have thought a brownie would upset you."

"She didn't."

Questions swam in my mind and a newfound excitement tingled across my skin. The riots had brought with them a new world order based on fear, but I was being shown much more. It was a huge leap of faith for them to share their secrets with me.

But why me? I kept coming back to that.

He kissed my neck.

Rose stepped in front of us. Her gaze focused on me, but she spoke to Erick. "Arlea needs to meet her. It's imperative." Her tone had switched from friendly and casual to deadly serious, sending a chill down my spine. Who was Arlea? Why did she need to see me?

"She's not ready." Erick's voice rumbled behind me.

"For what?" I asked, but neither answered me.

"We can't afford to wait. If she's the one, another point on the star can be filled. We need to know—for the Sisters' protection and her own." Rose's eyes darkened, her honey-brown irises becoming a dark merlot color.

"I know," Erick hissed. "But not today."

I tried to step from between the two semi-snarling beings, but Erick's hands latched onto my hips and held me against his body. The kitchen noise had quieted and all eyes were on the three of us. For several seconds, I don't think anyone even breathed.

"Tomorrow morning," Rose countered.

"Fine." The mumble was barely audible. I felt it more

than heard it. In seconds, he'd swept me out of the kitchen and into the dining room. We took a seat at an empty booth and Erick slid in beside me instead of across the table. I pulled a menu from the stand at the end of the table and glanced over it. Eggs and bacon sounded pretty good to me right now. Maybe some fruit. Anything to distract me from the tension stiffening Erick's body.

"I'm sorry if we frightened you." His voice was soft again, the way I preferred. I had yet to see him truly angry, but if that little spat with Rose was any indication, I could wait.

"I don't want to cause a problem. If I need to meet this woman, Arlea. I can."

"It can wait, *kjaere*." His gaze softened and he kissed me gently, his lips lulling me into a contented bliss. Whatever he wanted, I would do.

"What was Rose talking about? A point on a star — what does that mean? Why am I important to the town?"

It might not be urgent, but it certainly piqued my curiosity. Why would some powerful supernatural think I was supposed to complete anything? I didn't belong in their world. I'd just tumbled in haphazardly.

Erick sighed. Whatever it was, he didn't want to tell me. Indecision was written in the furrowed lines on his forehead and his gaze stayed glued to the table. "Why don't you order something for dinner? I'll tell you about it later.

"Viking," a deep, male voice boomed from across the room. Miles' giant body slid into the seat across from us. "Bailey." He nodded toward me and smiled. I squirmed just a little when his knee brushed mine. Damn, he was a big man. Erick was tall and muscular, but this guy was built like a brick house. "Have you eaten yet?"

I shook my head.

He raised his hand and the same pink-haired pixie sidled over to the table.

"Hey, Miles." Her smile curved mischievously and a certain twinkle in her eye made it clear she had the hots for dragon-guy Miles. "Hi, Erick. Bailey, right?"

I nodded again, still unable to make sound come out of my mouth.

"Sweetheart, can you bring us out the house special for tonight? Bailey looks like she could use some protein." Miles caught my darting gaze and winked.

A low rumble started in Erick's chest. He rubbed his palm up and down my thigh and heat rushed to my sex and then ricocheted through my whole body. Flames licked at my skin. Food sounded good, but really all I could think about was getting back into bed with him. What was wrong with me?

"Do you like barbecue?" Erick asked.

The question jarred me from my naughty thoughts. "Yes," I managed to squeak.

"Good," he squeezed my thigh and slid his hand farther up.

Heat rose in my cheeks. If the blush wasn't a tell-all, Miles' and Erick's flaring nostrils were a dead giveaway that my arousal was being broadcast to the entire room. I wanted to crawl under the table. Only that wouldn't help either, because it was a maze of masculine legs. Why couldn't I just have dinner without feeling like I was going to be the dessert? I wasn't under the impression that Erick had any intention of sharing me. He'd said as much already. But the dragon's obvious interest was difficult to ignore.

"So when are you bringing her over to the Castle? I bet she would look just scrumptious on one of our St. Andrew's crosses. You've got to be itching for a good session. It's been weeks since you dropped in."

A cross? What? No way. I'm not interested in kink. I like Erick's big, fluffy bed, maybe his big shower, but that's it. I don't want to be strung out on anything. My mind raced in time with my heartbeat and my breathing sped up, too.

Both men's gazes zeroed in on me. I could feel their questions without looking up from the spot on the table I was trying to set ablaze with my laser vision. The table was silent.

"Bailey, I apologize." Miles' comment seemed genuine. "I read into your arousal and went too far. Please don't be frightened."

"It's okay, *kjaere*. Miles is notorious for teasing."

Really? I wouldn't have thought that at all from the dragon's stoic, stony expression.

My racing heartbeat slowed just a hair and the arrival of our food helped break the uncomfortable tension. Several racks of ribs, fries, celery sticks, and ranch dressing. The barbecue smelled divine. I couldn't wait to taste it.

The bell on the door rang and I caught a glimpse of Garrett. Crap. Like it wasn't bad enough to have a vampire and a dragon sniffing at my pheromones, now there would be a wolf listening to my actual thoughts.

I starting saying the alphabet in my head. Maybe I

could make my thoughts so annoying that he wouldn't even try.

"Help yourself, darl'n. I won't bite." Miles chuckled and grabbed a celery stick. "Unlike the Viking sitting next to you, staring longingly at your carotid artery."

"He already —" I slapped my hand over my mouth. Heat rushed to my face again, turning it dark crimson for sure.

Erick and Miles laughed together and Erick leaned over and placed a reassuring kiss on the top of my head. "Don't worry. He baited you on purpose to find out if I had fed from you."

I took a deep breath and released another long sigh. If they were both laughing, I should be able to find a way to relax a little, too. They were friends. Maybe I could eventually count Miles as a friend, too. I wasn't very good at socializing, mostly from lack of practice. Keeping to myself and hiding had become an art form for me.

Taking a rib from the plate, I bit into the sauce-slathered meat and moaned. I hadn't eaten anything so good in years. "This is amazing." I ditched the cleaned bone and grabbed another piece from the plate in the middle.

"She's too skinny. You need to feed her more." Miles tossed a couple more ribs onto my plate.

"She's been on her own a long time. Give her a break," Erick shot back, leaning back in the booth.

"Uh, sitting right here," I said, waving my hand. I dropped another bone on my plate and went straight for more meat. I didn't usually eat this much, but maybe

Erick's feeding had made a difference. He'd acted like it would.

"Miles," I started, feeling a little more confident, "Why do you sound like a native Texan, but Erick still has a little bit of an accent?"

He tossed down a bone and wiped the corner of his mouth with a napkin. "He does not care to hide his accent. I, however, do." The style of his voice morphed instantly from a laid-back Texas drawl to a British accent. "I like everyone thinking I'm from around here. Simplifies life."

I smiled. Blending in was definitely something I understood.

After finishing a couple more ribs, not willing to let the ones he'd tossed my direction go to waste, I cleaned my fingers with a little towelette from the container at the end of the table. I wanted to lick my fingers clean. The sweet, tangy bite of the barbecue sauce was so good, but I'd had enough teasing for one day. Licking my fingers at the table with two men staring at me was not an option.

I leaned back against the booth and Erick's shoulder, listening to them talk about his sister's wedding. Apparently, she wasn't Erick's real sister, but he'd saved her life several centuries ago and she'd called him brother ever since.

When Miles asked what had happened with the Djinn, I sat up. Erick glanced at me briefly before continuing, as if trying to decide if he should let me in on this conversation. "He was there to bother Cyn. The wedding was out in the open, so we knew he'd try something."

"We've got to take care of that asshole," Miles said. "He's getting more brazen and I don't like it."

Miles snapped up the last piece of celery and licked his lips before chomping it down in one bite. "Oh, by the way." He looked straight at me, his brown eyes flickering with just a hint of honey. "Arlea told me to tell you hi, Bailey. She said she understands your hesitation to enter the Castle, but hopes you will visit soon."

"Miles," Erick growled.

"Hey, I'm just relaying a message from the Oracle. I don't know about you, but if Arlea tells me to do something, I sure as hell do it. I don't need any more bad karma. Me and Eli already have enough. Losing Diana pretty much kicked our collective asses."

"We will find her, Miles. Even the Sisters say that she will return to you."

"Yeah." He sighed. "That's what they've been saying for centuries." Moving from the booth, he stood slowly, his seven-foot frame looming over the table. "I have to go relieve my brother from dungeon duty, so I'll see you two lovebirds later," he said, a mischievous glint shining in his brown eyes. He nodded his head to me before heading out the front door.

I laughed and then slapped my hand over my mouth, staring down at the table in horror. Miles was already outside, but I couldn't believe I'd felt comfortable enough to laugh at him. But, he'd just used the words dungeon and lovebirds in the same sentence. As if it were perfectly normal for someone to have something called dungeon duty. I guess when a castle, dragons, and kinky sex are involved, having a dungeon isn't so far out of the realm of possibility.

Erick gave me a gentle smile. "It's good to hear you laugh."

"It feels strange." I glanced around the café. Lots of people were laughing and carrying on. Some were quiet. There were even a few couples tucked into the back of the room. "I haven't had friends since ... well ... even after the way they scared me at first, Miles seems like someone I can trust. Actually, I feel pretty comfortable with everyone I've met in town so far.

"Even Garrett?"

"He may not be your biggest fan, but yes, I think I can trust him. He protected me on the bus. Even though he continues to invade my personal thoughts from time to time, he seems like an okay guy."

"He is interested in you."

I nearly choked on my tongue. Interested? The art of flirtation was not one of my talents. In fact, I'd made quite an art of avoiding all such advances over the last few years. How had I missed Garrett's intentions?

"Ummm ..."

"Are you interested in him?"

"No! Not that way. I just ..."

Erick stared at me, waiting patiently. No jealousy, just persistence. He wanted an answer. What was I supposed to say? That I found Garrett attractive, but had no interest in being with him?

"Find him attractive?" he ventured.

"I, maybe, but ... I don't have feelings for him."

"I know." He slipped an arm around my waist and squeezed. "You shouldn't feel bad for being attracted to him or anyone in town. Appreciating someone's appearance isn't wrong."

"Oh."

"Humans are brainwashed into believing that appreciation or admiration is tantamount to cheating on their significant other. Many supernaturals feel the same way, but I am not one of them. Nor are my friends." He paused a moment and kissed the top of my head. "Garrett and his brother are not my friends," he whispered.

"But you trust them?"

"To protect the town? Yes." Erick's eyes darkened, pulling me into their inky blue depths. "To try and woo you away from me? Yes."

"I wouldn't ever ... why would he think ... ?"

"Men do not always follow logic and reason where women are concerned." He slid from his seat and stood, offering me his hand. His palm was cool and his grasp on my fingers was firm, but gentle.

No disgruntled Djinn, horny werewolf, or pissed-off ex would take me from Erick. I wanted this life. These friends.

Something about this town called to me.

It said I belonged.

CHAPTER 9

A warm summer breeze ruffled a few pieces of my hair that'd come loose from my braid. The moon and star-soaked sky shone brightly on Sanctuary. The gas street lamps along the main circle added a warm glow to the evening's natural light. The lamps complemented the style of the town—old, brick, with cobblestone streets. Only the sidewalks were made of smooth concrete, reminding me I hadn't stepped into a contraband history book.

I touched one of the lampposts as we walked. The finish made it look like an old wooden post, but it was solid metal. Such detail and beauty in this hidden-away sanctuary. Little things made it special, like the hand-painted signs above the shops. It was a world away from the grind of the most people's reality.

"Is the market still open?" I pointed toward the grocery store window. "It would be nice to have some eggs and juice in the morning."

"I'm sure Bella will let us in. She's usually there until all hours of the night."

"Is she a pixie? Rose said pixies ran the market."

"Yes. Sanctuary took in an entire grove of pixies when we first started building the town," he answered, putting his hand around my waist as we walked along the winding sidewalk. "They came with the stream and oak forest that lie just west of the town border."

"They came with it?" How could people come from a river? Or some old trees?

"Pixies, or fairies as some call them, are from nature. There isn't an easy way to explain it, but they lived in the trees and in the water. When we arrived and started building, they would trash our camp every night, trying to scare us off."

"Didn't that irritate you?"

"Of course it did. On the third night, we caught a few of them and they had a heart-to-heart with Rose. After that, the pixies mostly stayed with us. There are a few who still live outside the town in their natural form, but most joined us."

I stopped at the window and looked in. The market looked like any other small grocery store I'd been in, except in the back. I could see lights and ... bushes ... trees. What was in there? I squinted.

"We could go in and ask Bella to give you a tour." The amusement in his voice was not masked, and I couldn't help but smile. I nearly had my nose pressed to the glass, trying to get a closer look.

"That would probably be better."

He chuckled. "I thought it might."

Before he grabbed the handle, the door swung open and a petite woman with short, sky blue hair stood in the entrance. Her skin was ivory and as smooth as porcelain. But it was her eyes that really stood out. Green— greener than a freshly budded leaf in springtime. No glowing or sparkling, just color in its purest form. Spectacular, really.

"Bella, this is Bailey." The rumble of his voice jarred me from my thoughts.

"Hi," I answered, extending my hand.

She smiled and leaned forward to hug me instead. The quick squeeze was surprising but not unpleasant. "Hi, sweetie. I knew you'd be by eventually. A girl likes to have at least a little food in the house, am I right?"

"Yes." The pixie's easygoing attitude put me completely at ease.

"Come on in then. You won't get far trying to dematerialize and come through the window pane." She giggled and led us into the store.

Heat flared in my cheeks. She'd seen me peering in the window.

"Do you want to see the plants in the back first? I think that's what caught your eye, wasn't it?" I caught sight of a smirk on her face before she trotted through the store and back to the area where I thought I'd seen shrubbery.

"How do you grow them inside?" I walked forward, grateful to feel Erick's hand at the small of my back. It was exciting to see new things and not be afraid of talking to people. I could see myself staying and making friends with the people in Sanctuary. As long as they would tolerate me —a human.

"We have skylights." She gestured to the ceiling and I

looked up. Indeed, there were skylights. In fact, the entire roof was made of glass. Only the front of the store was covered. "Well, technically it's more of a greenhouse." She twirled and smiled. "I love seeing the reaction on people's faces when they see it for the first time." She waved her hands and iridescent water droplets rained from the glass ceiling onto the variety of plants. Some I recognized and others looked like miniatures of larger trees.

"It's like magick." The words slipped from my mouth without hesitation. I sounded so infantile. Magick? Really. But, they were supernatural beings with extraordinary powers ... and the siren made enchanted, self-cleaning clothes. Were pixies with a supernatural greenhouse so outlandish?

Bella's face beamed. I could have sworn I saw an effervescent glow surround her. "It is magick. Fae dust, to be precise. Mixed into the water we give the plants, it allows us to completely control the essence of the plant, down to its atomic structure. Any plant anyone brings me, we can grow here." She waved her hands again and the glowing mist ceased to fall. Lights brightened in the room until it appeared as though it was noon outside. "Now, tell me. What's your favorite fruit?"

"Pineapple."

"Oh, good one! Follow me." She scurried down an aisle beckoning us to follow.

I glanced back at Erick.

"I'll wait here for you. Go see," he answered, grinning.

My hesitation lasted only a second before I darted after her. She'd stopped in the back corner and had picked up a pot from the floor and set it on an empty table in the middle of the aisle. Maybe it was a pineapple plant. I couldn't be sure. I didn't really know what they grew on.

She looked up and caught my gaze. "Watch the bud in the center of the plant."

Nodding, I focused on the reddish-pink ball in the middle. It was the size of a tennis ball and looked like it was covered with reptilian scales. A flick of her wrist surrounded us in the fine glowing mist again. I gasped. The plant moved, growing and changing right in front of me. The bud got bigger and brighter. It was bigger than my fist in seconds and then started changing colors, fading from the bright pink red to a rich green. The scales started to widen and stretch. Then I began to see a faint yellow outline around each one. It was ripe. A pineapple had grown and ripened in front of me in a matter of seconds.

"How?"

"Like you said earlier." She grabbed the fruit and cut it from the stem. "It's magick."

"So all the plants here ... they grow just as you need them?"

Bella nodded. "Except for meat and packaged food, though why anyone would ever want to eat something called a Twinkie is beyond me, the town is completely self-sufficient. We provide produce for everyone's home, including the café."

"I don't know what to say." The whole place was overwhelming.

"Just tell me what you need for breakfast and I'll set you up with a quick basket. I can show you more another time."

"I would like that. If there's anything I can do to help

in the store, please let me know. I'm not really sure where they think I'm going to fit in around here. I'd really like to have something to keep me busy."

She waggled a pointer finger at me and clicked her tongue. "Be careful what you ask for, I may just hold you to that offer."

"Thank you."

"What do you need?"

"Oh, some eggs, orange juice, maybe a little bacon would be good. Any fresh fruit you are willing to part with would be appreciated."

"Excellent. I'll meet you at the front."

"Thank you, again."

"Phffft. No trouble, sweetie." She flitted away, plucking this and that from different plants.

I walked back to the front of the store where Erick stood. His gaze darkened as it fell on me and I felt his hunger in the air between us like a sparking live wire. His wasn't the only energy. My arousal spiked right along with his. I wanted nothing more than to be naked and wrapped in his arms.

"*Kjaere*," his accent oozed sex. I'd met dozens of vampires since I'd moved to Texas, but Erick was a whole different variety. Hell, he was a whole different variety of man, too. "Did you enjoy the tour?"

"Yes," I nodded, licking my lips. "She showed me how the fae dust feeds the plants."

He stepped forward and pulled me into his arms. His peppermint scent filled my lungs just as his mouth captured my lips. He tasted like honey and smelled like peppermint. Where did he get the candy? He drove his tongue into my mouth and all thoughts of missing the bowl of mints vanished. He crushed my lips with his, all the while cradling my head in his large palms. His thumbs caressed the rise of my cheeks and I moaned into his mouth.

My body burned and my sex throbbed. I could feel my pulse everywhere. Moisture soaked my panties and my breasts were heavy. It was like we'd been in bed touching each other for hours, instead of only a few seconds.

"Erick Thorson, take your tongue out of her mouth and get her into a proper bed before you spread her across the counter next to the cash register."

I squeaked and tried to pull away, but he held me tight, licking the edges of my lips before slowly releasing me from his grasp.

Bella held up a basket of groceries and flashed me a quick smile before looking back at Erick. "She had a nice dowsing of dust. You can thank me later by helping me build some new tables for the back."

"Will do." He took the basket and guided me out of the store with his other hand at my back. "Night, Bella," he called out before she closed the door after us.

"What was that? What did she mean I got dowsed? I thought that stuff was just for the plants."

"Fae dust has a unique effect on humans," he finally answered as we turned off the main town circle. "It heightens their senses and libido."

"It makes us horny?" I giggled. I certainly felt horny and absolutely ready to strip naked in the street. Damn, we needed to hurry. I pushed into a faster walk and felt his arm encircle my waist. My feet lifted from the ground and we rushed forward. Air whipped against my face. The scent of honeysuckle was on the breeze and a second later we were at his door.

He set me down in the center of his foyer and left my side in a blur. The lights flashed in the kitchen for only a few seconds before he was back and carrying me up the stairs, cradled in his arms like a precious treasure.

Shouldering open the double doors to his bedroom, he walked to the edge of the bed and let me slide slowly to my feet. I kicked off the ballet flats and raised my arms in the air over my head, allowing him to pull off my shirt. It sailed across the room and moments later, my bra followed.

He paused and kissed each breast before unsnapping my jeans and pushing them gently over my hips. I shimmied until they fell to the floor. The underwear was next and I breathed a sigh of relief when he let me step out of them instead of tearing them from my body. I really liked these clothes. I would hate to have to ask Calliope for more so soon.

His lips seared my skin, leaving a hot trail from my neck down to my breasts. I pulled at the hem of his shirt, begging him to join me skin to skin. He obliged and I ran my hands over his solid pecs and taut, eight-pack abs. I wanted to bite and nip at his body. He smelled so good.

He lifted me like a feather and laid me gently on the bed. I sat up and crawled toward him on my knees. He shucked his pants and underwear and gestured with a hand for me to turn. My pussy creamed at the thought of him behind me and I twisted to present my ass. He gave each cheek a quick smack and I yelped. Before I could move, he grabbed my hips and drove into me from behind with one thrust.

So full. So much pressure.

My heart leapt into my throat and I strangled a moan. He held me there several moments before slowly pulling out and then pushing back in. The movement was torturously slow. I tried to push back against him to get a better rhythm, but he held my hips still.

"Am I hurting you?"

"No," I gasped. Nerve endings surged with electricity as he drew his cock in and out of my slick pussy. Every moment was pure pleasure. One of his hands slid down from my hips and between the folds of my sex, finding the tiny swollen nub that thrummed with need and circling it with a finger ever so slowly. "Ahhh," I whimpered and pushed back against his cock. Struggling against his grip, I fought to take him harder and faster, but he wouldn't be rushed. His thrusts remained slow, and just his one hand on my hip held me firmly in place.

As his cock slid in and out, his talented fingers tortured my clit until a sheen of sweat coated my skin and my entire body shook. The release I needed was just out of reach. Every time I would rise to the crest, he slowed down, keeping me on an edge that bordered on painful.

"Please." My arms threatened to collapse. Soon I would just be a writhing mass, crying for an orgasm to soothe my humming body. "I need you."

He released my hips, slid from my body. I cried out. The emptiness was worse than the desire to come had been.

"Shhh, *kjaere*. I am here." He turned me over and

spread me out on my back. Kneeling between my legs, his form was truly spectacular. His tanned skin glowed in the low lamplight of the bedroom, and his blond hair caught the light and shone like strands of spun gold. A god among men.

He was overwhelmingly male ... protector, predator, and lover.

His blue eyes were as dark as the night sky and I caught a glimpse of crimson sparkling from them. My skin tingled in anticipation of his bite. I knew it was coming. I wanted it to come.

I smiled and reached up to embrace him.

My hands slid along his arms and up over his shoulders as he lowered himself onto me. He guided his cock back to my entrance and sank inside me. I made a noise that sounded like the purr of a cat, enjoying every inch of his hardness as it returned to my wet pussy, filling me once again.

His chest rubbed against my sensitive breasts and I arched into his mouth as he suckled first one nipple and then the other. Every surface of my body throbbed with my pounding pulse. He raised his head and looked up at me.

"May I?"

I nodded and turned my head to the side, baring my neck. He leaned down and licked my neck, then kissed along my collarbone and back up to the soft hollow just where my neck and shoulder came together.

His thrusts sped up and my focus returned to my throbbing sex and all-consuming desire to find release. An orgasm started building within me again, swirling inside and heating my skin until the touch of his skin to mine was like fire on ice. My need only grew more and I rocked my hips, matching his rhythm. He ground his pelvis against mine and it set me off like he'd struck a match.

A scream tore from my throat and I arched my back, pressing against him as hard as my human body was able. Muscles tightened and I wrapped my legs around his waist, digging in my heels and pulling him deeper.

A slight pinch on my shoulder made me flinch just slightly, and then the pain faded to pleasure as I felt the pull of blood. I moaned as he drank. Being the one to feed him filled me with a sense of empowerment. He asked. He didn't take. He made sure I knew it was a gift to be given, not a debt I owed. I loved him for that.

I'd known him two days. Could I love someone that fast? My mind soared to a place of euphoria and I contemplated my realization. His cock moved slowly inside me as he drank. When he finished I felt the swipe of his tongue as he sealed the bite and licked away any trace of blood.

His strokes increased their speed and depth, pushing against my womb and sending me spiraling toward a second orgasm. I couldn't come again. Not so soon. Not so hard.

"Fly, *min kjaereste*. Let go and soar again for me." He reached between us and pressed hard on my clit. Everything went white. My body contracted as if it were made of one single muscle. A deeper, huskier scream, almost like a growl came from my throat and I dug my fingers into his arms. I rode the wave of pleasure higher than I'd ever gone before.

He roared as his body went rigid against mine. After

finding his release, he lowered his chest down on top of me, pulling his cock free of my slick sex. He rolled to the side and moved me to lie in the crook of his shoulder.

I snuggled closer, throwing a leg over his thigh. It was unexplainable, but I loved him. He'd stolen my heart in that cold bus station and brought it to a sanctuary. What we'd done together over the last two days, I hadn't done with another man ... ever. I hadn't wanted to, either. With Erick, I wanted it. Wanted everything. I was alive again, truly alive for the first time in four years. At his side, anything was possible.

"I'm glad you are happy, *kjaere*." His chest rose and fell as he spoke. "You fill me with a joy I thought I'd never find again."

I smiled against his skin and rubbed my thumb back and forth over one of his ribs, tracing a small arc back and forth. "There you go reading my mind again."

A chuckle shook his shoulder, jostling my head ever so slightly.

"I don't think I've ever felt this happy before, Erick. I ..." I snapped my mouth shut before I said too much. I couldn't tell him I loved him now. He was a thousand years old and I'd known him two days. Whether I loved him or not, I couldn't say it out loud, yet. "You feel like home," I whispered.

He squeezed me tighter and I craned my neck to look up at him. I was rewarded with a soft kiss on the lips. "As do you, my beautiful Bailey. As do you." He rubbed his hand through my hair and I leaned into the caress. His thumb traced figure eights on my scalp and my eyes drooped. Sleep was calling, but I wanted to enjoy just being with him a little longer.

"You'll stay with me ... tonight? I don't want to wake up and find you gone."

"I'm not going anywhere," he assured me. "Sleep, *min kjaereste*."

I could have sworn he said something about a busy day after telling me to sleep. But, tomorrow would just have to wait. Tonight I was snuggled in the arms of a man who offered me a chance at a fresh start. A chance to love and just maybe, be loved in return.

I was taking it.

CHAPTER 10

T he gentle, but persistent prodding of Erick's cock against my ass awakened me from a contented sleep and I shivered in anticipation. One of his arms was draped over my waist with the palm holding one of my breasts hostage. I wiggled my hips, rubbing against his hardness.

He shifted behind me and trailed his lips along my bare shoulder. Chuckling, his breath tickled the hairs along the back of my neck.

Wait. "Why does it feel like you are breathing?"

He moved his hand from my breast and lifted my leg, sliding into my wet sex without a hitch. I took a deep breath, surprised that I was so ready for him. A moan slipped from my lips as he slowly pumped in and out, stroking the folds of my sex and building a burn deep in my belly.

"It's something I did long before I became a vampire. Motor memory. The act of drawing air in and out of my lungs serves no physical purpose, but it does give me a more human appearance."

He thrust in and out, grabbing my hips to give himself more leverage. Another moan slipped out and I leaned back against his chest, quite content to let him have his way with me.

My body was still sore from the night's escapades, but he had no intention of allowing me to be lazy. One of his hands slipped from my hip to my slick folds and rubbed directly across my clit.

I gasped and jerked, digging my nails into his arms. Fire burns in my belly, and an orgasm rushes forward with unusual speed. How does he do this to me? He pressed again on my now-throbbing clit and I grasped at the sheets in front of me, fisting handfuls. I heard myself screaming his name as my body contracted, squeezing his cock for everything it was worth. He drove into me once more, growling into my ear and taking his release as my mind and body continued to soar in ecstasy.

As my panting returned to normal breathing, he rolled away and got up from the bed. He walked around to my side and scooped me into his arms. I started to protest, but then decided that being carried against his hard, sexy chest was exactly where I wanted to be. Why walk when a sexy man insisted on carrying me?

He pushed through the bathroom door, put me down on the edge of his large soaker tub, continuing across to the shower. A few turns of the hardware had water coming out of all the spigots, including the ones on the wall. I stood, my legs still a little wobbly, and moved to his side.

"You should have waited."

"I can walk." A slight smirk twisted my mouth, but my legs wobble like gelatin, betraying how much he'd affected me.

"Barely," he answered, a smartass grin splitting his face. Taking my hand, he led me into the steaming hot water. The streams pounded against my body.

I sighed. "I'll just stand here if that's okay with you."

He laughed.

I closed my eyes and leaned my head back, letting the rain-like spray from the showerhead directly above me smooth my mussed hair away from my face. Ecstasy. That's what Erick's shower was –a marbled room of perfect bliss.

The squeak of a lever made me open my eyes. A draft of cool air wrapped around my wet body as all the flowing water stopped on my side of the shower. Then his hands were on me, running up and down my body, creating a silky lather from neck to toes, chasing away all thoughts of the cold. He took special care with all of my most intimate parts.

A moment later, he pushed a button on the wall next to me and the massaging jets of water returned, along with the steady stream from the overhead spigot. The water temperature was warm enough to keep the chill at bay, but not hot enough to fog the glass wall of the enclosure. He rubbed and guided the water over my soap-slicked body until every trace had been washed away.

"Feel better?"

"What a lovely way to begin the morning." I licked away some of the water from the top of my lip.

He returned my grin. "There are towels on the warmer. I'll be out in just a moment."

I followed the line of his hand across the bathroom and saw several black towels hanging over a chrome frame. Stepping carefully out of the shower, I tiptoed across the black marble floors and grabbed one of the oversized, fluffy towels.

After pressing as much water out of my hair as I could, I wrapped the damp towel around my torso and set the hairdryer to my long tresses. A few minutes later, the water turned off in the shower.

He grabbed a towel and wrapped it around his waist. Via the mirror, I watched water droplets fall from the ends of his blond hair and run in rivulets down his muscled chest. I couldn't help but wet my lips. An urge to toss down the hair dryer and lick the water from his chest crossed my mind. I caught his naughty smirk in the mirror. Heat crept into my cheeks, and it wasn't due to the hair dryer.

He disappeared into his closet, returning with an armful of clothing. "Be careful how you look at me, Bailey Ross, or I'll take you right back to bed."

The way he'd used my full name made me giggle like a naughty school girl. He made me laugh—made me feel like I could just be me. I didn't have to be afraid of what was around the corner in his world. Granted, there were all kinds of crazy, supernatural creatures here, but they seemed like decent people, unlike most of those I'd encountered since my parents died.

I continued drying my hair, greedily watching for glimpses of his bare body in the mirror as he dressed. My efforts were rewarded when he let the towel drop to the floor. My heart leapt into my throat and moisture pooled yet again between my thighs.

"I can smell you, *kjaere*."

I turned off the hairdryer and lay it on the counter, picking up a bottle of leave-in conditioner instead. I spritzed a healthy amount over the length of my hair and smiled back at him in the mirror. "I can't help it."

My stomach chose just that moment to growl and gurgle as loudly as it possibly could. Heat raced to my cheeks, turning my face bright red yet again. Way to ruin the moment. What was wrong with my stomach? I was starving, but still. Why did it have to be so loud?

He appeared beside me, dressed and ready for the day. A pair of dark, loose-fitting jeans rode low on his hips and a short-sleeved t-shirt covered his spectacular chest, leaving his arms on full display. Arms that any human man would envy.

"Here." He handed me a colorful stack of clothing items. A bright pink bra and panty set and a tank-style maxi dress in royal purple. "I pulled these from the closet. We'll have to stop by Calliope's later today and let you pick out a few more things. I'm afraid all I got you are these two outfits."

"Thank you. They are lovely. I'm sure I don't need anything else right now. I've made do with a pair of jeans and little else for a long time. You don't have to keep getting me—"

His finger touched my lips. "I will do as I please."

"But—"

He pushed harder. "Say, yes sir, thank you."

"Yes s-sir, thank you," I repeated slowly, tilting my head

to the side. Sir? Was he just playing with me or was he asserting a little more dominance than I'd seen so far? He knew I was uncomfortable with that type of role-playing, yet just that little demand made my heart speed up and stoked my seemingly constant state of arousal.

"Good, *kjaere*. Now why don't you put these on?" He smiled, gave me a soft kiss on the lips and then pressed the clothes into my arms. I stood frozen, still absorbing our small exchange. He stepped back slowly and sat on the edge of the tub in the center of the bathroom.

"Are you going to just sit there and watch?" I asked, when words finally returned to my brain.

"Yes." He nodded and grinned, a wicked sparkle shining in his bright blue eyes.

Two could play this game. I plopped the clothes on the counter and unhooked the towel, letting it pool to the floor at my feet. My eyes never left his face and I smiled when his eyes widened. My dare excited him and I felt a sense of power I'd never experienced.

I slowly slipped on the panties and then the bra, the underwear cinched and stretched in all the right places until they fit better than a glove. I grabbed the hem of the dress and pulled the large loose garment over my head. It hung on my body like a sack until the enchantment began working. The upper part of the dress tightened around my torso and bust until it fit like a second skin. At my hips, it flared into a full skirt and lengthened until it just brushed the tops of my feet. I twirled, watching myself in the mirror.

It was beautiful. I couldn't wait to actually go into Calliope's shop myself and look around.

"The color is perfect on you."

"Thank you."

He rose from the edge of the tub and followed me out the bathroom door. Grabbing the hem of my dress, I went barefoot down the stairs and padded into the kitchen.

The black and white color scheme was clean and modern, but lacked personality. It was cold in more ways than one. Goose bumps populated my arms as I opened a cabinet to look for a frying pan.

Nothing. Completely empty.

I opened another door. Same thing.

"Shit." He growled behind me. "I forgot to grab a pan and some cooking utensils last night at Bella's."

I closed another empty cabinet and turned to face him.

"I'm sorry. It's been so long since I fed anyone."

"It's okay." The idea that he wouldn't have any pans or dishes hadn't even crossed my mind.

"I'll stop while we are out today and pick up a few more things."

I flashed him a supportive smile. At that moment he looked more like an embarrassed boyfriend than a millennia-old vampire who'd seen empires rise and fall. I liked it. It made him seem more real.

He took my hand and led me toward the front door. I slipped on a pair of sandals as he opened it. "We'll get you some breakfast and then—" His words stopped suddenly and he turned, looking down to meet my gaze. "Rose wants you to meet Arlea today. Do you think you are up for that? If not, I will insist it wait."

"I don't want you fighting with Rose. If I need to meet this woman today, then that's what I'll do. It can't be that bad." I searched his eyes for some hint of reassurance. What I saw was uncertainty. He knew this Arlea woman. Why would he be so against my meeting her? "Is she mean?"

He looked away and shook his head. "No, she's not mean. Just old and …"

"And what?"

"Arlea is an Oracle. She sees fates." A long sigh slipped from his lips and he shrugged his shoulders. "All the Sisters are seers of some variety. You need to be prepared."

"For what?"

"For something you may not like."

Well that wasn't vague at all. Something I might not like? Was she going to read my palm and tell me my fortune? That was all such bull. No one could see the future. Though only a few days ago I would have said dragons and pixies didn't exist either.

We exited his apartment and walked down the stairs to the sidewalk. Across the street stood two tall men, one with short brown hair and the other with shoulder-length black curls. The first was in loose jeans and a white t-shirt. The one with black hair sported Western jeans, boots, and a flannel shirt with the sleeves rolled up just a little, showing muscular forearms. They glanced up when we reached the bottom step and nodded toward us before going back to their conversation.

"Are they vampires?"

He took my hand and led me around the corner to the town circle. "Yes. Marcus lives in the apartment they were standing in front of. The one dressed like a cowboy is

Javier. His place is next door to mine. They are Protectors, like me."

"So they have the tattoo that protects them from the sun, too, I guess." I mentally pinched myself. That was a stupid question, seeing as how we were all outside and the sun was up.

"Yes."

"Are all the Protectors vampires?"

"Yes."

"Why?"

"We are stronger and faster than many supernaturals. Also, we don't grow old."

"So it makes you the perfect soldier." There were definite advantages to being a vampire. But not being able to enjoy the taste of food ever again had to be high on the list of cons. And for most of them, daylight wasn't an option either.

"It certainly makes us difficult to replace. The Protectors are chosen by the Oracle of Lamidae, Arlea. Rose bestows the magick needed to gift us with immunity against the sunlight."

"Are there other vampires in town who aren't Protectors?"

"No."

We turned onto the main circle of town and passed Calliope's shop. A pretty, ocean blue dress in the window caught my eye and I couldn't help but stare, if only for a moment. The color of the dress reminded me of Erick's eyes.

"Vampires, as a rule, prefer their space. You won't find them in groups. That Sanctuary is the home to four of us already is quite stressful because we need to feed. In a small town, there are not many options. No hospitals and clinics mean no blood banks. Most vampires keep to large metropolises and stay as anonymous as possible."

"So then do they all feed from Rose? She was going to let you drink her blood."

"Several of the Protectors have taken up with other people in town. That helps with the feeding, but Rose still provides when we need extra. Though she has not fed me since you arrived."

"Do I taste different?"

"Very." He nuzzled my ear and opened the café door. "Your blood is sweeter and lighter."

He made it sound enticing. I couldn't imagine the draw. I'd tasted my blood before, several times after being beaten by Kevin. All I remembered was a bitter, metallic taste and the pain I'd associated with the taste. It was the furthest thing from sweet and light. Still, it made me curious.

"What does Rose taste like?"

The bell rang, announcing our arrival into the dining room. "Her blood is rich and potent, like a perfectly aged scotch. A very little will go a long way."

"So you need more of my blood to be satisfied than hers?" My jealousy surprised me.

His hand guided me forward and toward an empty booth. I sat, sliding to the center and adjusting my dress so it fell neatly over my legs. "So many questions, *kjaere*." He smiled at me from across the table. "And, yes. I do require a larger dose of your blood than Rose's to be sated. It would be the same if I drank from most any supernatural. Human blood is sweeter, but not as potent."

The delightful scent of baking bread and sugar wafted from the window behind the breakfast bar. The food coming out to others in the dining room made my mouth water and my brain forget about what I'd asked. A large plate of what looked like a cross between a cinnamon bun and some type of bread loaf was delivered to the table just across from us.

"Bailey?"

I glanced back at Erick's laughing, blue eyes. A smirk curved his mouth and pulled up the corners of his eyes.

"Sorry. The food distracted me. You were saying how sweet I tasted and then I saw a mutant cinnamon roll slash pound cake." I gave him a quick wink and sat back against the cushion of my seat.

He waved at Raven and pointed to the concoction on the table next to us. Minutes later, I was devouring my own plate of sticky, sweet cinnamon goodness and washing it down with a glass of OJ. She'd also brought me a small plate of eggs and bacon, which Erick insisted I consume as well. There's no way I would have been able to eat everything, but his regular feedings kept my body in a constant state of hunger, besides the unnatural libido I'd developed. I polished off the sweetbread and the plate of protein in record time.

When I looked up, he sat quietly, watching. His bright blue irises caressed my face with a glance and heated my skin as his gaze traveled down to my cleavage, which I had to say looked quite nice, thanks to Calliope's designs.

Now *she* was a woman who knew how to pick the

perfect fabric and weave an amazing enchantment. I'd never worn anything so amazing. Between the attention Erick lavished on me and the confidence the new clothes provided, I started to believe Sanctuary might be just that —a safe haven for me. Somewhere I could stay. Make friends. Build some semblance of a life.

It almost felt like it could be a home ... almost.

"I need to speak to Rose for a minute before we leave. Will you wait for me here?"

"Sure." I nodded and took a sip from my water glass. I took a quick glance at his fine ass as he moved quickly to the counter and then disappeared into the kitchen. Shaking my head, I sighed. It was strange. I never thought I could enjoy sex again or even want it, for that matter. But with Erick, lustful thoughts were never far from the front of my mind.

An old jukebox on the far wall caught my eye. I'd seen pictures of them before, but I had never seen one in person. Music with words, like literature, was now government-controlled in most places. Most of it was dry and boring. Instrumental music was mostly what I'd grown up listening to. I couldn't believe they'd been able to keep this from being confiscated.

My curiosity got the better of me and I rose from my seat and walked over to it. There was a list of songs, none familiar. Titles like *I Walk the Line, Your Cheatin' Heart, Coal Miner's Daughter, I Fall to Pieces* and dozens more. Some of them sounded terrible. Why would anyone sing about a cheating heart or falling to pieces?

"Rose always liked classic country." Raven's voice piped up beside me. "You can pick one. She has it fixed to play without putting in money. Just push the button for the corresponding song number." She pointed to a row of silver buttons below the glass display area.

"No one will mind?"

"Course not."

I stared back at the list and looked for a title that sounded pleasant, finally deciding on *I Can't Stop Loving You* by Kitty Wells. Arms and levers moved inside the juke-box. I watched, fascinated, as a circular black disk was placed on a tray and began to spin. A raspy woman's voice rolled out from the machine slowly. The soft lilting sound made me want to rock back and forth. I'd never heard music like this before. I'd heard about concerts and singers in the newspapers, but unless you were rich and part of the elite or well-versed in black-market trading, you never got to hear them.

"Ahh, pretty girl, you can't play a song like that and not dance," an unfamiliar, deep bass voice rumbled next to me.

I turned toward the man and took a step back. Where the hell had he come from? Before I could squeak out a response, he grabbed my hand and twirled me around. A moment later I was flush to his hard, cool body, held in place with his other arm. I recognized his plaid shirt and long black hair. He was one of the vampires I'd seen outside Erick's apartment that morning.

I looked across the dining room and gave Raven a pleading glance. She stood frozen by the counter with her mouth hanging open. Everyone was staring.

"Please let me go." I spoke firmly, but quietly, not wanting to make a scene. He wasn't hurting me. I just didn't really want to dance with him. I especially didn't want to be this close to his body. Unlike Erick, this giant of a vampire made me nervous. "I don't want to dance."

"By the way Erick's scent coats your sweet skin, I'd say you're more than comfortable in a man's arms."

What a nerve! I reeled backward, pushing against his chest. He dropped his arm from where it was wrapped around my waist and cocked an arrogant eyebrow, which only served to further infuriate me. My palm connected with his face. The terrifying crack echoed through the already silent dining room.

Fear shot through my body, freezing me in place. What had I done? What kind of stupid human slaps a vampire across the face? Me, apparently. I'd only been here a couple of days and already my brain had gone to mush.

I waited for him to snarl and attack. His lip curled a bit, but he made no move to retaliate.

"Your chica packs a bit of a temper, no?" He grinned and glanced toward the counter.

Erick stood next to the counter, his eyes black as night and his fangs fully descended. His body strained against a hand wrapped around his wrist. Rose held him with one hand. There was a bit more to this Sentinel than anyone had shared with me. I'd seen what a vampire was capable of doing. One woman didn't have a shot in hell of holding back an angry vampire, yet she stood calmly, holding his wrist, without appearing to exert much effort.

"Javier, you shame yourself with such behavior," Rose's soft voice broke the silence. "You know very well Erick has claimed Bailey."

He licked his fangs and took a step toward me, making a crude gesture toward my groin. "Maybe she likes a little variety between her legs. I bet a good smack or two in the right place would get her all hot and bothered."

Air rushed from my lungs and anger simmered beneath my skin, mixing with terror. His comment brought old memories rushing forward. Tears burned down my cheeks and a scream tore from my throat as I lunged toward the giant vampire.

Seconds later I was surrounded by Raven, Maven, and Rose. A blur of bodies exited the café. The door closed behind them with an ominous thud. I squeezed my hands into fists and winced in pain. I opened my palm, surprised to find a steak knife in my right hand. Somewhere in the rush of the moment, I'd grabbed the utensil from one of the tables next to me. Blood flowed from a deep gash where I'd gripped the blade. Damn.

"What the hell?" I dropped the knife and swallowed nervously as it clattered to the floor.

"That, my dear, was a bit of a brawl," Rose said, patting my shoulder. "Just give them a few minutes, they'll work it out or I'll do it for them. Let's get your hand tended to before they come back."

"They'll both come in? Together?" Shock didn't even begin to describe my feelings.

"Javier is several hundred years Erick's senior. In fact, he is the eldest Protector in Sanctuary. I did not think he would try to take you from Erick, though. Your very presence in the town was not by chance. The claim was clear."

"I'm not going anywhere with Javier. Why would he think I would?"

She grabbed my wrist and pulled me through the dining room to the kitchen. "You are not marked. To a vampire that means you are available. Erick was foolish to heal all his bite marks."

I knew he'd healed them so I wouldn't have any extra scars. His thoughtfulness had only endeared him to me more.

Rose dragged me to the sink and started running cold water over the wound on my palm. The water ran red with my blood and slowly became clear again as the bleeding slowed. "I have bandages in my office. Raven, would you fetch the first aid kit from my desk?"

The colorful pixie dashed off, and I turned back to Rose. "I'm not going anywhere with Javier."

"Shhh, I know, darling. Everything will be fine. I'm proud of you for standing up for yourself. I know that must've been very difficult for you."

"How?" The pain in my hand had dulled to a throb under the ice-cold flow of water, and my mind tried to comprehend just exactly how much she knew about my history.

"How what?"

"How do you know that was difficult? Did Erick say something?"

"No, he would never betray your confidence, but the Oracle spoke of your suffering."

"The Oracle? Arlea? The woman I'm supposed to meet with today? How does she know anything about me?"

"She is the Oracle. She sees for the Sisters and those who protect them. And you have been on a path to us for quite some time."

The bell above the door in the dining room rang, then

the building shuddered as the door slammed closed. I caught Rose's gaze and she smiled.

"Erick's back."

Relief washed over me and my tense muscles relaxed. Before I could turn he was next to me, breathing over my shoulder, and whispering apologies in my ear as he nibbled on the bottom of the lobe.

Rose released my hand and stepped back to the sink to wash her hands. "Do I need to speak to Javier?"

"No," Erick growled. "Everything is fine."

"Very good." Rose moved toward the prep counter, slipped on a pair of plastic gloves, and joined two other women rolling out dough.

"What happened to your hand?"

"She thought she'd stab Javier," Raven piped up, returning from Rose's office. She held up the bright red box. "Found the kit. We'll get you all fixed up."

"No," Erick growled again. Raven backed away without another word, taking the box with her. He raised his wrist to his mouth and bit down. A trickle of dark red blood ran across his skin. He moved his wrist toward my mouth.

I raised my hands and blocked. "What are you doing?"

"Just a little of my blood will heal you quickly. I don't want you walking around with a gash like that. It will attract—"

"The other Protectors?" As far as I knew, vampires were the only species of Other that drank blood.

"Yes. And I do not care to fight again today."

"Did he hurt you?"

A smile broke the stern features of his face. "No, *kjaere*. I am perfectly well. I will let you check for wounds later."

"Oh, really?" I snorted. Sure he would. Like either of us needed a reason to be naked with each other.

"Please, Bailey." He pushed his wrist closer again. "Just a little will completely heal you."

I relented, dropping my hands to my side. He pressed his wrist to my mouth and closed my mouth over the small puncture wounds he'd made. His blood was cool and metallic. Not pleasant in the least. I swallowed three times before my stomach turned and I pushed his arm away.

He nodded toward the sink and I watched in amazement as the gash in my hand disappeared in front of my eyes. The water rinsed the last trace of blood from my palm, leaving my skin completely clean. I pulled it from the water. There was no trace of the cut. No scar. Nothing.

CHAPTER 11

T he double doors of the Castle loomed ahead—
tall and menacing. Dark iron twisted into the
outline of a dragon on each. The doors were
easily twice my height, probably making them close to
twelve feet tall. The curved handles were fashioned from
wrought iron as well, and were thicker around than my
wrist.

Erick knocked and a few seconds passed before both
doors swung open. A giant of a man barred the opening
and it took a moment for me to recognize him as Miles.
His body was bare from the waist up, displaying abs and a
cut chest that would make any man envious. Except maybe
Erick.

Heat rushed to my face, and I knew my cheeks must
be as red as the roses in the Castle gardens we'd passed.
From the waist down, he wore black leather pants, tight
enough to detail the lines of muscle in his thighs and the
bulge in his crotch. My throat went dry. Crap.

"G-good morning." I sounded like I'd swallowed a toad. My mind refused to quit daydreaming about how beautiful the men of this town were.

To my horror, both men chuckled loudly. Miles stepped back and Erick's hand at my back slipped lower. His fingers pinched my ass before urging me through the open door.

He knew. Of course he knew. I was flushed and aroused, the damn man could smell it. Could Miles tell, too?

I tried to take a step back, but trying to move against Erick's hand was futile. He guided me forward, leaning down to my ear and whispering how beautiful I looked and how delicious I smelled. My knees went weak and my body responded by soaking my panties yet again.

With only a few faltering steps, I stood speechless in the center of a round room. Three grand staircases spiraled up to a second floor, each appearing to lead into a different hallway. The floors were black marble and the walls were made of multi-colored dark stone. White and gold-colored, crushed velvet drapes hung across several openings on the ground floor. There were more than enough chandeliers and wall sconces to keep the huge place well-lit, even pleasant. Seeing it from the outside, I'd been afraid that without windows, the Castle would be like walking into a cave.

"It's beautiful." The awe in my voice must have pleased Miles.

His face split into a welcoming grin. "Thank you. The Sisters complain it's too dark, but we try to brighten it as much as we can during the day. Though, I rather prefer it dark."

"Why?"

He leaned down, his face inches from mine. The irises of his eyes elongated and changed colors, from a dark amber to a bright orange gold. I took a step back and leaned against Erick's chest, my heart pounding so loud in my ears I couldn't hear anything else.

"My dragon can see better in the dark."

"Miles!" Erick's growl vibrated through my back, reassuring me of his presence and protection. Though, I didn't truly believe Miles would hurt me.

The other man straightened to his full height and scoffed. "Scaring little humans is fun. I don't get to do it nearly often enough anymore." He gestured to the opening to our left. "Straight through the courtyard. Arlea is in the garden."

"Thanks," Erick said as he looped his arm through mine and led me away from the smiling dragon of a man. He'd scared me on purpose. Hot or not, I found myself wishing it'd been his brother Eli at the door. Equally built and sexy, Eli had exhibited more compassion toward me than his brother in the few times we'd seen each other. I wasn't even sure Miles knew the definition of consideration, much less compassion.

Erick pushed back the drapes and we continued down a hallway brightened by chandeliers that sparkled like diamonds. We reached a set of glass French doors that opened into a stunning garden courtyard. Flagstone paths twisted and turned between lush foliage and flowers, leading to various gazebos and sitting areas.

Several women waved and passed us on their way out of the garden. They were beautiful, and all were wearing loose, flowing dresses like the one I wore from Calliope's shop. But theirs were all white with a shimmering silver sheen, almost like the fabric was woven with fine silver strands. The two women who passed us were probably in their early twenties, but then I caught sight of several elderly women across the courtyard pruning a purple flowering bush.

"The Sisters ... they age?"

"Yes, the Sisters are human, sort of, but for their gift of sight." He gently pressed me toward the center of the garden. He stopped at the steps of a large, white gazebo. "Oracle, I've brought Bailey to meet you."

"Took you long enough," an elderly woman quipped.

Erick chuckled. "Nothing ever goes fast enough for you, Sister."

"When you're my age, people need to hurry a little. I might not be around if they dawdle."

I turned to face the woman's voice and paused. She was ancient. Her skin was wrinkled and sagged on her face. The bones beneath her paper-thin skin were high and she had an elegant nose. She'd been gorgeous in her day, no doubt, but her advanced years had left her bent and worn. Her long, silvery-gray hair fell over her shoulders like a waterfall. She wore a loose, white robe with bell-shaped sleeves over her silver dress.

"Not quite what you expected, eh?" Her brown eyes flashed and she smiled, waving me to come nearer. "A hundred and two will do a number on a gal."

I shook my head in disbelief. I'd never met anyone

who'd lived past seventy, much less a hundred. Healthcare was almost nonexistent for most of the U.S. population. Medicine was for the wealthy. No one else could afford it.

"Fae dust does wonders for your health, among other things." She gave me a telltale wink and motioned toward the empty chair next to hers. "Please come sit with me, child. I've been waiting a long time to meet you."

I took a few steps and stopped when I no longer felt Erick's form behind me. Looking over my shoulder, he shook his head.

"I don't bite, Viking, at least not anymore."

Her statement confused and surprised me, but had a completely different effect on Erick.

Laughter rumbled from behind me. I turned back. Erick leaned against the opening of the gazebo frame. "You always were a sassy wench, Arlea." He caught my gaze and flashed me a reassuring smile, dimples showing in both his cheeks. "You have but to desire my presence, *kjaere*, and I will be at your side." He bowed and turned to leave. His long strides ate up the stone walk and soon he disappeared, leaving me alone with the ancient seer.

"Come, child. There is much to say and I don't stay awake as long as I used to."

I moved to the large, cushioned chair opposite Arlea. Tucking my legs beneath my body, I sighed. What could she possibly have to say to me? And why did I keep getting hints that my arrival in Sanctuary was expected?

Her brown eyes sparkled with a fire that surprised me. For one so old, she spoke and acted decades younger. That dust must really be something.

"You and Erick make a good match. I'm glad he found you and not one of the other Protectors."

"Were they looking? I thought our meeting was chance."

"Oh it was. Even when he found you, the Viking had no idea who you were."

Who I was? I scrunched my face. She wasn't making sense. They were looking, but not really? He didn't know who I was? "You aren't making sense."

"You have been on a path to find Sanctuary since you were born. I had a vision of you twenty-six years ago. Since then, I've seen you in my dreams many times over the years. I never knew your name or where you were, but I knew you were meant for us. Can I ask your full name?"

"Bailey Ross. Meant for you how? This town is full of Others. I'm human."

"What is your true name, the one your parents passed down. Ross isn't right."

"D'Roth," I answered slowly. How could she have known Ross wasn't my real name?

"Ah, the D'Roth family goes back centuries. Your ancestors were not human. You come from a family line steeped in the old magick. The bloodline is diluted enough that you don't have powers any longer, but your soul spoke to me when you entered this world. Your sacrifice will put the House of Lamidae one step closer to freedom."

Sacrifice? Nothing about a sacrifice sounded pleasant. I shivered and silently wished for Erick to return, hoping he had been telling the truth about returning to me with only a thought. Just then, a whir of air stirred my hair and he appeared at my side, kneeling next to my chair.

"What is wrong?"

"Nothing," Arlea snapped at him. Her demeanor changed from friendly, old woman to angry shrew in a matter of seconds. "She's scared."

"Sister Arlea, there is no need for cruelty. Bailey has had more than her fair share of it in her short life."

"I know exactly what her life was. It is in the past. She is the next piece of the star of Shamesh. She will be Sanctuary's fifth Protector. There is no time for tiptoeing around the topic. Xerxes grows bolder each year. She is irreplaceable."

A Protector? I couldn't be. I'd have to ... die.

"You can't expect her to just give up her life on command. The other Protectors were already vampires when we were called. She deserves to live. To have a family. Children. New vampires are not created on a whim. Even yours." Erick's fury sent a chill through my body.

"Tread carefully, Viking. I know you care for her, but you do serve me."

"I protect the House, Oracle. But, I am not a slave to your whims."

The old woman's voice sharpened, becoming colder than a steel blade. "It is her destiny. I do not choose this for her, Erick. I only see it, but she cannot escape it, no matter what you do."

They were both angry, but it was more than just me they were arguing about. I didn't care, though. Their voices were drowned out in the sea of my raging thoughts. What the hell? She thought I was supposed to be a Protector ... like Erick? She thought I'd willingly become a vampire? That I didn't have a choice. How could I not have a choice? What had she seen?

I didn't have a lot to lose. I had no human family or friends. Nothing truly tied me to my old life except pain and fear. But dying and becoming a night-walking, blood-sucking, immortal, hated by most of the human race hadn't really been in my plans, either.

Besides, what kind of person tells a stranger their destiny is to die and become an immortal warrior for some out-of-the-way West Texas town no one's ever heard of. And to fight for what? These carefree women who lived in the lap of luxury behind the walls of a massive castle having dreams of the future? What were they so afraid of?

I stood from my chair and stared down at the small woman still arguing with Erick. Maybe I'd taken too quickly to this town. Something felt wrong about this whole conversation. "You have the wrong person, ma'am. Sanctuary is nice and all, but sooner or later I will have to leave. I never stay anywhere for long."

Arlea turned her bright, brown eyes on me and laid a hand on my arm. A cold tingle shot across my skin, making me shudder like the air around me was freezing cold instead of tropically warm. Erick said she was human, but the glint of something else in her eyes made me question it. "I've dreamed your face since you were born, child. This is your fate, whether you choose to accept it or not. It's not something from which you can run."

Maybe, maybe not, but it didn't mean I had to lay back and just take it either. I yanked my arm away from her vise-like fingers and fled the gazebo.

She had no right to ask for what she did. At least Erick

had stood up for me. But would that be enough if the whole town sided with Arlea? She was a respected elder. I wasn't stupid. I knew her words carried weight. Even Rose, the all-powerful Sentinel, had pushed for me to meet and hear out the seer. Or Oracle. Whatever they called her. It didn't matter. I wasn't going to just let them turn me into a vampire.

But, just because Erick didn't want to follow Arlea's orders didn't mean one of the other Protectors wouldn't step up and do the deed. I'd been beaten and tortured to within an inch of my life and I'd survived. This old woman was not going to get the better of me with her "it's your destiny" crap.

The stone path before me split into a Y and I followed it to the left. I was long past lost. All the arched doorways along the outer edges of the garden looked the same. I picked one and slipped inside.

The room was barely lit and the thudding bass of music I'd never heard before reverberated from the walls and ceiling—so loud the very air in the room seemed to pulse.

There were quite a few people in the room. Some dressed as Sisters in long, flowing silver dresses, some naked as the day they were born. I averted my eyes when one of the Sisters walked past with a mountain of a man following close behind her, naked but for the wide, black, leather collar around his neck. She gave me a sultry wink and walked to the corner of the room.

Now that my eyes adjusted to the low light, I could make out furniture along the walls. A crowd was gathering to one side and the telltale snap of a whip made the bile in my stomach rise to my mouth. But the burning in my throat was nothing compared to the phantom pain racing across my skin every time the whip found its target. Each stripe on my body came alive, burning as if it were fresh.

My breathing grew ragged and I dropped to my knees. The cold stone seared like ice on my palms. I could see my terrified reflection in the polished finish.

I thought I had more control, but that sound brought everything crashing down, threatening to suffocate me in my memories. Erick's cool hands were on my shoulders seconds later. He really could feel when I needed him.

I sucked in a breath and tried to speak, but managed no more than a choked cough. All I wanted was to get away. I wanted to be free of this pain. Of the memories that haunted me. But it would never happen. My scars would always be there. Even if Erick thought they were beautiful ... they were still reminders of what *he* had done to me. For now, I just needed to get away from the sound of that bullwhip slicing through the air.

Several unfamiliar voices asked if I was all right. I couldn't answer. Erick's arms surrounded me and lifted me from the floor. Air rushed past us. He was moving so fast. The darkness of the Castle disappeared. We were outside again. Then we weren't.

When he finally came to a stop, I sighed. We were in his bedroom. He lowered me gently onto silky sheets of the large bed we'd been sharing since I'd arrived. The familiar peppermint scent soothed my raw nerves and I reached for one of the many pillows against the head-board, pulling it close to my chest and burying my face in it.

"I'll be right back, I'm going to get you a drink."

I nodded my head and mumbled an okay through the pillow.

A few seconds later, his fingers stroked my upper arm. "Sit up and drink this."

I did as he asked and shoved the pillow behind my back before turning to face his gorgeous, blue eyes. He placed the highball glass in my hand. I touched it to my lips and the fumes from the alcohol hit my eyes with a blast. Seconds later the liquid fire scorched a path down my esophagus, but at least it burned away the acrid taste of bile. Nothing like a good scotch to wipe a slate clean.

"It's not even lunchtime yet, and I'm already drinking." I tried to manage a half smile as I handed him the empty glass.

He took the glass and set it softly on the nightstand. "It's been a crapshoot of a morning. I think the etiquette gods will look kindly on you for this indulgence."

"Will you hold me?"

"Of course, *min kjaereste.*" He shucked his shoes and crawled over my body, settling into the center of the bed. I moved to the offered shoulder, releasing a deep sigh as the arm beneath my head curled around my back and pulled me snugly to his chest.

He pressed his lips to my forehead and inhaled deeply. "You are so special to me. I can't imagine living without you. You touch my heart the way only one other woman in centuries has done."

The idea that he felt so strongly for me wasn't scary. My feelings for him were strong, too. He'd found a way to get past the walls I'd put around my heart after I thought Kevin had destroyed it.

"You have the heart of a warrior, Bailey. To have fought and survived what your visible wounds proclaim is an untold feat in itself. I can only imagine the pain and scars you have yet to share with me. You must understand. I will protect you with everything I possess. No matter what the Oracle said, you have a choice. No one is turned against their will."

Did that mean I would choose to die?

CHAPTER 12

A quiet buzz stirred my mind from where it floated listlessly between consciousness and dream. Erick's voice rumbled from deep in his chest. I could hear another male voice on the other end of the phone, but couldn't tell who it was.

"She's fine ... No, it was the whip." A low growl made me turn my head to look up at him. He avoided my gaze. "If I hadn't been arguing with the Oracle, I would've been with her ... No ... She'll deal when she's ready ... Fine. Give me a few minutes."

"What is it?"

"There was a fire in the Lycans' neighborhood."

"Is everyone okay?"

"Yes, everyone is fine, but Rose felt a Djinn presence just before it happened."

My heart leapt to my throat. Already? I didn't want to leave him ... any of them. Even with the weird crap with the Oracle woman, this place felt right. She'd recognized my parent's family name and running from her may have been a mistake, but it had been a knee-jerk reaction. I'd always solved my problems by running.

It tore at me to think about leaving, but there was no other option. I couldn't let a psychopath roam their streets hurting others just to get to me.

"Breathe, Bailey. I'm taking you to Calliope's. You can pick out a few more clothes while I take care of business. She can sense other supernaturals, too. She'll feel him coming long before he's there. Other than Rose, she's the best companion for you until we eliminate the threat."

"Can't I just stay with you?" I sat up and looked down at him.

"I want you inside a warded building. If not Calliope's, then the Castle, but after what happened this morning, that's not an option."

I swallowed at the mention of the dragons' lair. It truly was a lair, with its dark floors and walls, old-style chandeliers, and wall sconces designed to look like candles. Decadence and elegance mixed with darkness. Going back to that place definitely wasn't *an option*, as he'd put it. Not for a while.

"Calliope's."

Dimples showed on both cheeks as he smiled. "I thought as much." He lifted his hand and caressed my cheek. "I'm here when you want to talk about it. I can help you."

"Perhaps."

TEN MINUTES LATER, HE WAS KISSING ME ON THE CHEEK and leaving me in the cutest boutique. Clothes hung everywhere, bolts of fabric lined the back wall and shoes lined another. It was enough to make any woman forget her worries, and I was no different.

The woman standing a few feet away was gorgeous and scary at the same time. Her eyes were golden brown and her creamy white skin was as flawless as porcelain. Long, black hair hung in smooth shiny waves well past her waist. She winked at me as a mischievous grin tugged at her lips.

Erick said she was a siren. What exactly that was, I didn't know, but the woman made clothes to die for. The entire shop was filled with things that would make even the wealthiest women in the world swoon.

"Let her pick anything she wants, Calliope."

"Oh, honey, I will shower her with things her mind can't even conceive."

He chuckled and slipped out the front door of the shop. The familiar blue shimmer of the warding spell dropped into place as the door closed behind him.

Calliope strolled over and turned the deadbolt. "Private shopping is my specialty. We don't need any uninvited visitors." A flick of her hand in the air drew the curtains closed on both front windows. "Now, what do you like to wear?"

I stared at the curtains. She'd moved them with a mere gesture. Maybe the citizens of Sanctuary really were capable of protecting themselves ... and me. A little of the guilt I'd been carrying around slipped from my shoulders. I had been safely tucked away in this amazing boutique and told to shop to my heart's content. My inner girly girl wanted to squeal out loud, but I contained myself and let my fingers run down a sparkly top, enjoying the silky feel of the fabric.

"Can you tell me more about the Sisters?" Erick hadn't really explained a lot and neither had Rose. Maybe I could get a little more out of Calliope. It wouldn't hurt. Especially with what they wanted me to do, I more than deserved the full history lesson.

"The House of Lamidae? They are seers."

I chuckled and pulled a soft tank from a hanger. "That, I know."

"I think the red would look better with your coloring, doll." She pulled another tank from a shelf next to me and offered it up. I put down the brown one and took the red from her. "So, the Sisters are a strange group. They are human in every aspect that we know. They age. They die. They don't heal like other supernaturals. But, they never have male children and most of them are more sexually active than rabbits."

My mouth dropped open at the last comment, but somehow them living inside a fetish club made a lot more sense now. "Being horny doesn't make them Others."

"No, of course not, but the only female baby thing is kinda strange."

"Who fathers their children?"

"Strangers mostly. The Castle is quite the destination for people in the lifestyle. The brothers have visitor day twice a month where humans and supernaturals from outside Sanctuary can visit and play."

Play? Why would anyone consider being tortured play? Though I hadn't seen anyone upset while I was in the

Castle. Maybe there was a bit more to this whole thing than I knew. Even so, I had no desire to ever feel another pair of cuffs or hear the clink of a chain or the crack of a whip. I shook my head and refocused back on Calliope. "Do the men just agree to father children?"

"I don't know the particulars, but contracts are signed and the men are never told if they father a child or not."

"But they only sleep with human men, right? Because otherwise, wouldn't the children be ... something else?"

Calliope belted out a laugh and wrapped her arms around her stomach. "Oh, honey, those nymphomaniacs will sleep with humans or supernaturals. It doesn't matter to them. Whatever makes them a Sister makes sure any children are just like them. Default programming or some strange shit. Like I said, they appear human and claim to be human, but most of us aren't fooled at all."

"And they see the future?"

"Sometimes." Calliope shrugged. "Personally, I think the future is a lot more fun if you don't know it ahead of time."

"Do you know why Erick is called a Protector? And Rose a Sentinel? The woman, Arlea said I am to become the fifth Protector."

"Shit! Really? But you're human!" Calliope's eyes widened. "Why don't we go sit down and chat? Since the Protector bomb has been dropped, I'm guessing that clears you to know just about everything."

Everything? How much more was there to know? I followed her to the wall of shoes, trying not to drool in the process. They were a pleasant distraction from the questions and fears swirling in my mind.

"Pretty aren't they?"

I nodded. "They don't sell shoes like these at ValueMart."

She made an ugly face and shuddered. "Gods, I should hope not."

A giggle slipped out and I sank into a soft, velvet armchair. The fabric soothed my frazzled nerves as I rubbed my fingertips over the smooth arm of the chair.

"So, what else did the old bitty say? I know she's been spouting for years about the fifth Protector, but this doesn't make sense. All Protectors have to be vampire. It's part of the spell."

"She said I would become the Protector. That it was my destiny."

"So you have to die?"

"That was my understanding."

"Do you want to die?" She cocked her head to the side, studying me, waiting.

"No!"

"Okay, don't get your panties in a wad. I was just asking." She crossed her legs and sighed. "Well damn, girl. I can see why Erick was so testy."

"Erick said no one would turn me against my will."

"He'll make sure of it, too. I can vouch for that." She rolled her head from side to side, vertebrae popping loudly. "Now Rose is something called a Lamassu, if she hasn't already explained. She's a really powerful supernatural being that was worshiped back in ancient Babylon."

"Babylon?"

"Shit, they don't teach y'all history anymore. I keep forgetting the U.S. dropped into the Dark Ages after the

L.A. riots. All right. So Babylon was a city that existed thousands of years ago and a world away."

"Is everyone in town really old?"

A snort of a laugh erupted from her mouth and she nodded. "Pretty much. I'm from around 1600 BCE."

I scrunched my forehead, again not really grasping what she'd said. I'd never heard the acronym BCE.

"Like it's 2096 right now. If you counted the years backward to zero and then kept going into the negative numbers you would eventually get to 1600 BCE."

"You're almost four-thousand years old?"

"Shhhh, don't say it out loud like that. Damn, girl, you're making me feel old. Anyway, Rose is from a species of supernatural that guarded a kingdom called Babylon and the portal to a place called the Veil, the original home of everything supernatural. One of her kind betrayed them and she and her husband were the only ones who escaped the massacre. Her brother-in-law, Xerxes, was the betrayer. He freed the king of the Djinn from his prison and helped him lead an army that succeeded in destroying Babylon for good."

"Why would he want to destroy people who worshiped him? And what is the Veil?"

"The Veil is a Garden of Eden, of sorts. Untouched by humans. Beautiful. Perfect." She looked at me and waited, but I didn't know what to say. I'd never heard of a Garden of Eden, either. "You need to read some books, girl. Anyway, it's a secret realm you can only get into with a key. We'll talk about it later. As far as Xerxes goes, I just think he's crazy. But the common story is that Babylon wasn't enough for him. He wanted to sire half-Lamassu, half-seers, control the world, and wipe out humanity completely. He's pretty much as crazy as the Djinn king he freed."

"I thought the Sisters couldn't have supernatural children."

"There's always a loophole when it comes to the supernatural and the Lamassu are it. They are powerful enough to get around whatever it is that keeps the Sisters' children from being hybrids. This is just what I've been told, but before all this went down and Xerxes betrayed the Sentinels, which was what the Lamassu were called in Babylon, he fell in love with one of the Sisters and got her pregnant. They broke all kinds of rules and traditions. The baby was a boy and he was recognized as a hybrid from infancy. The mother died in childbirth and Rose and the rest of the Lamassu hid the child from Xerxes."

"So really it's more of a revenge thing for him with a side of taking over the world?"

"Yeah, that sums it up nicely."

"What are the Protectors for exactly? What spell were you talking about?"

"The Protectors are warriors dedicated to protecting the House of Lamadae. I don't know the specifics of the spell, other than it will be permanent. Oh, and they need eight Protectors to complete it."

"And Arlea says I'm number five."

"Apparently so." She stood from her chair abruptly. "You want a drink? I think it's late enough for a glass of wine."

"No, I'm good. Thanks."

"Okay." She shrugged and disappeared through a swinging black door into the back room of her shop.

I got up and walked over to look at a cute pair of red sandals. When she reappeared, a wineglass was in one hand and a bottle was in the other. She set them both on the counter and joined me by the shoes.

"You like?"

"I like a lot of things. That doesn't mean I need them."

"Pfshht, you are spending someone else's money and he hasn't paid attention to a particular woman for more than a fleeting one-nighter since the late Middle Ages."

"When was that?" I asked, trying not to sound too eager.

Another heavy sigh preceded her answer. "I think he was married to her during the 14th century."

"Has he ever talked about her?"

"Elinor? Some ... I know she was very small, fair-haired, and stubborn. He always carried on about how stubborn she was. But I think that's also what he liked about her. She was the only human he's ever wanted to turn that forbade him from doing it."

"Has he turned people?" I knew that's how vampires were made. Other vampires turned them. But it couldn't just be a bite or there would be a lot more vampires running around than there were.

"A few, I think, before he met Elinor. After she passed away, he went off grid for a while. Rose couldn't find him. No one could. A few centuries later, he reappeared and rejoined Sanctuary ... He doesn't talk much about when he was gone, but I know he never had the chance to have a real family or kids and it eats at him. Elinor was a taste of what he missed out on."

Calliope smiled and pulled the red flats from their display shelf. "You should see him though when one of the couples in town has a baby. That big, scary Viking is the first one on their doorstep with gifts and well wishes, waiting patiently to hold the new bundle of joy."

My heart warmed at the image of Erick cradling a baby. It sounded like he would've made a good father. He certainly was compassionate and caring enough. Sure, he had a rough exterior. Who wouldn't after living as long as he had, but I felt completely safe with him. And after only one night. Hell, I left a bus station with him in a matter of hours after meeting him. Both were miracles, since I'd made a concerted effort to avoid the male species altogether, if possible.

"I think you should try on those shoes."

"But they'll form to me?"

"Exactly. Then we can pick out an outfit to go with them."

Chuckling, I set the red flats on the floor in front of me and slid my feet out of the shoes I wore. Then slipped my feet into the red ones and watched, still awed by the magick as the shoes shrank to my size and width, fitting so perfectly I'd never want to take them off.

"Now, come this way." She guided me to a line of racks and proceeded to walk up and down each, pulling off garment after garment—blouses, skirts, dresses, pants, and several pieces I didn't think were meant for use in public. When my arms were sagging beneath the load, she threw a couple pairs of jeans on top and pointed me toward a curtained area on the other side of her shop. "Go get undressed and I'll grab you a few more bra and panty sets, too."

"This is too much."

"Nope, you'll need it. You're gonna be here a while, doll."

"But it's too much money."

"Erick has more money than he knows what to do with. Don't worry about price tags. Plus, he specifically told me to spoil you."

"He did not," I shot back, pulling the curtain across the dressing area. I dropped the mound of clothing on a nearby armchair and pulled off the purple dress I was wearing.

"Yes he did, you just didn't hear him." Her voice was close, right on the other side of the curtain. Her arm came through the gap near the wall, holding out a variety of bras and panties. "Found these, too."

Two hours later, after trying on and modeling each piece of fantastic clothing, she took all of them, wrapped them in tissue, and put them in three large recyclable bags. I couldn't believe how many beautiful things were in those bags just for me. It was more clothing than I'd ever owned in my entire life and certainly nicer than anything I could afford.

"Hungry?" she asked, tucking the bags behind the counter. "We could head over to Rose's. Erick texted a little while ago that they were still working."

"What are they doing?"

"A Djinn has been popping in and out of Sanctuary all day. I get faint reads on him and then nothing."

"How can you tell?"

"I'm a siren. We have a sixth sense about supernatural individuals. Kinda like a warning radar. Helps us with hunting." She grinned. "Rose has it, too. If we can't smell them, we can usually sense them another way."

"Erick said that was one reason he was willing to leave you with me."

She belted out a laugh. "Yeah, that and I'm a bitch with claws." Her eyes darkened and I watched, spellbound, as her bright red nails lengthened into what could literally be described as claws. Holy crap!

I choked a little and took a step back.

"Sorry," she giggled out. "I love doing that."

"Let me guess, you don't get to scare humans very often anymore."

"Oh, touché!" She laughed again as her eyes and nails changed back to normal. "You saw Miles today. Did he breathe fire?"

"F-fire? He can do that?"

"Of course. He and Eli are both fire dragons."

"No, he just leaned in and did something with his eyes. It was creepy, like what you just did."

"Well, you should ask him to breathe fire for you sometime. It's an amazing thing to see."

"I'm sure it is. I think I'd rather keep all my hair unsinged for now. Thanks for the heads up, though."

Calliope grabbed a small yellow purse from behind the counter and waved toward the door. "Come on, let's get some lunch. I'm starved."

"Sure." I could eat again. Though if they kept feeding me three meals a day, my clothes would have to readjust for my growing waistline. "Don't y'all ever get bored of eating at just one restaurant?"

I stepped to the side and waited while Calliope locked the door to her shop. "Nope. The brownies and pixies are always changing things up. The menu rarely stays the same for more than two weeks at a time. Now, if there's something specific you want. You can always ask for a special order." She turned toward me and we strolled down the concrete sidewalk toward Rose's Café. "The café is like home. You never get tired of home cooking."

"How long have you lived in this town?"

She sighed and swiped her dark chocolate bangs to the side. "I've been here since the 1920s. I was between husbands at the time and Rose convinced me there could be more purpose to my life than finding my next sugar daddy."

"How many husbands have you had?"

"Dozens by now. I lost count years ago, though I haven't married anyone since moving to Sanctuary. Most humans who visit the Castle are already attached to a partner. I'm not really interested in developing an attachment to anyone who lives in town, and my reputation keeps me pretty single. I stick to out-of-towners."

"What reputation would that be?"

"Everyone I develop a lasting sexual relationship with dies."

"W-why?"

"I'm a siren. I fall madly in love, but it's never allowed to last long. One day I'm happy, then the next I wake up and they're dead beside me in bed. The longest relationship I've had lasted five years. I knew every day I stayed with him put him in danger, but I just couldn't leave."

"So it's not really intentional?"

"Well ... it's complicated. But, like I said, there's no one in town who would risk a relationship with me and certainly no man who would spend an entire night in my bed knowing I was a siren."

"You must be lonely." I couldn't imagine living with that kind of curse hanging over my head. The thought of killing the person you loved while you slept ...

"Being single this last century has been good for me. The cravings for a relationship have gotten easier to ignore. Rose and this town and the people in it have filled an emptiness in my soul I could never do on my own." She paused in front of the café door and turned, catching my gaze. "Plus, if I need a good fucking from time to time, the Castle is right across the circle."

I swallowed. "You sleep with—?"

"Ah, ah, ah, I do not sleep with anyone. I do, however, fuck several sexy older gentlemen when they visit from out of town. It's a mutually beneficial arrangement. They enjoy it and it helps me stay satisfied ... sexually."

I reached for the café door and shook my head as I pulled it open. "I never would have believed all of this only a few days ago. Now, it's one weird story after another. Are there others like you?"

"Of course. We aren't a prolific species, but there are others. I've only met a handful of other sirens in my lifetime."

She entered the café first and I followed her over to sit

at the bar. Raven walked up on the other side, her flowing locks every color of the rainbow.

"Love the new colors, girly," Calliope said, opening the menu lying on the counter in front of her.

"Thanks. It was time to freshen it up. You should see Maven's. Prettiest solid purple."

"Cool."

"How are you settling in, Bailey? Did you hear about the Djinn setting fires over in the Lycan neighborhood?"

"That's why she's with me, pixie. Her ever-protective vampire actually had to work today."

"Garrett came in earlier, said it's not going well," Raven added. "The Djinn keeps jumping, never staying in one place long enough for anyone to get a good look at him. But, he did say the scent was familiar."

"Meaning it's the same one who followed me from Fort Worth," I muttered. Every muscle in my body tensed and the fear I'd managed to push away came roaring back like a tidal wave, threatening to drown me. What use was running? The Djinn would always be coming for me. He'd never stop … just like Kevin.

"Doesn't matter, sweetie. We've got you covered. He's just trying to get on people's nerves. Rose will have him bottled soon enough."

Bottled?

Raven turned to Calliope. "Oh, Charles popped in this morning and said to let you know to come see him when you got a chance."

"He wasn't supposed to be here for another week. Why didn't he come to the shop?"

"Said you had company and he didn't want to interrupt. Something about the shop being closed."

"Oh." Calliope grinned. "Guess Bailey and I were a little distracted earlier." She turned in her stool and winked. "Charles is one of my friends from out of town."

I nodded. "I can stay here in the café if you want to go see him."

"Nope. I'm on duty. Charles will understand. Plus, he's the one who showed up unscheduled. The Sisters will keep him entertained until I get there."

CHAPTER 13

Calliope might be *on* duty, but I couldn't help glancing at the door every time the bell rang. Always watchful. Always worried. Always waiting to be caught. That feeling never left me.

This time it was just Garrett, the mind-reading, sexy-as-hell werewolf who preferred to be called a Lycan. I really wished I didn't know about the mind reading. Ignorance really was bliss sometimes.

The door swung closed behind him and I waited patiently for Erick to come through after, but the door didn't budge again.

"Afternoon, Rose. I'm here for the guys' lunch order," he called out. Then he walked straight to the table where Calliope and I were eating, pulled up a chair and sat.

A strange hissing sound came from Calliope and I covered my mouth to avoid snorting water all over my plate. What kind of noise was that?

"Beat it, wolf boy." Calliope spat out. "I prefer to eat

without smelling sweaty dog." Her voice was low, but playfully menacing. Almost like a tease.

"You like it, siren. Stop whining." He didn't even blink when he turned his gaze onto me. "Sexy as hell? Good to know." His mouth curled into an arrogant, self-satisfactory smile as his eyes swept from my face down to my chest and then back. "If you get tired of your Protector, just let me know. My brother and I would take really good care of you."

My jaw dropped and heat rushed to my cheeks. Presumptuous much? Not only had he he invaded my private thoughts again, he'd had the nerve to proposition me in the middle of a diner. And he'd proposed that I sleep with him and his brother—a man I'd never met! What the hell was he smoking?

A chuckle rolled from his chest and he leaned back in his chair. "You may not have met Travis, but he got a peek at you already. If you think I'm attractive, I don't think you'll complain about him."

"Stop! Stay out of my head!" I glanced at Calliope. Her eyes were black and her fingernails had lengthened into claws around the white porcelain coffee cup. *Holy shit!* "Calliope?" My voice faltered. She didn't look like she was playing anymore.

"Djinn," she whispered.

My heart fell into my stomach and nausea clawed its way up my throat in return. This was it. Darius would kidnap, torture, and kill me.

Garrett's eyes flashed gold and a growl rumbled in his chest. "I won't let that happen, even if you don't want to sleep with me and my brother." He grinned before dashing to the door and slipping outside.

A moment later, Rose ran into the dining room from the kitchen. "Bailey!" She and Calliope exchanged some sort of look. Then I heard a thud on the sidewalk out front.

Outside the front windows, I saw him. The Djinn from the bus station. Darius. He smiled and waved, disappearing just as Garrett's body came flying through the air. Garrett landed with a familiar sounding thump on the sidewalk.

He appeared again, but this time had a gas can in his hands and was sloshing it all over the windows and walls outside the diner. Garrett leapt again, this time fast enough to catch hold of him before he teleported.

I stood and stared at the fight, just like everyone else in the diner. We just waited.

A second later, they came crashing through the front window. Glass shattered and people ran. Calliope moved to stand in front of me and Rose started shouting for everyone to go out the back door.

Garrett growled, but Darius stood and stared at me over Calliope's shoulder, ignoring the menacing rumble. His purple eyes sliced straight to my soul. Terror laced its way through my body, clamping down on my lungs and making it difficult to breathe.

"I'll get you, bitch. Just you wait. They can't watch you every second of the day." His voice was cold. Angry.

I gasped a breath and took a step backward, bumping into the table behind me. Trapped.

Another barreling charge from Garrett sent Darius

flying. Unable to teleport, he hit the ground with a thud and scrambled to his feet.

"Damn spells!" He snarled, leaping for the opening.

Garrett caught his leg before he got through and tugged him back to the floor. He threw a few punches before Darius heaved him off, sending Garrett crashing into several tables, splintering them into a thousand pieces on impact and sending their contents straight at me and Calliope, hitting us both.

A glass hit her in the face and she hissed, jumping at Darius with a roar unlike anything I'd heard before. Her cry reverberated around the room and made my head ache.

Rose stepped forward before Calliope reached the Djinn and laid a hand on his shoulder. She started chanting something I couldn't make out and he screamed like she'd stuck him with a hot poker.

Out of the corner of my eye, I saw Garrett get up and run straight for Darius again.

Time stretched out, moving slower. Voices became indistinct and delayed. I sucked in a deep breath and moaned in pain. Then I heard the strangest sound and turned my attention back to Rose and the Djinn. My vision was blurry, but I could tell he was laughing now, not screaming.

I squinted, trying to focus. An evil smile spread across his face. He shoved Rose to the ground and looked at me again.

"I like the color red on you."

Nausea crept over me, and bile rose into my mouth. Then something else did. Coppery, metallic liquid gurgled up into my mouth and ran between my lips. I coughed and pain radiated from my stomach. Looking down, I could see the handle of a steak knife protruding from my upper abdomen. The front of my dress was wet and stained.

Wet with my blood.

When I looked up again, Darius leapt out the window and everyone else turned to stare at me. Black spots invaded my vision as the world began spinning. Forms rushed at me and their voices became nothing more than a loud roar in my head.

The Djinn was gone.

It was over.

Was I dying?

People were still shouting all around me. My head throbbed and then a fiery burst of pain made me attempt a scream, but all I managed was a gurgled moan. The pain was quickly followed by pressure on my stomach. It took a few moments, but my mind finally registered that they'd probably removed the knife.

All I wanted was Erick. I wanted his quiet. His comfort. His way of making me feel like I was the most important person in his world. If I was dying, I wanted to be with him when I breathed my last.

Seconds later, a rush of air stirred around me just before familiar male arms scooped me up off the floor.

He cradled my head and pressed his face to mine.

I breathed in his sweet scent. He was speaking, but I still couldn't make anything out. The world around me was cold and fuzzy. A moment later, his wrist was pressed against my lips. I knew what he wanted and I did my best to swallow, but there was so much blood in my mouth, I couldn't tell what was mine and what was his.

Then everything went black.

♦❦♦

I OPENED MY EYES AND STARED UP AT A WHITE, coffered ceiling. Sitting up straight, I gasped for breath and rubbed my stomach, feeling for a bandage.

Nothing was there.

Nothing hurt.

Had I imagined the whole thing? Was it all a dream?

I wasn't wearing the blue dress anymore, just a t-shirt and panties.

I scanned the semi-lit room. Only one lamp on the dresser across the room was on. A new digital clock next to it read eight thirty. The last thing I remembered was dropping to the floor of the diner with a knife in my stomach at lunchtime.

I rolled to the edge of the bed and slid my feet to the carpet. Then hurried into the bathroom, flipping on the light as I went through the door.

Stopping in front of the mirror, I pulled up the t-shirt.

My mouth went dry. No wound. Not even a scar from the knife. On top of that, several other older scars were nearly gone. The dark pink, raised, whip lines that had crisscrossed my body for four years were smooth and white. Some were gone completely.

It had all happened.

The fight. The diner. The knife. Erick had fed me his blood. I vaguely remembered that. I looked at my bare stomach in the mirror again. How much blood had he fed me to heal this much? It didn't matter now. I was alive and apparently in much better shape than I had been before the incident. Talk about a well-kept secret. The medical community would lose their shit if they knew how powerful vampire blood was.

I caught sight of a wad of blue fabric in his tub. It was the dress I'd been wearing earlier. It was completely clean, thanks to Calliope's spell. I draped it over my arm, scanning the dress. A small inch-long slice in the front near the bust-line still remained from where the knife had entered.

Voices rumbled from below, pulling me out of my state of shock. At first it sounded like Erick might be on the phone, but the deep rumble of other male voices soon mixed with his. It sounded like the two dragon brothers again. They seemed to be a tight little trio, merely adding to my discomfort since they ran the Castle. Sooner or later, I'd have to face that can of worms. I certainly hoped it would be later.

Dropping the dress back into the tub, I scanned the bathroom for something to wear. I wasn't putting that dress back on again ... ever, but I wasn't about to walk downstairs in a t-shirt and panties in front of company, either. Walking to the closet, I pulled open both doors and took a breath. There had to be something. He'd mentioned robes. Sure enough, a white robe hung on a hook just inside.

I stepped forward, reaching up to pull it down and stubbed my toe on a heavy canvas bag. "Shit." I jumped back, grabbing for the throbbing toe. The robe slipped from the hook and fell in front of me, covering the offending bag. I landed on the floor next to it and snatched up the robe. Heaving a sigh, I stood and threw it around my shoulders, tying the band around my waist.

The bag was open and a pink strap lay across the top. Curiosity got the better of me and I knelt back down. I pulled out the pink strap, which was connected to a tangle of other straps and a ... dildo. I dropped it back in the bag and pulled the zipper open further. My hands trembled. A large bullwhip lay coiled on top of several other items Kevin used to use on me regularly—paddle, crop, and a gag.

Shit. Shit. Shit.

How could I have been so stupid? Erick had been lying to me this whole time. He wanted to tie me up and beat me, too. Why else would he have this bag of stuff?

My heart was racing and my palms were sweaty. I took a deep gulp of air, but nothing would stop the trembling of my body. Had it been his plan all along? Were his dragon pals in on it, too? He'd said he wouldn't share me though ... but how could I trust anything he'd ever said now?

I shut the closet doors and glanced up at the mirror.

The whole town knew him. Calliope, Rose, Raven, Maven—surely they would have said something. I'd believed them all when they said they wanted to protect me. They had to have known what he was like. What he liked ... *He* knew how much those things frightened me.

My heart still screamed that I could trust him, but my head knew I was being foolish. No one kept a bag like that without planning to use it.

Was I condemning him for something he used to do? Maybe he hadn't lied to me. Maybe I was just lying to myself.

Walking from the bathroom, I padded quietly across the room to the partially open doorway, pausing to listen.

"You can't possibly think you'll be happy. You are a Dom, Erick. There's no getting around that fact." It was Eli's gravelly voice telling Erick I wasn't the right girl for him. "It's not fair to either of you. She'd be better off with Jav—."

"She'll be better off with me because I care about her," Erick snapped back at him. "Javier can go to hell. He'd use her and then put her aside a week later. He's a jackass."

Eli grunted but didn't speak any intelligible words.

"You won't be satisfied." Miles' voice added, echoing his brother's sentiments. My heart sank. Apparently Erick really was more interested in kink than he had led me to believe, though he was putting up a pretty good fight on my behalf.

"I don't give a shit if I never pick up a whip again. Or if I never use another set of cuffs. Being a Dom isn't about the *things* you use, and you both know it."

The dragons grumbled something I couldn't quite understand.

"We understand, Erick," Eli continued. "But we can't help feeling a little skeptical at the idea of not using restraints or pain ... ever. But you are right. It is not about the power we hold, but the power a sub offers us."

Sub? Offered power? That didn't sound like any of the crap Kevin spouted while he held me captive and tortured me. Still, the dragons sounded like they were in favor of pain. Who would volunteer to be beaten by two men at the same time?

I leaned against the door and it creaked. The men below silenced and Erick was in front of me in an instant.

"I thought you still slept, *min kjaereste.*" He leaned down and kissed my cheek.

His candy-sweet scent filled my lungs and I momentarily forgot the confusion swirling in my brain. I leaned against him as he wrapped his long arms around my body and nuzzled my neck. His very touch brought me peace. How could I think he would also bring pain?

He pulled back suddenly. "What's wrong?"

I stiffened in his arms. "I ... you all sound so angry." What was I supposed to say? I found your bag of torture items in the closet. Did you plan to use them on me?

"We're not angry, Bailey. Just loud. " Eli shouted from below in the living room. "Please forgive our insensitive conversation."

A snarl cut off Eli's apology and I couldn't help the small giggle that escaped. Miles' disgust for his brother's politeness was obvious.

No matter how freaked out I was, these men truly acted as if they were just oversized boys.

"You're laughing." Erick lifted my chin so our gazes met.

"I don't understand, either. Those two guys scare the crap out of me, but they are funny when they are together. Miles is so gruff and Eli is so polite and they can't stand each other for it."

A chuckle rolled up from Erick's chest. His lips curved into a smile that showed in his bright, blue eyes. So beautiful. I almost wished I hadn't seen the bag and didn't know what he really wanted from me.

He took a deep breath and I saw the ring of scarlet red appear around his blue irises. Hunger. Desire. Need. They all swirled in his gaze, making it even easier to forget what I knew and pretend I was still in heaven with a man who adored me and would never hurt me.

But, I couldn't. And there was no heaven for me. No matter how badly I wanted it. And I did want it. The wetness between my thighs validated my desires.

"There will be time for us to play later, *kjaere*. I promise. First, come eat. You missed your evening meal. I don't want you feeling weak."

"Especially since you are feeling hungry," I threw back, trying to mask my anxiety. I knew he could probably still smell it, but I could at least try to hide it.

He flashed a wicked grin, making my insides melt and the self-cleaning panties work overtime. I was crazy about him, but scared what he wanted from me would be more than I could give.

He took my hand and led me down the stairs. "You can both leave now," he said as we stepped off the last stair. "I think she's heard quite enough."

Eli stepped forward first. "We were—." He paused, licking his lips and giving me a once over that would've made the boldest whore blush.

I pulled the robe tighter.

"Leaving." He snapped his jaw shut, grabbed his brother by the shoulder, and hauled them both through the door. Miles grumbled until the door shut behind them and I turned, glancing up to Erick.

His eyes were darker and the red ring around the iris was bright.

"Was he okay?"

"Yes, that was just Eli making a smart choice." Erick chuckled. "Now, let's get you something to eat before I strip you right here where you stand." His smiled faded and he cocked his head to the side. "Something is still bothering you ... how much did you hear at the top of the stairs?"

"Enough to know that you probably want to use that bag up in your closet." There. I'd just thrown it out into the open. Until seeing that bag, I thought Erick had been honest with me. I wanted that back. I wanted him to tell me it was a mistake. That he hadn't used that stuff in years and didn't care if he ever did again.

A snarl tore from his throat and his fangs descended. Then he sighed and sank down onto the couch, letting his head rest in his hands. He stayed like that for several minutes and I just stood ... waiting.

Regret surged through me. I'd just ruined the best thing I'd had going for me. I wanted him. I was pretty sure I loved him. But I was terrified of what he might want from me. Being beaten in the name of affection was not something I could go through again.

He would end it before he would hurt me. I knew it in my heart. All that was left was to say goodbye. "I'm sure Calliope or Rose can find me somewhere else in town to stay."

Another snarl came from his chest. His blue eyes flashed completely red, power radiating from him like heat from a furnace. "No! You are mine."

Instead of being scared, like I should've been, I recognized his outburst as raw pain. The agony in his voice over the thought of losing me, pulled at my heart. I wanted to be his. I liked belonging to him. I wanted him to strip me naked right there and take me. I wanted to forget about everything else and just be with him, but I couldn't.

"I can't be yours if that bag is what you want."

"I don't care about the fucking bag, Bailey. Didn't you hear me tell Miles that? I want you, no matter what."

"But he said you're a Dom. Doesn't that mean—?"

"It means a lot of things. Things you don't understand. Things that your ex didn't understand. He was an abusive asshole who used objects to hurt you."

"Those things are what hurt me!"

"No, he hurt you. The whip didn't get up of its own accord and hit you. *He* hit you."

"I don't want to like those things, Erick. I don't ever want to see or feel whips or cuffs again. The thought of them makes my skin crawl and my stomach heave. It's bad enough there's a club literally down the street, run by your friends." This conversation was going somewhere I'd been afraid to go with him since I found out about the Castle. Found out he was friends with the two men who ran it. Saw how familiar the Sisters were with him when we visited the other day. "You'll miss it. If you settle for me."

"Bailey," he answered. "I'm not settling. If I never do another scene, it won't matter as long as you are happy. But ..."

Here it was. The catch.

"I will be very honest with you. I want to work through some play scenes to help eliminate your anxiety. You shouldn't fear objects. It is only the people behind the objects that hold the true power."

A tear rolled down my cheek. Why was he asking me this? I just said I couldn't do it. "I can't."

"Do you trust me?"

I did. "Yes, but—"

He grabbed my hand and tugged me to his lap. "No pain, *kjaere*. Not even the slightest pinch unless you ask me for it. I give you my word."

Then what was the point? Isn't that what the kink was about? Pain? Taking pleasure in hurting the person you had power over? "But ... I don't get it. What could we do that wouldn't hurt? Everything Kevin ever did hurt." A lot. I had the scars and healed broken bones to prove it.

Erick's arms gently squeezed me tighter and he kissed the top of my head again. "I'll kill him, *kjaere*. When I see him, I'll rip out his heart while it still beats and feed it to him."

I didn't consider myself a mean person. Or cruel and vengeful. But the picture Erick had just painted filled me with a strange sense of calm. I wanted Kevin dead. I'd wanted it the second I decided to leave that bus station with Erick. It was the only way my torture would end. The only way I could move forward from the horrors of my past and have any kind of future.

He was right. I shouldn't have to live in fear of objects. When he spelled it out that way, I could see it for the crazy it was. But letting those particular objects anywhere near my body was still going to be astronomically hard. I trusted Erick to keep me safe and not to break his word, but I would be trapped. There was no recourse once the chains went on. Mercy was something I'd cried for and hoped to get from Kevin, but never did. Everything inside me said not to give a man that much power willingly again.

I'd learned the hard way that life had no guarantees.

"These activities ... would they happen here or at the Castle?"

"It needs to be there. You fear it because of what it is."

"Would I be chained?"

"No."

"We're not going to have sex in front of anyone, right?"

"No." He spoke slowly. "Unless you ask for that."

Unless I ask. Wow. Most of me was terrified, but there was this little corner of my brain that wanted to know what he thought he could do to get me past my fears. And part of me wanted to get past them.

"Can I think about it?"

"Of course." He kissed me softly and a low moan rumbled in his throat, almost like the purr of a lion. Pleasure sparked through my body as he ran one of his hands up my thigh. Then he jerked back and shook his head, like he was trying to wake from a trance. "I promised to feed you. Be right back." He set me on the cushion next to him and got up.

His body moved silently from the living room to the kitchen. Even though he was fully clothed, I could appreciate the beauty of his broad, muscular shoulders, tapered waist, and tight butt. Damn, those jeans really did fit perfectly. Definitely owed Calliope a huge thank you for the bountiful view in front of me.

He disappeared around the corner and I moved to follow him into the cool, dimly lit kitchen. A shiver ran up my spine as my bare feet touched the slate tile on the floor. My eyes adjusted to the dark and I grinned at the nice view of his frame. He was bent over, digging in the refrigerator, his body silhouetted by the light. Mostly what I could see was a nice view of his ass.

"There's grilled chicken breasts. Bella put some fresh bread in here for you and a few other vegetables, too. How about I make you a sandwich?"

My brain took several seconds to register the question, but I still didn't speak.

"Bailey, please. Try to focus on something else or you aren't going to get anything to eat right now." He groaned and closed the fridge door holding an armful of groceries.

"Sorry. Bad pheromones." I grinned and snapped my attention to his face. For now I was willing to forget what I knew he wanted from me. Right now, it didn't matter. I'd almost died today. All I wanted was to have his arms around me again. Feel him inside me.

"Yes, very bad pheromones." A glint of amusement flickered in his eyes, but he hid it quickly. Flip the switch by your shoulder, please." He nodded his head toward the wall and I moved my hand in the dark until I felt the small lever.

Light flooded the kitchen from the stainless steel lamps hanging from the ceiling. I blinked a few times and then rubbed my eyes and leaned against the opposite side of the counter where he'd dropped all the sandwich stuff.

"Erick," I pleaded. I wasn't going to last. My appetite for food had vanished. All I could think about was being with him. I prayed he would get past the "feeding me" thing and let me eat afterward. My face was hot, my palms were damp, and I could feel my pulse in my sex. "Please." I tried again.

The desperation in my voice should've been embarrassing, but it wasn't. All I was waiting on was a nod or a look or anything that said I could leap into his arms. He was holding himself back. I knew he was.

CHAPTER 14

A moment later I was in his arms and pushed up against the kitchen wall with a soft thud. Even in the midst of his passion, he could be gentle. I didn't need to fear him or whatever he had planned for me. My heart wanted to think he might one day love me, but I was a human and he was a vampire. It wasn't in the stars for us to be together for long, but perhaps I could have a short time in heaven with him on earth.

I sighed as he trailed his lips up my neck, over my jawline, and then crushed his mouth over mine. He plunged his tongue inside and swept it through my mouth. His hands slid down to my ass and he squeezed before pulling my legs out from under me and guiding them around his waist. My pussy throbbed against his hard cock and I locked my ankles behind his back. He was so strong that he held me in place with little effort.

I reached down between our bodies and fumbled with

his pants until they came undone. He pushed them down, along with his boxers, until his cock sprang free.

The robe came open easily, leaving only my soaked panties between him and my swollen pussy. I couldn't get them off though, not with my legs firmly clasped around his waist.

"You are amazing," he growled, pulling his mouth from mine.

I watched his eyes turn from their normal bright blue to the color of midnight rimmed with scarlet. "You make me feel again, *kjaere*. Things I never thought to find with another woman as long as I lived."

How did I respond to that? I couldn't blurt out that I was falling in love with him. Not when I knew I'd have to leave. Not when I knew he wouldn't be satisfied with what I could give him. My broken soul and body would never be enough.

I wanted to stay with him, though. I wanted to tell him he made me feel safe and loved and valued. Something I hadn't felt in a really long time. And something I wanted to keep feeling. I wanted to tell him I loved his overprotective nature. Craved it, even.

"I need you. Please," I whispered. Those four words were all I could get out.

His hand slipped between my legs and tore my panties from my body like they were made of tissue. A shiver ran through me as I anticipated him filling me. He shifted me against the wall and used his hand to guide his length to my wet and wanting opening. The tip brushed my slick entrance and I moaned as nerves shot streaks of fire throughout my body. I was so warm against his cool, rock-hard body.

More. I wanted more. So much more. I was on the cusp of an orgasm and he wasn't even inside me yet.

"My beautiful Bailey." His voice was deep and held a tenderness that shattered what was left of my defenses. He hadn't said he loved me, but the affection in his words and actions spoke louder than any declaration ever could.

He drove into me, pushing me harder against the kitchen wall. My breasts pressed into his chest and my pussy clamped down hard on his swollen cock as it filled me completely. His mouth went to my neck and I felt the slight pinch as he bit into me.

The sensation of him drinking was just enough to push me over the edge and my orgasm came crashing down on us both like huge waves in a storm. I cried out and clung to him as he pumped in and out, driving me higher and higher, all the while drinking from me, sending delightful sensations throughout my already overstimulated body.

Yes.

It was the only word on my mind as he moved me from the wall and sped us up to the bed I wanted to call mine, if given the chance.

I OPENED MY EYES AND STRETCHED, GROANING AT THE soreness in my girly parts. Even my nipples were still sensitive. I lifted the sheet gingerly and sat up on the edge of the bed.

Erick had asked me last night, after making love to me

for hours, if he could take me to the Castle today. Of course I'd agreed ... to think about it. The man had just plied me with a half-dozen orgasms. Any woman would have said yes to anything he requested.

Like I was really up for "activities" at a BDSM club. I'd almost died yesterday from a stab wound. I wasn't stupid.

Darius was still out there. Waiting. Watching. Even I knew the fires he was setting all over town were just a distraction to get me alone and separated—vulnerable. I was no stranger to being hunted by a psychopath. The asshole Djinn could get in line. Mostly, I hated that I was putting my new friends in danger. People who barely knew me were fighting to protect me—risking their lives.

Instead of hunting down the crazy psycho, Erick wanted to go "play" at the Castle. What did he really think he was going to accomplish? He'd promised no pain and no restraints. What was left? Was there any point?

But, I did hate that just the sound of that whip had brought me to my knees. It pissed me off. I wanted to believe I was stronger than that. If there was something Erick could do to help me regain my confidence and lose some of my anxiety, maybe I should give it a try.

After a hot shower, I opened the closet doors to grab a robe. My gaze flew to where the black canvas bag had been. It was gone. In its place were shoeboxes. Every pair Calliope and I had chosen the day before was neatly stacked in rows. A smile spread across my face at his thoughtfulness. When he'd had time to get them, I had no idea. He likely snuck them in that morning while I was sleeping.

Then I looked further and realized he'd also hung up

every piece of clothing from the bags of things she'd told me I needed to have. I stepped forward and ran my hand along the edges of the beautiful clothes. A tear welled up and ran down my cheek.

He was determined.

Was I going to be able to say goodbye? Years ago, I had accepted that I didn't get a happy ending. It just wasn't in the cards for me. Why was Erick torturing me with the hope that it could be different? Kevin wouldn't let it happen. I wouldn't stay in Sanctuary if he found me. He'd hurt my friends. Even if he couldn't do it personally, he'd find a way to ruin this beautiful place.

Taking a deep breath, I took a matching pair of black panties and a bra from a small basket he'd put next to the stack of shoeboxes. A little note was stuck at the top in his scribble—*not sure where you would want these.* I grinned, glad I hadn't had to hunt through his dresser in the bedroom.

After slipping the perfectly fitting bits of lace into place, I took a pair of soft, denim shorts and an aqua blue tank from the rail. The clothes fit perfectly in moments, as expected. The shorts clung to my ass in a way I knew Erick would appreciate, and the neck of the tank was just low enough to give a peek at the cleavage the bra helped to showcase.

Time to play. Maybe ...

I pulled out a pair of slip-on sandals and headed to the sink to brush my teeth and my hair. Another note was stuck to the mirror—*be right back, went to Rose's to get you some breakfast. Looking forward to playing.*

"Awfully confidant my answer will be yes, aren't you?" I huffed and ran a comb through my wet hair before braiding it into a long tail. I hadn't actually agreed to more than considering it, but Erick was right. He knew my answer would be yes, because he knew I trusted him completely.

"Yes to what, Bailey? Spreading your legs for that undead *thing* again? Are you letting it drink from you?"

I looked up into the mirror, dropped the comb, and froze. Kevin stared back at me in the reflection. I whirled around to face him and felt sick. My stomach crawled into my throat.

"H-how?"

"You're not as smart as you think, bitch."

"I am, you just have a badge you use unfairly." Where had that come from?

A cruel smile twisted his face. "You think since you hooked up with an Other, I can't get to you." He made a clucking sound with his tongue and shook his head. "I have to admit, your coming all the way out here to nowhere did slow me down just a hair."

I swallowed and took another step backward. "Erick!" I screamed at the top of my lungs. "Help!"

Kevin rushed and I dodged around the tub in the center of the bathroom, but he jumped it and tackled me to the floor. Air rushed from my lungs as his weight pushed down on me. I kicked and screamed. Erick wouldn't let him take me. He would protect me.

"Stupid, bitch. He's not coming to help you, Bailey. I made sure he met up with the Djinn that stalked you to the bus station. Apparently you are a popular commodity. Plus, we had a common enemy."

Erick! *No. No. No.* Kevin had always hated Others. Why

would he work with a Djinn? Why would Darius work with him? How had they even met?

"No, please!" I screamed again, landing a good kick to his gut. But, he returned the hit with one to my ribs and I heard something crack. Pain like a hot poker shot through my chest.

He straddled me on the floor, pinning me down. At six-feet, heavily-muscled, and angry, I didn't have a shot in hell, but I wouldn't stop fighting. I had never given up on anything. I knew I wasn't getting out of this, though.

Another punch struck the other side of my torso, pushing an agonizing wail from my chest. Another shot of pain ripped through my chest. Breathing was difficult and the familiar taste of blood reappeared in my mouth.

"Even the Djinn was stupid. He thought I'd share you with him, but I didn't come all this way to let someone else have you." He grabbed my wrists and held them above my head with one hand as he squeezed and pinched my breasts.

"He'll k-kill you." I coughed, struggling to draw a breath. Of course if the Djinn didn't kill him, Erick would.

Kevin's brown eyes were dark, reflecting what I could only imagine were the depths of hell itself. My heart skipped a beat. He'd come to kill me this time. Gone was his desire to take me and lock me away.

"By the time he realizes I decided against our arrangement, I'll be gone and your vampire won't know I was ever here."

Arrogance and evil wrapped into one. I couldn't believe he would consider double-crossing a Djinn, not that I was going to complain. I didn't want to see Darius any more than I wanted to see Kevin.

"He will kn-know and he'll hunt you until he finds you." My anger helped me growl out the words. He was wrong if he thought he could get away with this. I had vampires, dragons, and all kinds of Others who would avenge my death. I knew they would. He wouldn't survive for long after I was dead. That knowledge gave me some satisfaction.

His fist connected with my ribcage again and I gasped as the small amount of air I'd been pulling in was knocked from my struggling lungs. I twisted on the floor, opening my mouth to scream and was unable to produce any sound.

I couldn't breathe. My lungs refused to expand.

My pulse roared in my ears and all my senses reeled from the fiery pain radiating out from the ribs he'd broken and rammed into my lungs. He had let go of my wrists, but I didn't have the strength left to raise them from the floor.

I saw a flash of metal a second before I felt it draw across my neck. Warmth seeped from my body and my blurring vision faded to darkness.

The pain was fading, but so was my life.

CHAPTER 15

Erick's voice rumbled next to me.

How was that possible? Hadn't I died? Didn't Kevin cut my throat?

I opened my eyes and winced at the light flooding into the far end of the room. The smell of peppermint on Erick's breath was pleasant, but more overwhelming than usual. I could also smell Calliope's spicy perfume and Rose's honey oatmeal shampoo, but I didn't see them in the room. They had been there, though. Maybe a few hours ago.

"Bailey." Erick laid a hand on my wrist and I growled.

Growled? What the hell? What was wrong with me?!

I sat up. The urge to eat was overwhelming. "I'm starving," I croaked, my voice hoarse and cracking. I buried my face in my hands. My head felt like it was about to split in half.

"Here."

Looking between my fingers, I watched Erick pick up a

cup from the nightstand and offer it to me. I took the cup and scrunched my face. It was filled with a dark red, thick liquid.

Oh, God! No!

"I'm ... I died. H-he killed me!"

"He paid for what he did to you, Bailey. I tore his beating heart from his chest, just as I promised I would." Erick knelt at the side of the bed, his eyes glassy. "Forgive me for failing you, *min kjaereste*."

I did.

It wasn't his fault.

Even the Oracle had said he couldn't change my fate. Apparently, she was correct. Score one for the crotchety, old know-it-all.

"I couldn't get to you in time. I tried, Bailey. You must believe I tried. Darius was working with him. I heard you calling and he kept me from you." His anger and guilt showed in his red-rimmed eyes.

Not quite ready to down blood like water, I set the glass back on the nightstand and reached for him, pulling him close. He crawled into the bed next to me and nuzzled my neck before kissing my lips softly. We settled back against the pillows and I snuggled into the crook of his shoulder. He smelled sweet and the scent of his blood made my mouth water. I felt my fangs lengthen in my mouth and I shook my head, trying to clear away the sensation.

"I know, Erick. He told me Darius was keeping you away. I told him you'd kill him."

"I did." He buried his face in my hair and took a deep breath. "Gods, Bailey. It'd been so many hours since you had my blood. There was no guarantee you would turn."

"I'm here." I wasn't sure exactly what it meant to be what I was, but if I had survived the trauma of my human life, I could survive being an Other, too.

We lay quietly for a while. I don't know how long. He let me have the time I needed to process.

꧁꧂

KEVIN HAD KILLED ME.

I was a vampire.

All my running had been for nothing ... and yet, I was here in this little town called Sanctuary, wrapped in the arms of the strongest, kindest man, one who would go to the ends of the earth to protect and care for me. The Oracle said I'd been on a path to them for a long time. That my ancestors had magick in their blood.

I wasn't sure I believed in fate, but the stars had truly aligned for me to end up where I was right now.

An unfamiliar pain surged from a place deep inside.

Blood. I couldn't deny the craving any longer.

I pushed against Erick's chest and sat up again. "I think I need that cup after all."

He sat up next to me and handed me the glass.

I took a small sip, expecting it to be terrible. Instead, it was sweet and I gulped it down, wishing there was more. Running my tongue across my teeth, I paused, surprised to find fangs. I shouldn't have been surprised. I'd felt them descend earlier. I knew I was a vampire and vampires had fangs. But it still brought tears to my eyes. Fear of the unknown. I knew how to survive as a human. What was the world going to be like as a vampire?

"What's going to happen to me?"

"You will stay with me in Sanctuary ... if you choose."

"I have a choice?" Wouldn't Rose and the Sisters have a bit to say about me leaving? That Arlea woman had seemed quite confident I was supposed to be part of their little system.

"Yes. But, taking on the role of Protector is not something you should agree to lightly. This is a cause we have been fighting for millennia."

"Where would I go?"

"Anywhere you wanted to go. I would make sure you had everything you could ever want."

"You would do that? Go against your friends? Go against the Oracle? You would let me leave?"

"I don't want you to go, Bailey. But I would let you, if that is what would make you happy." His eyes were focused on the bedding, refusing to make contact with my gaze.

"What about Darius? He'll keep coming back."

"One step at a time, *kjaere*." He drew his hand over mine and finally looked up at me. "There is no hurry."

It was so much to consider.

I stared at the rays of sunlight across the room, creating a pattern of light on the wall. It seemed brighter than usual and I squinted.

"I'll burn in the sun, won't I?"

"Yes, unless you accept the role as a Protector and Rose enchants your tattoo. There are witches that can cast sun protection charms as well, but they are hard to find."

What was there to think about? I had no intention of leaving Erick or Sanctuary. This was my home.

I jumped from the bed, intending only to stand, but I flew through the air and landed near the doorway instead. "Holy crap!"

Erick chuckled. "Think slow. You can move much faster now, and your strength is fifty times what the average human possesses." He stood and walked toward me, his voice calm and sexy as hell. "Move deliberately. Think about where your foot needs to go before you lift it. Every cell in your body is perfectly attuned to your every desire and responds in turn."

I took a few more steps, carefully making my way down the flight of stairs to the entryway, but a large swath of sunlight from the living room blocked me from going any farther.

"Wait here. I'll pull the drapes." He went ahead, and soon the apartment was dimmed and sunlight was nowhere to be seen. He flipped on a few ceiling lights, though I found I could see perfectly in the shadows, and motioned for me to follow him to the kitchen.

I sat carefully in one of the polished, white leather barstools, worried that if I moved faster than the speed of a turtle, I might just break his furniture.

He opened the fridge and pulled out a blood bag. "Compliments of Raven and Maven. They got several cases off a donation van over in Fort Worth for you. Human blood will help ease you into your transition," he said, putting it on the counter in front of me. He pulled a couple of glasses from the cabinet to his left and then emptied the contents of the bag into both. "Cheers."

"Several cases?"

"You will need a lot at first. After a while, the hunger will fade to a more manageable level."

Picking up a glass, I took another sip and paused. It was different than the first glass. This blood was thinner, lighter, and almost had a fruity taste to it.

"Whose was in the glass upstairs?"

"Mine."

I set the glass down and stared at him while he downed his. "Why would you give me your blood?"

"The only way a vampire can complete the change is to drink the blood of their sire. If you had not, you would have died ... painfully."

"Oh." Not the answer I was expecting, but then this was all very new. Who was I to argue with how vampires were made? "I didn't know blood could taste so different. What did mine taste like?" The question popped out before I could stop it.

"*Kjaere*, your blood was like the finest, sweet, red wine. Thick and strong, with a healthy dose of sugar." He closed his eyes and smiled, as if reliving the memory of tasting me.

Strangely, it made me feel good to know he enjoyed my blood. Almost proud that I was that desirable. "I guess my destiny wasn't so easy to get away from after all."

"I'm sorry this happened to you, Bailey. If there was anything—"

"It wasn't your fault I died, Erick."

"No, but if it hadn't been for your previous injury ... I would have lost you. It's selfish, I know. Being semi-immortal is a hard life, and though I am happy to share it with you, there are things you can no longer have. I grieve that your choice was taken away."

"I'll miss food." My first thought was Rose's café. I hadn't eaten so well in years. I tried to lighten the mood and smile a little.

He frowned. "Food is negligible. And you can still eat, if you wish. But children," he said, taking another swig from him glass. "And family."

I sipped on the sweet liquid and considered his words. "Kevin stole my ability to have children years ago. I made peace with that already. My parents died when I was a teenager and I have no living relatives that I'm aware of. You ..." I gestured to the window. "You and this town are all I know. Arlea is the only person I've ever met that'd heard of my real family name. I still think I'm probably the last D'Roth on the planet. But maybe not."

"I heard you speak with Arlea, but I don't think you're the only one." He fell silent for a moment, staring so determinedly at his glass. "I'm sorry, though."

"For what?" It didn't surprise me that he'd listened in. I slipped from my chair and moved to stand next to him. "For being glad I'm still here and kind of alive? You only met me a few days ago. You can't possibly feel responsible for my life before that."

"I can. They should have sent us looking for you sooner. We could have protected you. Your family should've protected you."

"From life?" I leaned my head against his chest and sighed as he slipped his arm around me and squeezed. "I've had a shitty few years, but my entire life wasn't bad, Erick. I loved my parents and the time I had with them before they died. Granted, I could've skipped the foster system and the year with Kevin. I wouldn't mind having those memories permanently lasered from my brain, but like you said—I'm a fighter."

"A warrior," he whispered. "And I can help you research your family, *kjaere*. Don't be surprised if we find relatives somewhere in this vast world."

Turning to face him, I wrapped both my arms around his waist and looked up, waiting patiently for his beautiful, blue gaze to meet mine. "All in good time. Right now, in this moment, I'm glad that sonofabitch is dead. I'll sleep better at night because of it, but I've still got some fighting to do. Darius said he would be back."

"Let me worry about Darius. You just need to eat and get up your strength."

I giggled.

"What could you possibly find funny?" he asked.

"Nothing's changed. You're still trying to get me to eat."

A resounding laugh rumbled in his chest and he rubbed his hands up and down my back. "I really don't know what I would have done if I'd lost you."

"You didn't. Just focus on that."

He nodded. "You know Rose and Calliope were here earlier."

"Yes."

"She and Calliope worried I would leave town in a rage, but she needn't have. I wouldn't have left your side until I knew for sure if I'd lost you. Nothing in this world short of Rose locking me up would have kept me from hunting down Darius if you had died."

"I suppose Rose was also concerned that her future Protector might be dead."

"She means well, *kjaere*. She is just devoted. The House of Lamidae is the only thing she has left of her old world. She cares for everyone in Sanctuary, but in a special way, the Sisters are like her children."

"The Oracle did say one thing I've been wondering about."

"What?"

"She said my bloodline was magickal at one time. What exactly did she mean by that?"

"My family was descended from an ancient order of priests, probably witches. Javier and Marcus can also trace their lineage to gifted humans. Sita is another Protector whom you've not met, yet. She knows nothing of her family, but I would not be surprised if her family lines go back to witches as well. It seems to be a running theme."

"So, what? We're genetically predisposed to be part of this spell?"

"I don't know. Anything is possible when you are dealing with magick this old. I've personally not heard of the D'Roth name, but if Arlea knows something we will find out." He kissed the top of my head and released me from his embrace. "I've protected the House of Lamidae more years of my life than I haven't. I still do not understand them, but I know in my soul they need to be protected."

"I can see how an all-knowing, all-powerful supernatural who can control everyone could be a problem for the world."

"Hmm," he murmured his agreement.

"Could I have another glass of ... that ... um?"

"Blood?"

"Err ... yeah. It just doesn't sound right saying 'pass me a glass of blood'."

"Give it time."

"Will I want to bite everyone? Like, uncontrollably?" I leaned back against the counter, remembering how good he'd smelled and how my mouth had watered at the thought of drinking from him.

"You will be tempted, but no. It's not uncontrollable. Feeding often will also help control the urges."

"Can I have more now? Or do I need to wait a while?"

"Of course." He moved to the fridge and grabbed anther bag. Pulling out the top, he poured it into my empty glass. "There is more than enough to keep you sated for several weeks. Plus, we can supplement my blood as needed, too."

I took a deep breath and leaned back against the counter, sipping on my now-full glass. It tasted divine. No wonder vampires chose to drink from humans whenever possible. His blood had been good. Rich, thick, and filling. But human blood was like candy. Though, the fact that I'd just compared the taste of blood to candy was kind of gross.

Everything had happened so fast. Meeting him. Learning there was so much more to life than what the government let on. I couldn't imagine trying to live outside this town after being here. I felt a connection to the people I'd met here and committing to my predes-tined fate as a Protector felt like the right path. There were enough human tyrants already dominating the world. We didn't need unstoppable supernatural ones, too.

"How do I get my tattoo?"

Erick's eyes widened before a smile spread across his face. His two adorable dimples made me want to toss my glass aside and leap into his arms. He looked positively edible.

"Bailey." His voice brought me back from its preoccupied state of arousal.

"Yep." I blinked and tried to focus back on his face and not how I'd feel wrapped in his arms.

"Are you saying you want to stay? That you want to become a Protector? I told Rose I would not allow you to be pressured by her or anyone else."

"This is where I'm supposed to be." I put the glass down and stepped up to him again, wrapping my arms around his firm waist. "I can think of nowhere I'd rather be than by your side. If being a Protector comes along with that, then so be it. I can learn to be a vampire and a Protector at the same time."

He wrapped his arms around me and squeezed tightly. "I'll be with you through every step."

I nodded, taking a deep breath. It wasn't the air I needed, but the action was so familiar and comfortable I couldn't imagine feeling the way I did and not heaving a sigh. Human or not, some things would always be the same.

A buzzing caught my attention and I turned to the right. Rose's name was blinking on the face of his cell phone where it lay on the counter. Erick picked it up and answered.

"She's awake and has eaten … Yes …" He gazed into my eyes, a frown tugging at the corners of his mouth. "I know, but … He what?" Erick growled, his fangs descending. "We'll be right there." He pressed the red button on his screen and tossed the phone back onto the countertop.

"Darius?" My gut said it couldn't be anyone else.

"He tried to burn the library."

I blinked. A vague recollection of seeing a sign for a library rattled around in my brain somewhere. "Was anyone hurt?"

"No, thankfully Meredith was already home. Her wards protected the books, but the fire did quite a bit of damage to the building before Jared got there."

"Who are Meredith … and Jared?"

"Meredith is the redhead who helped us on the bus the day you came here."

An 'o' formed on my lips and I nodded, remembering the witch quite clearly.

"Jared is Sanctuary's fire chief, so to speak."

"But there's no engine or office. The sign makes it look like the fire and police share the same office." I remembered seeing the little brick building and wondering how they managed with such a small office for both departments.

"Alek Melos is sheriff and Jared MacKay is the fire chief. They take care of the town. Drama, accidents, etc. They make sure the town as a body of citizens gets along and everyone stays safe." He gestured to the front door and I walked ahead of him. A pair of my flats was sitting next to the wall. I slipped my bare feet into them.

"Are they human?" I hadn't met either of them but

wasn't surprised after hearing about their responsibilities. The poor men probably never had time to sit down.

"No. Alek is a Gryphon, and Jared is a Phoenix."

Neither species sounded familiar. "Do I even want to know?" I asked as we walked out the front door.

"Probably not right now." He chuckled, closing the door behind us and then taking my hand. "We are headed to the café. Why don't you try to run?"

I nodded and leapt into the first step. The wind rushed through my hair. A feeling of freedom swelled in my chest and I came to a sudden halt in front of Rose's café. Amazing. It felt like I'd only taken a few steps, but I knew from walking the path again and again over the last couple of days that I'd gone at least a quarter-mile.

A few yards down the sidewalk, a small crowd had gathered in front of a smoldering building. I recognized Miles and Eli's formidable figures. Both men were a good six inches taller than everyone around them. Several other men stood near them, but I didn't know them. Calliope was talking to Rose and another woman I'd yet to meet. Garrett caught my glance and nodded a hello before turning back to his conversation with some other men I didn't recognize.

"Why would Darius care about burning a library?"

Erick leaned down to my ear. "He's looking for the vault."

"Vault of what?" I scrunched my forehead.

"Bottled Djinn," Rose said, walking toward us. Calliope followed a step behind. "Over the course of several thousand years, I've caught and imprisoned nearly a thousand of their kind."

Rose had such strength in her presence, but I could tell she was tired this evening. Her eyes were reddened like she'd been crying, but maybe it was just irritation from the smoke clouding the air in the circle.

"Still, Xerxes keeps them loyal by promising to release them all when they help him take control of the Sisters."

"You can't bottle Darius because he's wearing your husband's ring," Erick said, rubbing his temple.

"True. At least Calliope and I can still sense when he teleports into town, but neither my powers nor Meredith's can affect him while he's wearing it." Rose sucked in a ragged breath. "I don't understand how they found it. It was lost so many years ago ..."

"We will make it right." Erick placed a reassuring hand on Rose's shoulder.

Rose nodded, but her gaze narrowed and veins in her neck bulged. Energy surged from her body like static electricity, sparking in the air like firecrackers.

Erick withdrew his hand like he'd been bitten.

Rose's voice doubled in volume, anger flowing like a river of white hot metal. "He's using my own husband's magick against me. Naram trusted Xerxes until the very end. Now his brother gives our sacred, binding ring to one of his psychotic flunkies." She fisted her hands at her sides and stomped a foot. I could've sworn the ground shook just a little.

At first glance, she was just a petite woman pitching a fit. A closer look showed the luminescent swirls of color in her eyes, the shimmer of gold on her sun-kissed skin, and the hint of fangs behind perfectly painted, mauve lips. Whatever Rose was, it was trying desperately to surface.

"Rose, take a deep breath," Calliope said, placing a hand on Rose's shoulder. "You can't let him get to you like this. You always tell us to keep our focus. Don't let him steal yours."

Rose shuddered. "Thank you, Calliope darling." The swirls of color in her eyes faded away and her hands relaxed at her sides. A moment later, she focused her gaze on me and I took a nervous step backward. She might be able to bottle Djinn, but she was keeping a whole lot of power bottled up just inside herself.

Calliope dropped her hand as Rose took several steps closer to me. Gooseflesh rose along my arms and the hair on the back of my neck stood on end. Nerves apparently didn't fade with death. The Sentinel of Sanctuary still made me quake in my shoes with just a glance—glowing eyes or not.

"Darius wouldn't even be here if it wasn't for me," I said.

"Oh, no." Rose waved her hand dismissively. "That arrogant Djinn has been hounding Sanctuary for centuries. Don't you dare think you're responsible."

I opened my mouth to object, but shut it again quickly when Garrett and another man walked up to the group.

"Bailey, you already know Garrett. This is his brother, Travis. If you are comfortable—"

Erick growled and pushed me behind his body, blocking me from the two wolves and Rose. "You said no pressure."

"I wasn't pressuring her. I was offering an option, Erick. I understand you claim her, but she is important to Sanctuary, too. We need her."

I brushed my fingertips along Erick's shoulder, surprised by how much I could feel—tension, anger, fear, then remorse and regret. In fact, I could smell the same things coming from most of the crowd. Pheromones? Wow. I took a deep breath and wanted to cry and then scream. It was too much. So many were upset by the fire. Others were angry. But some couldn't care less.

The wolves next to me were very different. Travis was devoted to Rose. I could see it in his gaze and smell it in his body chemistry, but Garrett held less concern for Rose and more for ... me. I narrowed my eyes and waited for a smart-ass comment to fall from his mouth like water through a sieve. Instead, he merely cocked his head to the side and stared.

He couldn't read my mind anymore.

Score one for being a vampire.

"How are you feeling?" Garrett asked, ignoring the slight rumble vibrating out from Erick's chest.

"Hungry," I answered, trying not to smile. He smelled delicious and I had to purse my lips together to keep from licking them. His pulse pounded in my ears, teasing my body into a state of arousal I wasn't used to. Actually, Calliope and Rose smelled just as good. The standing crowd outside the smoldering library was a feast my starving body couldn't ignore.

"You've got it bad," Calliope chuckled. "Better get her over to the café before she starts sampling all of us, Viking."

"I wouldn't!" Would I? Surely I had more control than that. I mean, the hunger was hard to ignore, but I wasn't about to go biting people without a second thought.

"Oh, Bailey. I know, sweetie," Calliope replied. "But you've got that look that says, dear gods in heaven and hell, please feed me!"

"I just ate."

"Your appetite is stronger for the first two weeks or so." Erick wrapped an arm around my waist and pulled me a step away from Garrett and Travis, both of whom were grinning at me without shame.

I wanted to bite them just for looking at me that way. A throaty growl tore its way between my lips and I lunged at them, even angrier that they could make me lose my cool.

Erick's arm cinched around my waist, yanking me back to the ground.

"When you're ready for your tattoo, let me know." Travis said, turning to leave.

His brother followed a moment later, but not before throwing one jab. "It's a shame I can't get into that pretty head of yours anymore."

"You are a mind-reading asshole," I spat back.

I sucked in a deep breath, taking a moment to process. My tattoo? The Protector tattoo. Travis did them ... I'd have to let Garrett's brother sit over me for hours with a needle full of ink!

Shit.

"I could always do your tat," Garrett answered, a grin splitting his face. "I'd even throw in a drink on the house. Bet you'd like to get a tas—"

"Garrett, that is quite enough." Rose's voice cut through the racket of voices like a sharp knife, making everyone turn and look. "Travis will be doing her tattoo and you will be on the far side of town helping clean up the mess Darius made of the Winters' place."

He snorted, but nodded his head and turned down a different road than his brother.

Rose looked back at me. "Get something to eat. Raven stashed some blood in our refrigerators as well. If you are agreeable, I'd like you to get the tattoo as soon as possible."

Erick started to speak, but she held up her hand and he snapped his jaw shut with a snarl.

"I promised I wouldn't pressure you, but we have a situation. Darius is untouchable with that ring and that is a very big problem for Sanctuary. The only thing we have besides the vault that he wants—"

"Is me," I whispered.

CHAPTER 16

I'd already decided I wanted the tattoo, wanted to
become a Protector, but hearing Rose point out that
I was the only bait they had to draw out Darius
made my skin crawl. The moonbeams highlighted the
gooseflesh pimpling my arm. I knew I was their best bet to
catch him, but it didn't make it any easier to swallow.

"I'm ready. Let's do it now before he shows up again."

Rose nodded. "Erick, take her to the shop. Travis was
headed that way. Call me when you finish. I'll meet you at
the Castle."

Erick's hand pressed against my lower back and turned
me across the circle until I was staring at the Castle. Why?
Why did she need me to go there? I'd already agreed to let
Erick help me work through my ... personal issues. I didn't
need to have any more exposure to the dragons' dungeon
than absolutely necessary.

"The tattoo shop is down a block behind the Castle."
He pointed to the street that cut between the monstrous

stone building and the strip of weather-beaten shops making up the face of the town circle.

"Wasn't I supposed to get to eat first?"

"I'll get you some after I get you situated at the shop."

"Okay." *Damn*. So much for avoiding the obvious.

We hurried across the grassy circle, avoiding the large, stone disk in the center, and down the dark alley next to the Castle. A light touch on my right shoulder guided me down a block and then around a turn. Another tap stopped me in my tracks in front of a small, white brick building. A large, blacked-out window covered most of the front wall, and a red neon light that read *Tattoos and Piercings* hung in the top right corner. The ratty, wooden front door was scuffed and most of its red paint had peeled.

I pulled open the door, expecting to see a messy shop I could balk at, a reason to refuse to get the tattoo. Instead, a pristine, white tile floor met my scrutinizing gaze. The walls were painted a bright, canary yellow and were decorated with gorgeous, life-sized photographs of completed tattoos in sharp, glossy black frames.

Shocked did not even begin to describe my state of mind. There was a small, glass counter to the side of the curtained-off hallway. The case held all styles and sizes of studs, rings, rods, and other things I didn't recognize.

I heard his heartbeat before Travis pushed aside the curtain and stepped into the main room of the shop. He glanced up and smiled at me. His scent was pleasant, earthy. I wondered what his blood would taste like. Would it be rich and thick like Erick's or sweeter, like the human blood from the bags?

"Ready?"

No, I wasn't.

All thoughts of hunger vanished as the reality of what I was taking on solidly slammed into my conscious mind. I gulped. Would it hurt? I took a step backward and grunted when my back hit Erick's solid chest. It couldn't hurt worse than anything I'd already been through. I stood a little taller and gathered myself.

I could do this.

Compared to everything my body had endured, a tattoo should be a walk in the park. "What do I do?"

He gestured back through the curtain. Erick's hand resting lightly on the curve of my ass propelled me forward. We turned a corner and ended up in another brightly lit room. White tile floors and white walls with floor-to ceiling mirrors were the only décor. A line of glossy, white base cabinets with a stone countertop lined the far wall. Two tinted windows gave a view out into a small green courtyard area.

The room was quite large and there were three different chairs. One looked like a massage table, another looked like a dental chair, and the last one was designed to straddle, facing away from the artist. That was the one Travis patted.

"Sit here, sweetheart. Let me get the straps."

"Straps?"

"Just to keep you from flinching and pulling away." He opened a drawer and pulled out several leather strips.

"I don't need them. I promise I won't move." My eyes blurred from the tears welling in them. "Erick, please. I can't ..." I started to back away from them both.

"It hurts, Bailey. It's just to help hold you steady."

Erick's voice cut through the panic flooding my brain, but it wasn't enough to stem the tide.

I felt my fangs descend and scrape against my dry tongue. My body was preparing to fight even though I wanted to turn and flee.

"You are strong enough to pull free of anything he uses. But the tie helps you focus on staying still."

"I've never seen anyone get strapped down for a tattoo," I snarled, taking another a step backward. How could he think I would be okay with this? He knew what I'd been through. He knew how I felt about restraints. This wasn't an option for me. Not now. Not ever.

I would never let anyone tie me down again.

"Hey, girl. It's okay." Travis dropped the ties back in the drawer and shoved it closed with his hip. "We can try without the ties, but it's gonna hurt like a hot poker in the eye. Vampires heal too fast. I have to use a special silver-plated needle to keep the wound open long enough for the ink to set."

The storm inside me calmed slightly at the explanation. My emotions were a rollercoaster between scared shitless and pissed off. Erick said everything would be enhanced, but this was far beyond anything I could've imagined.

My brain knew those ties didn't present a challenge to my new supernatural strength, but the wounds to my psyche screamed in protest, reminding me how stupid I'd been to trust Kevin.

"I'm going to need Erick to hold you, at least for the first few minutes until you adjust to the pain."

"No." I shook my head, clearing it of the raging storm

of emotions. "I won't move." Taking a few steps, I seated myself astride the chair and leaned against the chest panel. For such an odd looking contraption, it wasn't as uncomfortable as I thought it would be.

"*Kjaere*? Are you sure?" Genuine concern flowed from his ocean blue irises. He was worried about my well-being, not trying to chain me up and take advantage. It was consideration, not control I was shying away from. In my warped mind, control was all I'd learned to see.

"I won't move."

"All right," Travis answered. He sat on a stool and rolled up behind me. "You'll have to take off your shirt, the neck is too high."

No way was I stripping for the brother of the horniest werewolf in town. I'd never hear the end of it from Garrett.

I closed my eyes and willed the shirt to change. Calliope said the clothes would change for the person. Time to test that theory. The soft t-shirt fabric tightened around my waist and I felt the neck widen in the back and open up. In the front, it rose to my throat and I watched in the mirrors as the fabric in the back dropped into a loose cowl, baring all the skin above my bra. My skin was so ... smooth? How?

"Well, that works, too." Travis chuckled and leaned forward.

"Wait!" I jumped from the chair and grabbed the hem of my shirt, pulling it up baring most of my stomach and the bottom of my bra.

They were gone.

How had I not noticed?

I'd been dressed when I woke up, but still ... I should've felt different. Tracing my fingers across my skin, I felt for where the scars had been. But nothing remained. No discoloration. No raised scars. Nothing. It was as if it'd never happened.

But it had. I remembered where every single jagged white and red stripe had been. They would forever be imprinted in my mind.

"Bailey. Your transformation healed your human body. All imperfections are erased when you become a vampire."

I stared at Erick in the mirror. My once brown eyes were the same ocean blue as his.

So strange.

It was me, but it wasn't. Bailey Ross, or D'Roth, the human had ceased to exist. Kevin had killed her. Now I had the chance to have a different life. Maybe a better one.

I sat back down and Travis' hands brushed against my back. I sucked in a deep breath of air. His fingertips felt like fire against my cold skin.

Erick moved to stand in front of me as Travis continued.

"Did I feel like this when I touched you ... before?"

"Not to the same degree. Wolves run about ten degrees hotter than humans. It will pass as you get used to it."

"Sorry," Travis murmured.

"It's okay." My gaze flitted to one of the mirrors across from me and I watched him draw an outline. The design was a beautiful one. Almost a play on a sunburst, but with a lot of extra filigree and markings in a language I couldn't read. I'd studied Erick's, but never asked for any specifics about it.

"Will mine look just like yours?"

Erick nodded. "All our tattoos are the same, except yours will have the number five in it."

"What number are you?"

"Two." He folded his arms across his hard chest and I licked my lips. His nostrils flared and he narrowed his gaze, flashing me a wicked grin. No doubt even though I was a vampire, he could still smell my arousal.

"Who was first?"

"Sita. The Sisters found her in Greece before they fled to the north."

"Then you?"

"Yes."

"What about you, Travis? When did you join Sanctuary?"

"My pack was killed shortly after the Riots. My brother and I were deployed with the U.S. Army. When we got back ... there was nothing left. I may not be a Protector, but I owe Rose everything. She made me feel like I belonged somewhere again."

"I'm sorry. I know how hard it is to lose family."

He grunted something unintelligible.

A squeak of his chair and the absence of his hands on my back snapped me out of my thoughts.

"All right, sweetheart. Whatever you do, don't move." He reached for the needle on the counter and flipped a switch. A small motor whirred to life and I steeled myself.

The needle touched and pain radiated out from my neck in white-hot streaks. I screamed and cursed his name, but I did not move a millimeter. It hurt, but so had Kevin's whip, and his crop, and his cane, and his baseball bat. I'd been through so much. The fire of the needle felt cleansing in a way. My scars were gone. This was a new beginning.

I could start this new life with a group of people that needed me. Relied on me. Fought for me.

The tattoo wouldn't hurt forever. I wouldn't have a constant ache from it reminding me of my mistakes. It was a symbol of my rebirth. My new life. A life I would fight hard to protect.

The whirring sound was constant and time moved ever so slowly until the whole of my back felt like it was ablaze. I couldn't feel the needle so much as the heat of where the silver had been.

The tattoo would spread across the entire base of my neck. The long spires from the sun-shaped design would reach out along my shoulder blades and midway down my back and right up to my hairline. The circumference would be about the size of Erick's splayed-out hand when finished.

I closed my eyes and tried to focus outside the pain. He kept the needle moving, so at least the burn was constant instead of touch and go. I still wanted to scream, but it wasn't worse than Kevin's belt.

ERICK'S HAND ON MY CHEEK MADE ME OPEN MY EYES. Not sure how much time had passed. Probably hours. I hissed out a breath as Travis stopped and the room fell into silence. I glanced straight ahead and focused on the reflection of my back in the mirror behind me. My skin was smudged with blood, but I could see the outline of the intricate black tattoo beneath it.

Travis pulled a white washcloth from a lower cabinet next to him and dabbed at my back, removing the smeared blood.

"Good thing about vampires healing really fast, you won't have any redness or swelling. As soon as I wash you up, you're good to go." He turned the cloth several times, swabbing until my back was clean. "You were a trooper, sweetheart. The last vampire I tattooed destroyed my chair and I had to replace both of those windows."

I sighed, simply glad the pain had subsided. "What happened?"

"He threw the chair through the wall."

Erick chuckled, taking my hand. I stood and backed away from the contraption Travis called a chair. Stepping closer to the wall of mirrors, I turned and glanced over my shoulder, taking a closer look at the design that now covered the back of my neck and shoulders. At the center was a circle filled with markings I didn't understand. Parallel wavy lines extending outward from the edge of the ring, in between the eight points moving out from the sun. Between the wavy lines were more small inscriptions in the same foreign markings. It looked exactly the same as the one on Erick's neck and back. It was beautiful and it further cemented my place in this town.

Now I just had to get it activated, so I could be out in the sun.

"How do you feel?" Erick cupped my face in his palm.

"I'm good. The pain stopped as soon as it was done." I

leaned into his caress and breathed in his candied scent. "What's next?"

"Rose casts the spell that binds your tattoo with the rest of the Protectors and shields you from the sun." He dropped his hand and gestured to the doorway. "I'll call Rose and let her know we're on our way to the Castle."

"Why there?"

"Arlea has the spell book."

Of course she does. "Oh." I moved through the door and into the front of the shop, leaving Erick to walk with Travis. The last thing I wanted was to go into the Castle again. I'd agreed to *work* through my fears, but that wasn't really on my agenda for tonight.

"I'll be here if you need me," Travis called out as we exited the shop.

The Texas night air was warm, but pleasant without the sun beating down on our heads. I glanced up at the starry sky, surprised that I could see everything so clearly in the pitch-blackness of the night. The street we were on only had a single lamp on each cross street corner. Only Main Street Circle had lamps every few yards.

I could hear everything, from the bats flying high above my head to the crickets scrambling along the side-walks a dozen yards away. As we got closer to the Castle, I could hear voices, conversations even, and the heartbeats of the beings inside. The smells were so tantalizing. Each body had a specific scent and my mouth watered at the thought of tasting them.

Ewww! I'd just thought about drinking other people's blood. People I knew... and strangers.

"*Kjaere*, calm yourself. It's natural to be hungry when you smell food, is it not?"

"Yes, but they're people, not hamburgers." I turned and glanced over at him. "How did you know?"

"I could smell them, too. As soon as we turned the corner. It's natural. Don't be so hard on yourself." He grinned and slid a hand around my waist. "As long as you don't tell them you are thinking it, they'll never know."

I laughed. Full on, from-the-belly, cracked up. I'm sure the whole block could hear me, but I just didn't care. It felt so good to just let loose. The idea of walking around and imagining people as tasty treats was absolutely hilarious. Maybe I'd just lost my mind.

After I'd laughed enough to make the muscles of my abdomen hurt, I started to relax. The stress of everything that had happened over the last twenty-four hours had my body in knots and my mind overwhelmed.

I didn't have to run anymore.

I had a home.

I had people who wanted me to stick around, no matter what.

Erick's phone buzzed on his hip and he paused to answer it. His hand left my waist and I saw Calliope's name on the screen before something or someone else grabbed me around the waist and wrenched me away from him. Erick's growl was cut off and the world twisted in front of me and disappeared. My stomach flew to my throat and I felt worse than when I'd had food poisoning for a week.

In a flash of a millisecond I was somewhere else entirely. The smells in the air were different, the humidity, the altitude, everything. It wasn't Texas anymore and the man holding me wasn't Erick.

It was Darius.

I screamed and raked my fingers across his face. Blood flowed from the scratches and then everything went red. I could smell the sweetness coating my fingers, feel the energy in it as it ran down his cheeks. My vision changed and every sense I possessed focused on his body and the distinct beating of his heart.

"You bitch!" he yelled, releasing me and taking a step back. He touched his palm to his bloody cheek. "He turned you, damn vampire. He took my Nadia from me and I'll take you from him just like I took that bitch of his, Elinor."

He shook his head, flipping his long dark hair out of his face. Bright lavender eyes glared at me. I could smell his hate, his anger. It seeped from his skin like cheap cologne.

His fancy suit was crooked from our struggle. He pulled his tie from his neck and took a step forward this time. The snarl on his face changed to militant determination. Something shiny on his hand caught my eye and I remembered what needed to be done.

He didn't get to make me his victim. I would never be in that position again. I'd die first.

Something akin to a growl or snarl came from my mouth and I lunged, knocking him backward. His head hit the glass window directly behind him, shattering the glass and slicing up his scalp in the process.

More blood.

It was everywhere. My desire to feed roared through

my veins. His blood smelled so good. I licked my lips and brought my bloodstained fingers to my mouth—dark and rich. I wanted more.

His foot caught me in the stomach and hurled me backward. I landed on the coffee table in the middle of the room. Pain shot through my stomach, drawing a scream from my throat.

He leapt on top of me, laughing. "Vampires. Just a little blood and you can't even see straight." His hand went to my torso and more pain fired through my body in merciless waves.

I looked down and saw part of the coffee table's leg protruding from my right side. Oh, God—Really? Life seemed determined to continue stabbing me in the gut.

Would I die from this? It missed my heart. Lessons in school said only wood through the heart would kill a vampire. Or beheading.

Darius' hand on my breasts snapped me back to the present and I snarled. "Get off of me!"

"Oh, I have plans for you my sweet. Kevin just thought I was going to let him have you all to himself. Then the little fuck double-crossed me. If your Viking hadn't killed him, I would have ... but much slower and with a great deal more pain."

He pushed on the chunk of wood lodged in my side again and tears burned down my cheeks, but I held in the scream, not willing to give him the satisfaction.

"Tough girl, huh? That's not how Kevin described you. He said you'd whimper and cry for me." He pulled a blade from a sheath on his ankle and ran it across my face. The burn was like fire eating at my flesh.

That scream I couldn't stop and it rose from my throat like the pained sound of a dying animal. "There, there." He pulled the knife away and the pain faded. "That's more like it."

"Fuck you," I hissed between clenched teeth.

He shoved against the wood in my side again and I groaned as blinding pain traveled through every cell of my body at the speed of light.

"You think they care about you, little girl. They don't. Even your Viking only finds you attractive because you remind him of his dead wife. The wife I killed." His face parted into a sinister grin and fear clawed its way into my heart.

I refused to believe him.

"Now I get to take two women from him. Your blood looks just as good painting my floor as Elinor's did centuries ago."

"Why?"

"Thanks to Erick, your bitch of a Sentinel has my Nadia locked up in her vault. So I took the only thing he cared about in the world. Now I'm going to do it again."

There it was. That little slip gave me hope. I was only his target because Erick cared. Whether or not I reminded Erick of his lost wife, the adoration in his eyes and in his voice every time he'd called me *kjaere* didn't lie.

"You. Can't. Have. Me." My fangs descended and I grabbed his shoulders, pulling his neck to my mouth. I sank my fangs into his neck and drank deeply. His blood tasted like sweet revenge ... and power.

A lot of power.

He punched the side of my head, knocking himself

free for a moment. But he was no match for me now. His blood strengthened me and my anger pushed me harder. I had vowed never to be a victim again. This asshole was not going to make me break that promise.

I pushed him to the ground, yanked the hunk of wood from my side and fell on him again, drinking deeply and quickly.

So much blood.

So much anger.

His struggles slowed and soon he was a limp heap beneath me.

I pulled away, the shock of what I'd done registering in my blood-crazed brain. Had I killed him? No, please don't be dead. Even as nasty as he was, I didn't want to kill anyone. Kevin was the only person I'd ever wished death on. Even then, I wasn't sure I could've done it.

I pushed down the ferocious hunger flaming inside me. My vision went back to normal and I was able to detect a faint pulse within his limp form. Wiping the blood from my chin I glanced around the room.

It looked like a hotel suite. Nice carpets, plush bed, modern art on the walls. A tray of covered, silver food dishes.

Standing, I rushed to the table beside the door. A pamphlet lay next to a small bowl of mints. I picked up the paper, hoping for a clue. *The Levante Hotel, the secret gem of Austria.* Austria? Where the hell was that? Where had he taken me?

I ran back to his side and slapped his face. "Take me back! You bastard! Take me back."

He groaned and his eyes fluttered open for a second. "C-can't," he said, his voice gargling in his chest.

Damn it! His pulse was growing slower by the second.

I grabbed his right hand and slid the large gold signet ring from his finger and slipped it over my thumb. Then I bit my wrist and held it to his lips.

"Drink," I growled. "And take me back to Sanctuary."

He turned his head away from my dripping wrist and scoffed. "I w-won't help y-you, b-bitch."

"You will!" I grabbed the lapels of his suit jacket and pulled his face closer to mine. "Take. Me. Home."

The world flashed in front of me again and my stomach nearly flew out my open mouth. I wanted to puke so badly. When the earth stopped spinning, I looked around again and sighed in relief.

We were back.

The starry sky of Texas was spread above me. The smell of cut grass and oak trees swirled around me. The hint of wildflowers on the soft breeze and the soft glow of the Main Street Circle lamps cast an eerie shadow on Darius' bloody body. My clothes were unstained, but blood covered my hands, arms, neck, and face. I could feel it. Smell it. It was everywhere.

"Bailey!" Calliope's voice called from the dark.

"Here," I shouted into the night. We had teleported into the empty, grassy area in the middle of the circle. A few yards away from where the large, stone, stage thing glistened in the moonlight.

A second later, Erick was dragging me away from Darius and feeling me up and down. "Are you hurt?"

"I..." Feeling my stomach, I was shocked to find the

wound was already healed. Most of the blood that covered me now was the Djinn's. "It's his blood." I looked down at Darius again. He had a faint pulse, but it was fading rapidly. "He's going to die. I don't want to have killed him, Erick ... please."

"He deserves to die. He's a miserable being who has done nothing but bring suffering to this world."

"Please." I grabbed Erick's face in my hands and met his angry blue gaze. "Get Rose to lock him away instead."

I could smell and feel his emotions warring inside him. It was several minutes before he relaxed in my grasp and nodded.

"It shall be as you wish, *min kjaereste*."

"Thank you." I dropped my bloodstained hands to my sides, suddenly very heavy with the weight of what had just happened. He'd agreed. For me. To let the man who'd murdered his wife centuries ago ... live.

Rose appeared alongside Calliope. They stepped around Darius' body and hugged me, telling me how thankful they were that I was safe. Several others weren't far behind them. Soon I was being passed from one person's arms to the next. Even the dragons, Miles and Eli, weren't shy about giving me a quick squeeze and a kind word in my ear. By the end of the group hug, tears were running down my cheeks.

They all cared. Even people I hadn't met were patting me on the back and saying how grateful they were that Darius wouldn't terrorize the town again, and how much they appreciated my embracing the role of the fifth Protector.

Once the crowd had cleared and they'd left the circle, Rose approached me again.

"It took great strength not to kill the worthless miscreant lying at our feet. I'm very proud of you. Arlea told me you are descended from the D'Roth family. I knew some of your ancestors. They would be proud of the woman you've become." She turned to Erick. "And I am even more proud of you, my strong Viking. I know how much personal pain he has caused you."

Calliope, Miles, Eli and several others I didn't recognize stood a few yards away. Calliope stepped forward next when Rose glanced her way. She held out a small decorative black box with gold and silver inlay. Green jewels sparkled on the edges of the box.

Rose took it from her and Calliope returned to her place in line with the others. Turning to Erick and me, she spoke again. "He will spend eternity in the vault for his crimes. Death would be too sweet for one so evil." She traced her fingertips along Erick's shoulder. "Feed him just enough to start the healing process."

Erick nodded. He bit his wrist and knelt at Darius' side, pressing it into the Djinn's mouth. Only a few drops and then he pulled away.

It was enough, though. I could hear Darius' heartbeat strengthening immediately.

Rose opened the box and let her head fall back until it looked like she was speaking to the night sky. Strange words came from her lips over and over—*sikkaru awil pulhu*. She repeated them a dozen times before the little black box glowed bright white. Darius' body glowed white, too, and then turned to a wisp of radiant, white smoke.

His essence flowed slowly into the box. When the last trace of it was inside, Rose snapped the lid shut.

"*Sikkaru.*" She said once more and the box, no bigger than her fist, turned black once more.

Was it over?

Was he really gone?

CHAPTER 17

"What happened to him?"

Rose looked up. "Djinn are an interesting species. Because of their ability to dematerialize and teleport, they are vulnerable to being 'bottled', so to speak. He will be trapped, suspended in time and space. Unaware that he is inside a box and unaware that time is passing, but still imprisoned and unable to free himself."

"How do you keep others from opening the box and letting him out?" Surely she didn't just plan to put that little box on a shelf somewhere, like a trinket to display.

"Only a Lamassu can open or close a *quppu* box." She turned to face the large, stone disk behind her. At first glance, I had thought it was a round stage. Now I could see it was much more. Rose reached down to touch one of the marks on its edge. All the glyphs around the disk's rim glowed gold and the stone began to turn. Pieces moved inside it and the middle began to drop, creating a stairwell into the earth. The edge of each stair glowed with the same ethereal, yellow-gold light. "This is Sanctuary's vault, Bailey. This is what Darius hoped to find, using you as leverage."

She stepped over the edge of the main rim and down a couple of stairs. "Come."

I glanced up at Erick. He nodded and urged me toward Rose. I stepped over the rim and followed her down the curved, eerily glowing stairwell. We went at least three flights before I stepped into a cavernous room. The ceilings soared to fourteen, maybe even twenty feet high. The walls were stone, carved with amazingly detailed reliefs of dragons and other winged creatures I couldn't identify. Scenes of battles. Scenes of throne rooms. And at the end of the room, a painting depicted one of the most beautiful cities I could've ever imagined.

"Where is that?" I pointed.

She smiled and walked to a stack of black boxes very similar to the one she held in her hand.

"It was my home. The home of my people, Babylon. One of the most beautiful places on earth before its destruction." Her voice carried pain and longing. Even now, after so many thousands of years, I could tell she still considered that ancient city with a lot of love.

I glanced around the room a little more. Lamps hung from the ceiling, bathing the entire room in a soft glow. Stacks of those little black boxes were everywhere. Hundreds, maybe thousands of them.

"Do they all have a Djinn inside them?"

Rose turned back to me. "Yes."

"He said you locked up his wife ..."

She ran her fingertips across another black box. "Yes." Then walked a few paces and sat on a gilded, high-back chair. "Come, sit with me."

I joined her, taking a seat in the chair next to her. When I looked up, the painting directly in front of me was of a terrible battle. Bodies were strewn everywhere. Walls were crumbling. As I looked closer, I saw familiar structures from the painting of Babylon across the room.

This painting showed the fall of her home. My heart clenched in sympathy for what she must've gone through.

"We are at war, Bailey. A war that started millennia before you were born. So many years have passed, but I can still smell the fire. Feel the slick on the streets as I ran through the spilled blood of my family. Only three of the Sentinels escaped when Babylon fell to the Horde—my husband Naram and his brother Xerxes and myself."

She crossed her legs and leaned back in the chair. "We didn't know until much later that Xerxes was the betrayer. Naram and I watched our families and friends die, fighting to give us a chance to escape with the Sisters. They were our responsibility and the crown jewel of the city—the reason it was so great."

"Why didn't they see the war coming?"

Rose sighed. "They cannot *see* Lamassu. Our magick supersedes theirs. Anyone we collude with is also shielded."

"So the Djinn are working for your brother-in-law?"

"Yes."

"So, why do the Djinn fight for Xerxes?"

"He freed their king. My race bottled him thousands of years ago. Xerxes let him out."

"And after all these years, they still owe him?"

"Now they fight because they must. Over the centuries, I have decimated their numbers. There are only a few hundred Djinn left. If they hope to survive as a species ..." She gestured around the room at the thousands of jeweled black boxes. "Xerxes is the only one in the world besides me who can free their people."

I was trying hard to understand it all. "Why does he want the Sisters?"

"To sire children with them."

"Xerxes could have a child with one of them? A son? With powers?"

"Yes. Not only could he have a son, he could have a Lamassu son with powers of premonition. It could add an entirely new and powerful ability to our species. The Sisters are the only beings on earth, other than the Lamassu, with whom he could father a child."

Meaning Rose and Xerxes were the last of their kind.

"They look so normal."

"Doctors would be unable to tell the difference, so we allow the misinformation to perpetuate. It's less complicated for everyone."

"So they're *not* human at all?"

"No." Rose sighed. "In fact, humans are not allowed to live in Sanctuary. It's too dangerous."

"But you let me stay." I gasped. "That's why Miles and Eli were so upset I was staying with him."

She nodded. "I knew who you were. Arlea saw you in a vision the day before Erick arrived with you. I'm sorry, I hadn't had a chance to tell anyone else beside the pixies and brownies at the café." Rose met my gaze and I waited for her to go on. "When Erick called from the bus and told me he was bringing you to Sanctuary to stay with him, he was breaking our code. The only human visitors allowed in town are the ones who stay under lock and key at the Castle. They are vetted members of the club and understand that we are very secretive and private."

"So he knew I was supposed to be this Protector from almost the very beginning?" *Holy shit.*

Rose's eyes widened. "If you are doubting his affection, don't. I've only seen him care for a woman one other time in his life. Believe me, he would move mountains for you. In fact, he challenged me for your right to walk away if that was your choice."

Wow.

I leaned back in my chair and stared at the wall. My forefinger rolled the signet ring on my thumb. I'd forgotten it was there.

"You should probably keep this here." I removed the ring I'd taken from Darius and placed it in Rose's hand.

Tears made her eyes glassy, and she closed her fingers around the ring. "You got it back? Thank you." She got up and walked to a small table a few yards away. A jeweled, silver box sat centered on it. She opened it, kissed the signet ring, and then placed it inside. "I never thought I'd get that piece of him back. When I saw it on Darius' hand, it was like losing Naram all over again."

"I do want to stay, Rose. And I do want to help the Sisters to be free from Xerxes. I know I don't understand everything that's going on yet, but I can learn. I've never felt more at home than I do here in Sanctuary. The people who live here care about each other.."

"We are a family, in a sense." She turned back to face me, leaning against the edge of the table. "Even though, in other parts of the world certain Others wouldn't deem it safe to be within a hundred miles of one another, we've found a way to coexist and have become stronger for it."

I looked past her to the wall behind the table. Another large painting hung on the carved stone wall. A landscape so beautiful it took my breath away. Lush forests, mountains, and buildings unlike anything I'd ever seen on earth. They had spires that must've reached thousands of feet into the heavens, giving the residents of them the amazing sense of living among the clouds.

She turned and looked up at the painting as well. "The Veil. The original home of the Lamassu."

"Why aren't you there?" I asked, not able to imagine why anyone would want to live in Texas if they could live there. Calliope had mentioned it, but her description paled in comparison to this painting.

"In the chaos of the battle that destroyed Babylon, we also lost the key to the Veil."

"Are there people trapped on the other side?"

"I suppose for a long time there were. Eventually, we heard whispers that the Drakonae, the dragons, had the key and had taken over the Veil, leaving earth completely."

"If all the dragons left, how did Miles and Eli end up here?"

Rose shook her head. "That is not my story to tell. I wanted you to see where we come from—why this town is so important to us. Why we protect the Sisters at all costs. They are never allowed outside the castle. With Miles and Eli's aid, Xerxes can't get inside either."

"Is he scared of dragons?"

Rose's face split into a grin. "Very." She motioned toward the stairwell. "Dragons are the Lamassu's only equal in size, when shifted. And we can both fly. Lamassu have more magick, but dragon physiology creates a natural shield against it. However, their true advantage lies in their breath. Dragons are either born of fire or ice. Miles and Eli are both fire dragons. And one Lamassu against two fire dragons would be suicide."

"That's why he keeps sending Djinn."

She sighed. "He's trying to steal one of the Sisters."

I stood and followed her up the stairs. "Calliope said I should ask one of them to breathe fire for me." I heaved one foot in front of the other and peered up the seemingly never-ending stairwell. "Honestly, I thought she was kidding," I added.

"It is an amazing thing to see. Perhaps one day they will show you."

"Do any of you in town ever shift? Just because?"

Rose paused on the stairs above me. She looked back at me. I could see sorrow in her eyes. It haunted me, sending an icy chill across my already cool skin. "I haven't shifted in nearly a thousand years. With the advances in technology, it's just not safe. Some here are able to shift regularly. Wolves aren't a red flag to anyone in the country, but they have to be careful about the ranchers in the area. Many of them are trigger happy, even if their cattle haven't been disturbed."

She turned away and began climbing again. "Most of us hide in plain sight, trying our best not to draw extra attention to our existence. Even though the Texas Republic favors Others right now, there's no guarantee it will remain so."

Made sense. Still, I wondered what a Lamassu or a dragon really looked like. It would be amazing to see them in their element. Scary for sure, but I couldn't imagine that it was anything short of breathtaking. Having all that power locked inside for so long must be excruciating. But, they were right to do it. If people knew there were beings like them walking among humans, it would be the riots all over again. Maybe worse.

I ran my fingers along the stones as we climbed. The golden glow slowly faded and I saw the light from the moon above flooding the stairwell.

We stepped clear of the vault rim. Erick, Calliope, and several others stood a few yards away. The stone covering began moving again, closing up and returning to a solid, smooth disk. I stared carefully, searching for a crack or crevice that showed where the parts fit together.

"Amazing." I ran my hand over the smooth rock, tracing along the markings decorating the edge.

"Magick," Rose whispered. "Speaking of which, would you like to see the sunrise in a few hours?"

I nodded and smiled up at Erick who had already moved to my side.

He slipped an arm around my waist and squeezed me against his hip. I loved being close to him. His touch filled me with longing and comfort at the same time.

CHAPTER 18

After a quick detour to his apartment to wash the blood off my skin and change clothes, we walked slowly toward the Castle. Rose, Calliope, and the others were already there.

"What are you thinking, my precious Bailey?"

"That even though I've only known you a short time, I love you."

"Mmm," he rumbled. "Perhaps you should wait to declare your affections until after we have our time together in the Castle. I worry that you may not want to have anything to do with me afterward."

"Why do you want to go through with it then?"

"You deserve to go through your now-very-long life without coming undone at the smell of leather and the sound of a cracking whip. Submission can be a beautifully exquisite exchange and I want you to see that part of it."

"Oh." I shivered at the mention of the whip. He was right. It did bother me. I dreaded hearing or seeing it, even now. It didn't matter that I was a vampire with super-natural strength, fangs, and the ability to protect myself. I'd proved that by taking down Darius. Yet, the thought of restraints or a whip completely terrified me. Given the choice, I would hide from them still.

I had no clue how he thought he could get me over it. The idea that a scene in a place called a dungeon could be beautiful was doubtful in my mind, but I trusted him completely. If he really thought he could help, I was willing to let him try.

The great doors of the Castle opened and a wave of heat rolled over my cool body. When I looked up, Miles' honey brown eyes stared down at me from the gaping entryway. I knew it was Miles, even before I saw the tell-tale scar above his eye. Miles didn't smile. His brother, Eli, was always grinning, even though his eyes held great sorrow.

Both of them were saddened by something terrible, but they each dealt with it differently. Miles hid behind a gruff exterior and Eli behind a smile. I had a feeling it had to do with the woman Erick had mentioned when they confronted me in his house. Diana.

Miles bent to give me a hug. "Everyone is ready and waiting for you in the main courtyard."

"Thank you, Miles," I said, still a little shocked by the show of affection.

He and Erick nodded to each other and we paused to wait while Miles secured the huge front doors. I watched in awe, amazed he was moving them at all without any type of mechanical assistance. The doors were easily a foot thick and wrapped in wrought iron.

"Can anyone else open those doors?"

The light in the entryway dimmed as the door slid slowly into place, leaving only the soft glow from the chandeliers high above our heads. The dark floors and walls, while decadent and polished, still made the place seem more like a cave than a castle.

Miles pulled down a heavy bar from the side of the entrance and it dropped into place across both doors. The thump of the bar echoed ominously through the room. I swallowed, wondering if there were any other exits from the Castle that didn't require help to open.

"Rose can," Miles finally answered, bringing me back from my thoughts. "But it would take several vampires or wolves working together to get them to budge."

Wow. It was hard to believe Rose, so small physically, possessed as much or more strength than one of the giant Blackmoor brothers.

A few minutes later we were in a small, grassy area, separate from the large garden I remembered from before. Sisters lined the walls and Arlea stood with Rose in the center. The breeze had died down, but I could smell the grass underfoot and the scent of fresh water on the soil. Other smells mixed with the natural ones—oils, leather, sweat. No one would have suspected a group of women dressed in flowing, white dresses were the heart and soul of a sex club.

Erick stopped and I paused beside him. I felt a little underdressed in my white shorts, blue sparkly t-shirt, and flats. But no one looked upset. They were all smiling.

Rose caught my gaze and motioned me forward.

One of my feet stepped forward, but I hesitated when I realized Erick wasn't moving with me.

"I have to stay here. You will be fine, *kjaere*. I promise."

"It won't hurt?"

"It tingles a little, but nothing worse than a static shock."

I took a deep breath. The action relaxed my brain and I stepped forward. The Sisters parted, creating a straight path through the well-trimmed lawn to the center of the group.

When I reached them, Arlea took my hand and kissed the top of it. "Thank you for accepting the role as Protector of the House of Lamidae. We will forever be indebted to you."

"This is where I belong," I answered. "I know that now."

"I have dreamed of you since you were a baby. It has been so many years since a Protector was chosen. We are blessed by your presence, Bailey D'Roth. Welcome to Sanctuary."

"Thank you." I didn't know what else to say. I meant it, but the crowd was making me nervous. I wished they would just get whatever they were going to do over with.

Rose stepped forward and took my hand from Arlea. She turned me so that I was facing east. I could see the midnight blue of the sky starting to fade as morning approached. They better get their shit together soon, or I'd burn to a crisp before they ever started.

"You will see my wings surround you for a moment and then you will feel an influx of energy transferring to you."

"Your wings?" I squeaked.

She chuckled. "I don't have to fully shift to activate the spell, but you will see my wings."

I shivered and nodded.

Rose stepped behind me and laid her hands on my shoulders. She and Arlea began chanting a phrase I couldn't understand. The words ran together faster and faster. Then I felt it.

A jolt of energy passed through her hands and shocked my body, like touching a metal doorknob after rubbing your feet on the carpet. Then another jolt and another.

I focused on Erick and frowned. *A tingle my ass!*

The flow of energy increased and I gritted my teeth. The skin on my back heated, not uncomfortably so, but just enough to feel the outline of the tattoo in my mind's eye.

Her chanting changed and then I saw them.

Her wings.

They were beautiful. Golden feathers with highlights of ivory. Bigger than anything I could've imagined. Surely they would reach from one side of this grassy area to the other if she completely stretched them out, easily forty or fifty feet. Instead, they curled in front of me, blocking my view of the Sisters and the rest of the audience.

Time stood still as the golden color of her wings lightened more and more, until they were too bright to look at. I closed my eyes. She and Arlea stopped chanting and the energy exchange built to a climax. My body shook and I struggled to remain standing. Then her magick shot through me with one final burst. The overwhelming light, even through my closed eyelids, faded and I slowly opened my eyes.

Her wings were gone. The energy was gone. The heat from my tattoo had left. Instead, I felt the light and warmth from the morning sun shining on my face. More time had passed than I realized.

I held up my hand in the morning sunlight and smiled.

"Thank you," I said, spinning in place to face Rose and Arlea. "I hope someday I get to see you completely shift, Rose. I know your Lamassu form must be truly spectacular."

"One day, sweetie. One day." She pointed behind me. "I think someone is waiting for you now."

I looked over my shoulder and met Erick's bright gaze. Strength radiated from him toward me like the sun's rays warming the earth. His lips parted in a small smile and he whispered a few words in his foreign tongue. The only one I recognized was "*min.*"

Walking forward, I smiled and nodded. I was his. Whatever he had planned, I knew I was ready.

CHAPTER 19

ERICK

S o small, but so strong. A warrior in every sense of the word. Even my father would have approved, had I met her before I became what I am now.

A vampire.

A Protector for the House of Lamidae.

From the very first time I laid eyes her, I knew she was special. She wanted more than what the world had to offer. Her soul fought for something better, instead of giving in. When she agreed in the bus station to come to Sanctuary, I knew I would never be content again without her at my side and in my bed.

I could not pinpoint one thing exactly that had attracted me to her so strongly and so quickly, but I'd known without a shadow of a doubt that she was mine. Darius following her had only furthered my possessiveness.

He'd haunted my existence for more than a millennia already and had once again tried to steal the life of the woman I loved. I didn't heal or turn humans without permission—most didn't want to be vampires. My wife, Elinor, hadn't been an exception. Even as she lay dying in my arms from Darius' blade, she made me promise not to heal her.

Those were the hardest seconds in my very long life, up until the point when Kevin stabbed Bailey and I had to wait again, either for the second love of my life to leave me or come back as something she might detest.

A vampire.

I'd come to terms with it as the centuries passed. We weren't the glorified heroes the media played us up to be in the twenty-first century. We were just average men given the ability to learn and grow for as long as we could keep our heads. Some became better men and others became vicious monsters, no different than their human selves—just more powerful.

So far, I'd been surprised by how well Bailey had taken to her new state of being. Most new vampires were obsessed with feeding and couldn't stand to be in a room full of people. She behaved as if she'd been one of us for decades already. Her hunger was that of a newborn, but her control was beyond her years. I attributed it to the time she'd spent hiding from Kevin. She'd developed an awareness and fortitude most humans her age didn't have.

I watched her in silence as she wandered the private room of the Castle I'd requested for us to share. A luxurious, wrought iron, four-poster bed lay against the far wall, draped in a rich, red velvet coverlet.

She traced her fingers along the fabric and my skin warmed, imagining her fingers instead caressing my body. Holding myself back was going to be difficult. I wanted nothing more than to take her, body and soul, but she needed more. She needed a way to work through the pain her mind carried from her past.

Her hand traveled up one of the headboard posts and touched the chains hanging down from it. One of my favorite features of the beds in the Castle—used to restrain a sub at any point, heightening the intensity of the experience.

I took a step forward on the plush carpet, not making a sound, but her keen senses realized my movement and she cast a quick glance over her shoulder at me.

"Keep looking," I said, not wanting her to feel rushed.

She walked away from the bed, going over to the St. Andrew's cross I'd had Miles move to this room especially for this day. Usually the crosses were only used in the large common areas on the main floor and the more private dungeons on the lower level, but neither brother balked at having the large piece of equipment moved for me. This one, in particular, was constructed on a crank and could be moved from an upright inclined position to horizontal while the sub was bound in place.

I'd decided against having an audience for this. Not only did I not want to share the lush view of her naked body with anyone else just yet, I wanted her to feel comfortable. This scene wasn't for me. It was for her. Only her.

"You said no restraints," she whispered, touching the

padded leather cuffs attached to each of the four ends of the cross.

"We won't be using those, *kjaere*."

"Oh." She turned to face me and crossed her arms over her chest defensively.

No. That would never do.

I moved to stand in front of her and lifted her chin, placing a kiss on her soft, sweet lips. Even after the change, she still tasted just as sweet to me—perhaps even more so. Her resistance and defensive body language melted away. Her arms fell loose and she slipped them around my waist.

Her soft breasts pressed against my body and her hips tilted into mine, seeking out my growing erection. She was everything I wanted.

I couldn't fuck this up. Losing her was not an option.

I sucked her bottom lip between mine and nipped just enough to pinch. She growled and dug her nails into my back, but I could feel a smile curving over her face. I swept my tongue into her mouth, tasting her sweetness and wanting more. I wanted to taste her from head to foot.

Pulling back, I stepped forward, pushing her flush to the large X-shaped cross. She looked up nervously, her blue eyes flashing. Caribbean blue now. Just like mine. I would miss her soft brown eyes, mixed with flecks of green.

"Take off your shorts, *kjaere,* fold them, and lay them at your feet. But leave your shirt, bra, and panties."

She cocked her head at the instructions, but didn't say anything.

I went to a dresser a few feet away and pulled out

several silk scarves from a drawer, holding them up for her to see. She frowned, something I had anticipated, but I was pleased to see her following directions and slipping out of her shorts.

"Those still looks like restraints." She objected, setting her shoes precisely on top of her folded white denim shorts.

Her voice was firm, but I could hear the undercurrent of fear in her tone. Her hands were trembling and she wouldn't meet my gaze.

"Bailey, look at me." I moved to stand in front of her again. I tied the first scarf to the left upper leg of the cross and gestured to it. "Look."

She turned her head and stared.

"Slide your hand between the scarf and the cross. You are restrained only by yourself."

She did as I asked, but slid her hand in and out several times, testing the truth of my words. Or, she was worried the scarf would suddenly tighten on its own and bind her against her will. I tied the other three scarves in place and stepped back, waiting for her to comply.

She would.

I knew she would not back down from a scarf.

A few moments later she had slipped both her wrists and ankles beneath the loosely tied scarves and watched me warily, like an animal trying to avoid a trap.

Mentally cursing her bastard of an ex, I smiled encouragingly and stepped closer again, running my hand along her arm, up to her neck, and cupping her face with my palm.

"So beautiful. Are you ready to keep going?"

She took a deep breath and nodded, tension flowing from her body. "I am."

I tilted her chin up and stared into her deep blue eyes. There was fear, but there was also something else. Something I'd never thought to see in a woman's eyes again after losing Elinor. Love. "Are you sure, *kjaere*?" She'd already said it once, but I wanted to hear it again. Needed to.

"Yes. I am yours. Now and forever."

"I am honored by your trust. You are mine only because you choose it to be so. Just like you chose to place your hands beneath the scarves."

Her eyes widened as she contemplated the statement. She opened her mouth to respond but then hesitated for just a second. She wet her bottom lip with her tongue and I watched, enraptured by the seductive movement.

"It wouldn't matter if I were in cuffs, would it? One word and you would let me down."

"Everything we do in here is your choice. You must know, I will love and treasure you all of my days. Whether your choice is to move forward now, stop in five minutes, or finish the scene I have planned."

Her eyes watered and I leaned forward to press a soft kiss to her pink lips before continuing. "Say the word *red* and everything. Simply. Stops."

I could see the understanding blooming in her eyes like a flower. She was starting to see the bigger picture. The harmony that dominance and submission could offer to a relationship was unlike anything I'd found in my long lifetime. I wanted nothing more than to share it with her, but only if she made that choice on her own.

"Why red?"

Her question brought me back to the present. I should have been focused totally on her instead of wandering through my mind. "You might beg me to stop in the heat of the moment and not mean it." I smiled. "Pleasure can be overwhelming."

Her eyes widened, but she nodded. "Where is the appeal for you? If I can stop everything with one protest, then ... why do those women choose to be tortured? I heard that woman scream when he whipped her."

"*Min kjaereste*, only a select handful of people are sadists and masochists. The larger population of people in the lifestyle enjoy a modicum of pain meant only to enhance the pleasure of intimacy. As far as the appeal ..." I paused, ripping the shirt she was wearing from her body with one fluid downward motion. The fabric fluttered to the ground silently and I looked back at her horrified face. I waited instead of speaking. Either she would react well ... or terribly.

"I liked that shirt." She tried to hide it, but a smile tugged at the corners of her mouth.

The Dom in me roared to life at the idea that she might really enjoy what we were about to do. I'd prepped myself for the worst. For her to fall apart. To scream and storm out of the room. Anything but smile when I violently tore her shirt from her body.

"I'll have Calliope make you another."

"What am I going to tell her happened to it?"

"Tell her I ripped it off of you." I slid my hands behind her back and unsnapped the hooks of the strapless, white bra she wore. It popped loose and I tossed it to the side, letting her gorgeous, creamy breasts bounce free.

"I can't tell her that!" she shrieked, embarrassment coloring her face.

I smiled.

So cute. So innocent. So damn beautiful.

Leaning down, I took one nipple into my mouth and sucked and then the other, going back and forth until they were both erect and plump and dark. My cock strained against the jeans I was wearing, but my satisfaction would have to wait several hours.

Shrugging my shoulders, I bent a little farther, dropping to my knees, and kissed my way down to her navel. The muscles in her torso fluttered beneath my lips and little kitten-like mewls purred in her throat.

The lacy, black panties were next and tore away from her body like tissue. She protested only slightly before I slid two fingers into her wet vagina, rubbing against the front wall until she moaned even louder than before.

I teased her nipples with my free hand, pinching just hard enough to make her gasp, but pairing it with the teasing to her throbbing nubbin, she barely noticed the pain. Her head lolled forward and her fangs descended.

"Erick," she growled.

Her voice begged for more and I was more than obliged to provide. "Yes, *kjaere?*" I dropped the nipple I was torturing and kneaded the soft mound of one breast and then the other. Scissoring my fingers inside her, stretching her tight muscles, I slipped a third finger inside and thrust deep.

She rocked the cross, attempting to reach for me, but the bindings stopped her. Her eyes flew open and locked with mine.

This was a moment of realization for her. Even though the restraints were loose. They were there and she'd forgotten.

Instead of fear, her blue eyes darkened with desire and she leaned forward. I rose to my feet, meeting her lips with mine. The electric tension between us exploded and I growled, pressing her hard against the cross and devouring her mouth. Her sweetness was intoxicating and I wanted nothing more than to lose myself inside her.

I pulled back. There was more. She needed this exercise more than we needed to make love.

Her moan of frustration when I pulled back made my lips curve into a smile. Then I removed my fingers from within her and she arched her hips toward me. Good.

"Erick?"

"I going to add something."

"Okay," she answered, her gaze flitting to the dresser, probably wondering what I was going to get.

I moved, swiftly returning to her side with a pair of vinyl coated alligator clamps. They would hold firmly without sliding around, plus the little silver chain between them would tug with every movement, reminding her she was wearing them even after the initial pain dulled.

She took one look at the clamps and closed her eyes.

Brave, little warrior.

Taking one nipple in my mouth, I sucked and nipped until it was rock hard and swollen. As I slipped the first clamp into place, I took her other nipple into my mouth. A hiss of air came out of her mouth and she lurched away from me. She whined and threatened my dick with injury under her breath.

"You will do no such thing, *kjaere*," I said, my mouth still against her breast. Swirling her left nipple once more I pulled back and slipped the second clamp into place, the chain between them was just taut enough that even the slightest tug would deliver an exquisite sting.

"You are doing so good, my sweet Bailey."

"Please, take them off," she whimpered, leaning forward from the cross, her breasts swung back and forth beautifully, the chain catching and sparkling in the light that slipped between the mostly drawn curtains.

"Not just yet, when you are closer, I will."

She moaned again and closed her eyes. "Closer to what? I already feel like I'm going to come apart the second you touch me again."

"Good, that's exactly where I want you. Look at me, Bailey."

Her darkened blue eyes sprang open and she bared her fangs.

"Concentrate on me, *kjaere*. Are you going to use your safe word or are you going to let me lick your pretty pussy until you come undone?"

Her fangs disappeared and the hateful glare disappeared into a lustful pout. I sank to my knees in front of her and admired her clean-shaven mound. I parted the folds of her sex, baring her beautiful glistening pussy. The juices of her arousal already slicked the insides of her legs. She was more than ready for me. I leaned forward and licked the inside of one thigh, savoring the sweet taste of her honey.

She rewarded my affections with a loud mewl and a thrust of her hips toward my head. Needy little thing was trying to tell me what to do. I pinched her ass hard, pushing her need to orgasm away for just a little longer.

She flinched and squeaked in surprise.

The overwhelming scent of her did me in and I caved, flicking my tongue across her clit and then thrusting it deep inside her vagina, drinking in her sweetness. I wrapped my arms around her legs and dug my fingers into the curve of her ass, pulling her even closer. Sucking her clit and lapping at her slit drove her toward a huge orgasm. I could feel the contractions rippling through her body as it prepared to implode.

Not just yet, my sweet. I could only pray she would not hate me for this next move.

I dropped my hands from her backside and moved away from her mound. The cry that tore from her throat told me I was doing an excellent job of drawing out her pleasure. By now, her entire body was heavy and throbbing, desperate for a release. Exactly how I wanted her.

It was time to work through one other thing. I knew she would never like the sound or like the bite of a whip, but I hoped a flogger could be something she found pleasure in. First I wanted to work on just the sound. Even if I never used a whip on her, I wanted her comfortable around it.

I could feel her eyes boring a hole through my back as I walked toward the dresser. My short whip was in the bottom drawer. I retrieved it and a soft leather flogger, along with a padded blindfold and turned to face her.

"What the fuck? Erick!" She snarled, pulling her hands from the scarf bindings. I blurred to her side and forced her hands back into place. "You didn't say the safe word."

Her mouth parted to speak. I could hear the 'R' in red on the tip of her tongue.

"Think carefully, *kjaere*. Have I hurt you?"

She relaxed her arm and a tear ran down her cheek. "You promised." The pain in her glance tore at my heart, but I held her tightly. "But if this is what you need from me, then go ahead. I said I am yours and I meant it. Heart and soul ... and body."

Those last words nearly brought tears to my eyes. She was giving me permission to whip her. To hurt her. Something I'd promised I would never do. Something I would absolutely never do. I could see the terror she was bravely hiding behind those glassy, blue eyes. She needed to trust that I would not betray her. She did not trust in that, yet.

"Trust me, Bailey." I caught her panicked stare and held it. Some of the fire had left her eyes, but she nodded.

"Good girl. I love you, *min kjaereste*. For as long as you will have me." That admission drove the fear from her gaze and it changed into the most beautiful vision of submission I'd ever seen.

She closed her eyes and leaned back against the cross. I slipped the blindfold over her head and ran my hand down her torso. Her body arched into my touch as my hand fell lower and lower until it slipped between her wet nether lips and I slid two fingers into her slick vagina.

I held the short single tail whip in my hand. The snap would be loud enough to achieve the purpose I needed.

"You're going to hear the whip, but it won't touch you, *kjaere*. Tell me you trust me."

"I do."

I rubbed the inside wall of her vagina, finding just that

perfect spot to bring her hovering orgasm crashing down around her. She moaned and moved with my hand.

I flicked my wrist, snapping the short whip in the air a few feet away from her. The sharp crack echoed through the room. Every muscle in her body flinched and she whimpered, but I thrust my fingers a little faster and rubbed my thumb across her clit. Her muscles clenched again, but this time it was from her arousal. She moaned and jerked at her bindings, nearly ripping through one.

Snapping the whip again, I felt her body tense and her orgasm recede again. I worked her pussy, sliding my fingers in and out, rolling her clit with my thumb. Soon she was writhing on the cross again, and by the sixth snap of the whip, her reaction to it had lessened.

The only thing on her mind was reaching the climax I kept just out of her reach. There was one more thing I wanted her to experience and associate with pleasure. The flogger.

Dropping the short whip, I leaned over and picked up the butter-soft leather flogger from where it lay on the floor by her feet. Then I removed my fingers from her core. A tortured moan rose from her shuddering body.

"One last thing, *kjaere*." I drew the strands of the flogger across her stomach and watched the muscles in her body tense and then relax. She swallowed, a normal human reaction to stress, but she didn't object or use her safe word.

I continued to feather the flogger strands across different parts of her body. Over her thighs, up her torso, across her breasts, allowing the weight of the strands to tug gently on her chained nipples.

A quick gasp was her only response. She tracked every sound and movement. Her body was completely tuned in and ready. The smell of her arousal filled the room with a sweet, heavenly scent.

A little more.

I swung the flogger and lightly swept it across her stomach, picking up a slow but steady rhythm. She didn't flinch away and after the first few passes, began to lean into the stroke. Keeping the rhythm steady, I moved it lower giving her upper thighs a few soft swipes.

"How are you?"

"Mmmm," she moaned and nodded her head.

Moving my arm a little higher, I flicked strands across the bottom of her breasts, dragging them across the chain, and listened to her hiss. That should have burned just a little, but instead of panic, she pulled on her bonds and a slow tortured moan rose from her chest.

The sound was like seeing the sun come out for the first time after I'd been turned. I gave her stomach a few harder passes and again across her thighs, reveling in her mewls of pleasure. More moisture glistened on the insides of her thighs and I threw the flogger to the floor.

"*Min kjaereste*." I reached for the blindfold and pulled it from her face.

She blinked, adjusting to the light, and her gorgeous vampire blue eyes locked with mine. Gone was the fear. The uncertainty. She'd found her way through the blackness that pained her soul and came through cleansed and new. Her trust and submission was full and beautiful.

The contented smile that curved her lips upward warmed my heart.

It was a whole new beginning for her. For us both together.

I grasped one of her thighs and then the other, lifting her ankles free of the scarves. She slipped her hands from their bindings and cupped my face, pulling me close, and pressing her lips gently to mine.

I growled and swept her into my arms. Blurring to the bed, I shed my clothes in a quick movement, then parted her thighs and slipped between them. One more second and I thrust deep within her swollen pussy. Her arms came down onto my shoulders.

"Keep your arms above your head."

She complied immediately, her pussy clenching in response and my cock grew harder. I started to move inside her, holding her heated gaze and watching with pleasure and pride as her pupils dilated further.

"Please," she moaned.

I moved closer, pushing her legs up and over my shoulders until I could drive in deep and hard, her body nearly folded in half. Her hands fisted above her head, but neither arm moved from its place.

"Such beautiful submission, *min kjaereste*."

Her pussy clenched around my hard cock, every twitch and pulse driving me even closer to the release I was trying to prolong for both of us.

Sliding my hands up her torso, I slowed my thrusts and tugged gently at the chain dangling between her nipples. With a quick move, I squeezed the release on both clamps and a long howl tore from her throat. Tossing aside the chain and clamps, I thrust harder and dug my fingers into her hips, pulling her down hard, impaling her fully.

Once. Twice.

I moved one hand to her mound and rolled my thumb around her unhooded swollen clit then pressed down hard on top.

Another high pitched scream echoed through the room. Her pussy clamped down hard and her fingers dug into my shoulders. She bit my lip and growled into my mouth. Damn, she was pushing my buttons perfectly. My climax surged forward, building until it burst like a damn, rushing through every nerve until I filled her completely. I thrust deep and hard until she milked me dry.

Slowly, I pulled out, released, and guided her legs down flat on the bed again and lay down beside her. She rolled to her side and I slipped my arms around her, holding her tightly to my chest.

She curled into my body and sighed. "Thank you." The words were simple, but told me everything I needed to know. I was so proud of her. Of the risks she'd taken, the trust she'd placed in me. It was so much more than I thought possible.

I rubbed the soft pale skin of her shoulder with my thumb and then squeezed her even closer. "I love you, my precious Bailey D'Roth."

"I love you more, Erick Thorson," she replied and kissed my chest, her lips feathered lightly along my skin, giving me goose bumps. "My very own Viking vampire."

"Only yours."

⚜

I hope you enjoyed My Viking Vampire!

Thank you for spending time with me in my world. Please consider leaving a short review. Each one helps tremendously.

XOXO

Krystal Shannan

Turn the page to read part of book 2, MY DRAGON MASTERS!

MY DRAGON MASTERS
CHAPTER ONE

AFTER THOUSANDS OF YEARS, I STILL WANT ONLY ONE thing.

To be ruler of all the Veil and Earth. To be King.

—XERXES

BITS OF ROCK AND BRICK CRUNCHED AS I WALKED. I remembered when this roadway was paved and stunning. A smooth, red brick road leading into the heart of Orin. Now it was no more than crumbled bits and pieces.

The grinding of the gravel under each footstep reminded me of bones breaking beneath my paws in battles past, when I could fearlessly shift into my Lamassu form and tear apart my enemies with my teeth. Then walk across mounds of their bodies, my massive lion paws grinding them into the dirt.

I miss those days. It was kill or be killed. Winner take all.

Time had given the weak the ability to be strong in an annoying way. In the past, it had been easy to pit humans against each other and wipe out entire tribes or countries. Now, we had to play the humans' political games or the pathetic race might blow us all to hell, and both worlds along with it. The collapse began when an experimental drug exposed a half-dozen supernatural races.

Now "Others," as the humans called us, had to be more careful. We weren't worshiped or revered any longer. Instead, we were forced to hide our strengths.

It hadn't stopped me, though. I'd infiltrated and taken control of many global governments over the centuries. Humans were simple—their lives so short they were unable to see beyond the few decades of their existence.

It was the damn Drakonae that were giving me hell. They always had.

I stopped at the crest of a hill and looked down at the sprawling magnificence of Orin. The road might have gone to pieces, but the city shined like the gem it always had been—one of the greatest and most powerful cities in the Veil.

Eventually, it would be mine.

CHAPTER TWO

DIANA

IT WAS STARTING AGAIN. I COULD FEEL THE BEAST INSIDE

me, slithering around like a serpent. Sometimes it would rage, cooling the air around me and coating the walls with ice.

Despite this, I was never cold.

There were no windows in my cell, just a few furs to sleep on, a drain in the back corner, and walls of ice. I didn't know how to stop the ice. It was always there when I awoke.

It would have been pitch black were it not for the torch that burned brightly across the hall from my cell door. There were three small holes in the top half of the iron door that I could peer through, if I stretched on my toes.

Strangely enough, with just that bit of light I could see perfectly. I tried using a bit of rock to mark time with each meal, but the broken piece of stone had worn to the size of a pebble and I'd stopped counting when I reached ten-thousand days. What was the point?

I never saw anything but the torch. The guards passed by from time to time, but never spoke. They fed me by sliding a plate of gruel under the iron door. Perhaps it was once a day. Perhaps not. When I finished eating the glue they considered food, I always slid the plate back out. If I didn't, they wouldn't feed me the next time.

Time had ceased to exist for me.

Even sleep held no peace. Two faces appeared consistently in my dreams. They were beautiful, identical men. Twin brothers, for sure. They had square jawlines, long wavy black hair, and honey-brown eyes that made my body thrum with desire. I had no specific memories of them, just a very strong attraction. They had been significant to me at one point. Of this I was sure.

Other nights I would dream of hearing a baby wailing, but there was nothing visual. I would wake sobbing and my cell would be coated with an extra thick coat of the glaring white ice. I didn't remember birthing a child, but something in my heart said the cries in my dreams belonged to my child.

Beyond those two faint memories, there was nothing. Who was I? Where had I come from? I couldn't remember my name. Just that I'd been here—wherever here was—a long time. In this cell.

It was different today ... or this time. Usually, I felt the same all the time. But when I'd awakened, I was feverish— so warm that sweat ran in rivulets down my temples from my straggles of greasy, blond hair. I stood from the furs and walked to one wall of my cell. I touched the icy bricks, laying my hands against them. The ice soothed only a little.

I pressed my cheek to the wall and droplets of water trickled down to the slick floor, melting fast from the heat my body was generating.

"Hello?" I shouted and moved to the door. I flattened both palms on the cold iron and craned my neck to look out of the three small holes. The familiar orange light from the torch was all I could see. I had no idea how long it'd been since my last plate of gruel had been delivered, but I burned with fever and my stomach cramped with hunger.

"Please. I'm ill." I called out.

No one answered.

My heart leapt at the sound of boots on the stone floor. Food? Or would they help me?

I flinched with each step as they approached. There were multiple sets of feet, at least four people—three more than normal. This was different.

Hope swelled in my chest. Maybe they were going to let me out. They certainly didn't need four men to shove a plate of gruel and a bowl of water under the door.

I took a deep breath and drank in their scent, confused by my instant arousal. My body trembled with excitement, as bile rose in my throat at the thought of any of them actually touching me. Moisture pooled between my thighs underneath the thin, linen shift that covered me. My breasts were heavy and my nipples puckered against the soft fabric. My body had a mind of its own and behaved more like a bitch in heat than a woman. I felt like I should know why my body reacted this way, but I hadn't a clue.

Just one more frustration.

Keys rattled on the other side of the door. The tumblers on the lock clicked and opened. "Back away from the door," a gravelly voice commanded.

I did as he said, more from the shock of hearing someone speak to me than the willingness to follow orders. I wanted out of this cell more than anything.

The iron door screeched as it swung open and three enormous men marched through the doorway. They towered over me. Their chainmail armor clinked with each step, and their red tunics were strangely familiar.

My gaze traveled to their faces. Solemn, but handsome. Strong jawlines and rich, dark brown eyes. Their dark, almost black, hair was long and braided down their backs.

I took another deep breath and released it slowly, trying to control my urges. They smelled delicious and I wanted them. All of them.

Shaking my head, I refocused, taking another step backward instead of forward.

One of the men, probably the youngest of the three, gave me a wolfish grin and made a crude gesture at his crotch. The other two did not appreciate his behavior. One shoved the young man and he sailed across the room, slamming into the icy stone wall with a painful *thud.*

"You know the rules, Aldan. Don't be a fool," said the man who'd done the shoving.

The younger man picked himself up and grunted his acknowledgement, keeping his head bowed and his eyes on the floor.

"Come with us." The third man finally spoke, and my gaze locked with his.

His brown eyes glistened with desire, but he held back. Smart man.

The second man, who'd dealt out punishment to the youngest, growled deep in his throat and I glanced up at him. Part of his top lip was curled into a snarl, though I felt his anger was directed more at his companions than at me.

Toward me, I felt the slightest hint of ... pity.

He spoke again, but this time to me. "Will you walk freely or should we bind you, Milady?"

What did I have to lose? I didn't know who or where I was. All I had were icy walls, a painfully hot fever, and a traitorously aroused body.

I took a deep breath and nodded.

"Edith, lower the wards," said the third man. "But just enough so that we can pass through the doorway with her."

A moment later, a rush of white-hot energy knocked me back against the far wall of my cell. Air rushed from my lungs with an audible *umph*. The ice on the wall behind me melted on contact, soaking the fabric of my dress.

The thing ... the beast I'd felt inside me moved again and a growl tore from my throat unlike anything I'd ever heard. Power within me surged forward and I leapt at the youngest man, knocking him to the ground. His body and clothing iced solid within moments and I jumped back.

My head was spinning. Had I killed him? There wasn't time to contemplate guilt.

I could hear shouting, but the words were garbled in my racing mind. The other two men were backing slowly toward the open cell door. I refused to stay here any longer. The entity inside me was being pulled. The burning arousal that plagued my body was a mere pinprick compared to the stabbing pain I felt now.

Freeing myself from this icy prison was my only objective.

I lunged and the two men dove to either side of the cell. Instead of pursuing them, I ran through the open door and swung it closed. It locked in place with a heavy clank and I breathed a small sigh of relief.

I turned, running headlong into a small woman. She fell to the floor, but jumped back to her feet quickly.

Her bright, red hair hung in loose waves only to her shoulders and she was dressed in strange clothing. A loose, waist-length tunic covered her upper half, but on her lower body, she wore tightly fitting breeches that extended to her ankles, where the strangest looking furry boots covered her feet.

"No! Don't leave. They'll kill me!" The redhead extended her hand and I observed her in suspicious silence. I started to shake my head. Whatever she needed from me, I would not give. She carried no weapon that I could see, yet the beast inside my soul wanted absolutely nothing to do with her.

"I need to go."

"Go where? You don't even know where you are." Her voice was like velvet and dripped with honey, the fear had disappeared.

She was stalling me. That I did know. I couldn't let her steal this chance from me. My gut told me there wouldn't ever be another. Whatever she'd done to allow me out of that wretched cell had awakened more than even I understood. It was as if everything around and inside me came to life. It was like I'd been unchained. Like magick.

The redhead took a step forward and I threw up a hand, gesturing her to stop. Within seconds, a thick wall of ice separated us. Her muffled curses followed me as I made my way down the long, dimly lit hallway.

I passed many doors. Dozens of voices called after me, but I stopped for none. The rough gravel on the floor bit into my tender, bare feet and I winced with each step. The floor of my cell had been as smooth as glass, every inch covered in ice. How I wished for that smooth, cold surface now.

With the next step I took, the gravel was gone. I stared at the ground and saw my terrified expression in the dark, glassy surface. By the gods! The floors had iced over. I lifted one bloody foot and then the next, wiping off the gravel. Then I wiped my bloody hand on the side of my damp skirt. The smooth, cool floor was heaven to my throbbing feet. Hopefully, the cuts would stop bleeding soon.

More commotion carried down the tunnel from where the ice had formed between the redheaded woman and me. There was thunderous hammering and yelling. It wouldn't be long before they hacked their way through the frozen wall.

Confusion swirled in my mind like a howling snowstorm. Common sense said I'd created the ice, but then again, common sense also said that people could not create something from nothing. *Gods!* My stomach twisted in pain. Heat flamed through me like I'd been tossed on a funeral pyre, and the throbbing in my sex was bordering on maddening. I couldn't remember *ever* having sex with anyone, but my body knew exactly what it wanted.

It didn't matter. Right now, all that did matter was getting out of this dungeon. So unless propositioning one of the guards chasing me was a viable option, sex was just going to have to wait.

The beast inside me growled in frustration and my breath fogged in front of me as I ran.

I leaned against the wall to catch my breath. "Just pull yourself together and help me get out of this place," I told myself. A new surge of energy buzzed through my body. All my nerves stood on end. My skin was *so* warm; the ice beneath my feet was melting into puddles.

I slipped along the bare stone wall and peeked around

the next corner. There were several guards stationed at a gate that opened to the outside. Two guards stood on either side of the gate. How many were on the outside? I couldn't see anything past the glare of daylight. I'd been in the dark so long the light was uncomfortable. It was easier to focus in the darkness. In fact, the darker it was, the faster my eyes adjusted.

A bell sounded in the distance and the tunnel came to life. Dozens of guards poured in through the open gates and my heart dropped. I'd been so close. I could smell the fresh air, the scent of lavender on the breeze, and the tang of salt from an ocean.

Another emotion boiled from the center of my chest and the beast within pushed inside my mind. It wanted control and was refusing to give up. The single echoing thought in my head was *ice*.

Fine, then. *Take it.*

I stopped fighting the beast and let it guide me. I stepped out of the shadows and marched down the center of the tunnel. Several guards looked at me and then shouted. I raised my hands toward them and sheets of ice grew from the ground, trapping them. They hacked at the cold barrier with their swords, but it would take time for them to get free.

For a brief moment, I allowed myself hope. I threw up my hands and a wave of ice encased the group of men in my path. Running up the face of the frozen wave, I gasped, fear streaking along my spine as my fingernails lengthened into white claws. Though it made scaling the slippery face of the ice much easier, it further terrified my already confused mind. I slid down the other side and waved my arm to create more ice to smooth my descent. But I was a mere passenger in my body. The beast was controlling most of my actions.

A guard came out of nowhere and I threw him across the tunnel. His body slammed into the gray stone wall. My strength surprised me. The hit barely knocked the breath from my body.

No one was going to stop me. Not now.

I walked through the open gate unimpeded, drinking in the sights and scents around me. The salty breeze whipped through my long, white hair. I looked up at the azure sky and a roar tore from my chest that sounded inhuman. The beast receded, giving me full control once more over my body. My hands changed back to normal, claws retracted.

My eyesight adjusted to the bright sun and I scanned my surroundings. The landscape was eerily familiar, but no specific memories came to mind. I didn't know where I was or where I needed to go. The dungeon was isolated. I couldn't see a town or castle from this vantage point, but I could hear the tolling of the bells in the distance, raising the alarm. They were coming for me. I had to move.

The yearning inside me was stronger now. The call that had flared to life when they entered my cell pulled me to the left. I emerged from the shadow of the tower I'd escaped and stepped gingerly onto the soft, grassy turf. The green grass cushioned my aching feet. I looked behind me, glad to see I was no longer leaving bloody footprints. At least that would make tracking me somewhat harder for the soldiers I'd left frozen in the tunnels.

I hitched up the skirt of my shift, not worried about

showing a little leg. The pull inside me continued to grow; instinctively I knew it would lead me in the right direction. Every step I took pleased the beast within me.

Moments later, a large shadow passed over my head. I ducked to the ground. Terror clawed at my heart. I had no idea what kind of bird could make such a large shadow, but when I ventured a glance into the pure, blue sky, there was no bird. A creature that could only be described as a dragon had cast the shadow. It was big, reddish in color, and its wings were so large it easily could have covered an entire castle keep.

Where was I? And since when were dragons real?

The beast within me laughed and I shook my head. It could laugh all it wanted. There was no way I could stand up to a monster the size of a castle tower. The red dragon soared over the valley, exactly where I was headed.

Noises behind me pushed my feet into a run.

"Whatever gods or goddesses are out there, I could really use a hand right now." I half-slid, half-rolled down the face of a steep hill. I slipped through a thicket of trees and came out on the other side in time to see a man seemingly appear out of thin air inside a circle of large stones. A white mist hung in the air above the stones.

He walked out of the circle and looked around suspiciously. The mist vanished a few seconds later.

I flattened myself against a large pine and held my breath. Suspending my common sense, I realized this might be a good way to disappear. He was alone. Perhaps I could get him to take me away from this place. After singlehandedly escaping that horrid prison, one man didn't seem nearly as intimidating as he would have only hours ago.

I left the protection of the trees and walked toward him, taking a deep breath to try and calm my frayed nerves. The last thing I needed was him encased in a block of ice. I needed him to tell me how to escape. As I stepped closer, I noticed the odd cut of his clothing. He wore breeches that reached to his ankles and his coat only hung to his waist.

"Sir," I called out.

He looked at me and his eyes widened like he recognized me. But I had no knowledge of him.

The beast rumbled. Apparently, it recognized the stranger. I was the only one left in the dark.

"I need to leave this place. Can I go through the stones the same way you appeared? Where does it lead?" Only ten feet separated us now. Something about him gave me pause. Something I could feel surrounding him.

"You can't be alive. They said you died." He took a step forward and I backed up, keeping him at the same distance.

"I assure you I am alive, but I need your assistance to leave this place. I'm ill..." I wiped beads of sweat from my brow and refocused on him. "I need to go out the way you came. I cannot explain it." I could smell him now—his scent was masculine with a hint of cardamom. My senses were heightened and I could smell the moist dirt beneath my feet, the tangy scent of the grass. Salt hung in the air from an ocean I couldn't see. And then there was this man. Strange scents clung to his clothes—an unfamiliar musk of some type of animal. Sand? Perfume?

"You don't remember me?"

I opened my mouth to tell him I remembered no one, but then thought better of it. "I need to leave, sir. Those stones are a doorway. I don't know how or why, but they are, aren't they?"

He nodded and tightened his fingers around the handle of a small dagger he was holding. I hadn't noticed it before. It was short, no longer than the length of his hand. The blade was half that and triangular in shape. The hilt was gold, at least the part I could see. And his response to my question told me it was essential to using the gateway.

"If I let you out of the Veil, you have to promise to stay with me."

I narrowed my eyes and the beast within me pushed against my mind. The pain was so intense, as if someone were holding my face against hot iron. I screamed and fell to my knees. Something was happening that I couldn't stop. Ice flowed along the ground from me, spiraling outward in a circular pattern.

"Stop!" he shouted, running toward me with his hands raised.

An invisible force pushed on me and I screamed again. *He* was making the pain worse. Anger surged from deep within me and I stood, fighting through the searing pain and faced him. For a second, I saw hesitation in his pale gray eyes.

That was my moment. I lifted my hand and ice coated him from head to foot, except for the hand holding the small golden dagger. It amazed me that I could control this power with so little focus.

I should've been terrified, but instead it felt natural.

The ice and the beast were part of me. I'd just forgotten them.

That was a problem for later. Now, I needed to escape and return to my life—a life I couldn't remember, but a life I wanted desperately to find. And those handsome twins from my dreams—perhaps they could tell me what happened to the baby.

The ice around the stranger began to crack.

I wrenched the dagger from his hand and ran to the stone circle. The mist didn't reappear. Nothing happened. I could see him breaking his way out of the icy coating one chunk at a time. It would take him only a few more minutes to free himself completely.

I frantically searched the stones for markings, running my fingertips around the smooth surface looking for anything that might tell me how to open the doorway.

There were none.

I ran from one to another and then to the large pillar in the center. A bloody handprint stared back at me from the far side. It looked fresh. In fact, the entire pillar was covered with worn and faded handprints. All in shades of red and brown. All made with blood.

My fingers tightened around the handle of the dagger. It was worth trying. Nothing about this world made sense. Why wouldn't there be a magickal doorway? I dragged the blade across my left palm, wincing at the first burn of the cut. Blood pooled in my palm. I closed my hand into a fist to smear the blood and then slapped it onto the face of the pillar.

Energy shot through my body and the world moved around me. The pillar was gone. In its place was a waist-high altar of stacked stones held together by mortar. The towering pillars around the edge of the circle were also gone. Instead of large, freestanding rocks, there were smaller rocks stacked together to create a dozen pillars in a circle around the middle altar. And instead of rolling hills of green grass, I stood in the center of an unfamiliar forest.

I dropped to my knees and dug a hole at the base of the altar. After wiping my blood off the small dagger, I placed it into the hole and covered it quickly. The man would most certainly come looking for it and instinct told me it wasn't safe to carry it around.

My palm still bled from the cut so I tore a strip from the bottom of my shift and wrapped it around my left hand. I hoped it would be enough to stanch the flow of blood.

I closed my eyes and turned, listening to a force I couldn't explain tell me which direction to walk in a land I knew nothing about. Bloody hell of a mess this was.

Taking a deep breath, I opened my eyes and took several steps. The ground was rocky and cold here, not grassy and soft. My feet were already tender from running on the sharp rocks at the tower. I couldn't last long out here without shoes, and the terrain was too jagged to ice the ground. I'd be on my bum more than my feet.

Choosing each step carefully, I climbed away from the hidden stone circle and picked my way through the dense, pine forest. The dead needles on the ground stuck into my feet like slivers of glass, but I had to keep moving. The sun was falling and it would be dark in a few hours.

There was no telling what might come out hunting under the cover of darkness. I could protect myself to a point, but I could not just freeze everything that came near me. Or maybe I could, but I didn't want to. There had to be someone somewhere who could help me figure out who and what I was.

Someone who didn't want to hurt me.

Krystal Shannan, also known as Emma Roman, lives in a sprawling ranch style home with her husband, daughter, and a pack of rescue Basset Hounds. She is an advocate for Autism Awareness and shares the experiences and adventures she's been through with her daughter whenever she can.

Needless to say, life is never boring when you have an elementary-aged special needs child you are home-schooling and half a dozen 4-legged friends roaming the house. They keep her and her husband busy, smiling, and laughing.

Krystal writes magick and Emma doesn't. If you are looking for leisurely-paced sweet romance, her books are probably not for you. However, for those looking for a story filled with adventure, passion, and just enough humor to make you laugh out loud. Welcome home!

www.krystalshannan.com

Other Books By Krystal Shannan

Vegas Mates
Completed Series

Chasing Sam
Saving Margaret
Waking Sarah
Taking Nicole
Unwrapping Tess
Loving Hallie

Sanctuary, Texas
Completed Series

My Viking Vampire
My Dragon Masters
My Eternal Soldier
Mastered: Teagan
My Warrior Wolves
My Guardian Gryphon
My Vampire Knight

VonBrandt Family Pack
Part of the Somewhere, TX Saga

To Save A Mate
To Love A Mate
To Win A Mate
To Find A Mate
To Plan For A Mate (coming next)

MoonBound
Completed Series
Part of the Somewhere, TX Saga

The Werewolf Cowboy #1
The Werewolf Bodyguard #2
The Werewolf Ranger #3
Chasing A Wolf #4
Seducing A Wolf #5
Saving A Wolf #6
Broken Wolf #7
Hunted Wolf #8

The Moonbound wolves story continues in an epic way through the...

Courts of Draíochta
Part of the Somewhere, TX Saga

Of Spells And Shadows
Of Trial And Torment (coming next)

Pool of Souls

Open House
Finding Hope

Contemporary Romance by Krystal's alter ego, Emma Roman.

Bad Boys, Billionaires & Bachelors
Can't Get You Off My Mind
What's Love Got To Do With It
You're The One That I Want

Accidentally In Love
Must Be Santa (Coming Next)

<u>MacLaughlin Family</u>
Completed Series
Trevor
Caiden
Harvey
Lizzy

56328441R00187

Made in the USA
Middletown, DE
23 July 2019